BLAZE

has caught fire
with readers everywhere!

Last year Harlequin Temptation
launched a sizzling new special—
BLAZE. Romantic stories that
are sexy, sassy—*and* hot!

BLAZE was such a runaway success that
we've created this steamy collection
just for you!

Three sizzling love stories from
today's hottest writers!

And remember...each month there's a brand-new
BLAZE book in the Temptation lineup,
plus three more sexy, seductive romances
by your favorite authors.

BLAZE. It's hot...and it's out of control!

About the Authors

JoAnn Ross

The bestselling author of over fifty novels, JoAnn wrote her first story—a romance about two star-crossed mallard ducks—when she was just seven years old. She sold her first romance novel in 1982 and has an incredible eight million copies of her books in print. JoAnn married her high school sweetheart—twice—and makes her home in Arizona. A longtime contributor to the Harlequin Temptation series, she is thrilled about her next romance, #717 *Mackenzie's Woman*, to be published in February 1999. It's the launch book for an exciting new miniseries celebrating Harlequin's 50th anniversary! JoAnn also writes single titles for MIRA and Pocket Books.

Heather MacAllister

Most definitely a shining star in the romance genre, Heather has written twenty-three books for the Harlequin Temptation and Romance lines combined. Her unique ability to mix sexiness and humor in a love story has made her a reader favorite. Little wonder Heather's book *Bride Overboard* was nominated for a RITA Award for Best Short Contemporary by the Romance Writers of America. A former music teacher, Heather traded in her grand piano after deciding a computer keyboard was a *lot* quieter while her children napped. It's the perfect career for this Missouri native now living in Texas with her electrical engineer husband and two live-wire sons. Heather's next Temptation novel, #711 *Mr. December*, part of the MAIL ORDER MEN miniseries, will be on the stands in December 1998. Look for Harlequin Romance #3535, *Hand-Picked Husband*, to follow in January 1999.

Elda Minger

With over a decade's success in contemporary and historical romance fiction, bestselling author Elda Minger is known for her sensual writing, dynamite heroes *and* a wicked sense of humor. A longtime contributor to both Harlequin American Romance and Temptation, she enjoys writing a fun, sassy, sexy story. BLAZE is the perfect vehicle for her—watch for her next ultra-sexy Temptation, available in July 1999. Elda is a frequent speaker at writers' conferences and has also taught creative writing courses. She often appears on bestseller lists and has won several awards. Last year she received a RITA Award nomination for Best Short Contemporary for her novel *Christmas with Eve*. Elda lives in Southern California in a wonderful old house.

Temptation® BLAZE

JoAnn Ross
Heather MacAllister
Elda Minger

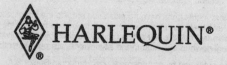

HARLEQUIN®

TORONTO • NEW YORK • LONDON
AMSTERDAM • PARIS • SYDNEY • HAMBURG
STOCKHOLM • ATHENS • TOKYO • MILAN • MADRID
PRAGUE • WARSAW • BUDAPEST • AUCKLAND

HARLEQUIN BOOKS
225 Duncan Mill Road, Don Mills
Ontario, Canada M3B 3K9

ISBN 0-373-83369-5

TEMPTATION BLAZE

The publisher acknowledges the copyright holders of
the individual works as follows:

MIDNIGHT HEAT
Copyright © 1998 by JoAnn Ross

A LARK IN THE DARK
Copyright © 1998 by Heather MacAllister

NIGHT FIRE
Copyright © 1998 by Elda Minger

CONTENTS

Midnight Heat
JoAnn Ross

With heartfelt appreciation to Garth Brooks, Leigh Reynolds and all the other country songwriters and singers who have provided both inspiration and enjoyment all these years.

And the Honeycutt family of Alamosa, Colorado, who put on a mighty fine rodeo and whose name I borrowed for my hero.

PROLOGUE

Daydreams about Night Things

ONE SUMMER MORNING, when Erin Montgomery was eight years old, she took a tumble off her horse while helping her daddy round up motherless calves in Arizona's high mountain country. Though Sunshine, a sweet-tempered mare who'd been retired from the rodeo circuit, immediately pulled up to keep from stepping on her young rider, Erin had feared that she was about to die.

Her daddy had always told her that being a cowgirl meant never saying it hurt. But sometimes, Erin thought, as she'd gasped for air, that was a whole lot easier said than done. As hard as she'd struggled, she couldn't breathe. As much as she'd wanted to, she couldn't cry.

John Montgomery had dismounted, ambled over to his daughter, who was flopping around like a grounded trout beneath the statue-still palomino, and assured her that she wasn't going to die anytime soon. She'd only had the wind knocked out of her. Confident that her larger-than-life daddy would never lie to her, Erin quit fighting her body.

Sure enough, pretty soon she was climbing back onto the docile golden mare and returning to work.

As the years passed, the memory of that feeling—as if Sunshine had all four hooves planted right in the middle of her chest—had nearly faded from Erin's mind. Until today.

The July morning had begun like any other, the only difference being the aftereffects she was feeling from last night's erotic dream. Dragging her still-tingling body from tangled cotton sheets, Erin had risen with the sun, dressed, fed the horses, fixed breakfast for her dad and C.J., written out some bills, and made up a list of things they needed in town. Since this was one of the three half-days a week that her four-year-old son went to preschool, she dropped C.J. off at the school on the way down the curving mountain road to the nearby town of Whiskey River.

Although Erin loved C.J. to pieces, he'd entered a new phase that had him demanding detailed answers to every question under the sun. Already today, she'd tried to explain why the sky was blue in the daytime and black at night, why Grandpa called his breakfast hotcakes but Kevin Blake's mother called them flapjacks, why little boys weren't allowed to ride bulls at the Fourth of July rodeo, and why woodpeckers had red heads. Which was why the solitude of the remote part of the country she'd been born and raised in was even more pleasurable on this sunny summer day.

Enjoying the vast robin's egg blue sky stretching out to far-distant horizons and the unexpected sight of a herd of elk grazing in a wildflower-dotted meadow, Erin began singing along with Alabama.

The tune was followed by a brief recorded interview with Faith Hill about how having a child had changed her life—something Erin could definitely identify with. And then, while she was still thinking about how C.J. was, hands down, the best thing that had ever happened to her, a painfully familiar baritone voice knocked the breath right out of Erin's lungs.

"Cinderella Cowgirl," the hit single on Jace Honeycutt's *Midnight Heat* album, had not only skyrocketed the country singing sensation to stardom, it had become his signature song. There had been a lot of speculation over the years that the tearjerker ballad about a bittersweet midnight romance between a struggling country singer and an innocent rancher's daughter was autobiographical. But speculation wasn't proof, and if some winsome cowgirl *had* stolen Jace's heart, the three-time AMC Entertainer of the Year wasn't talking.

And neither was the girl. Not back then, and not now. Unbidden, sensual memories flooded back, causing Erin's body to glow with a radiant heat. The poignant song that was, indeed, about her, conjured up in heartbreaking detail how he'd kissed her that night—lightly at first, then with increasing pressure. She remembered clearly the way his teeth had nipped at her lip, and how he'd soothed the reddened flesh with his tongue.

There had been a full moon that night, hanging in the star-spangled black velvet sky like a silver pendant as he'd slowly, almost reverently undressed her. He calmed her virginal nervousness with warm, deepening kisses, slow caresses, pretty words and extravagant compliments that almost had Erin believing that she was, indeed, the most beautiful girl in the world.

In the morning, Jace had moved on, as she'd known all along he would, taking her heart with him. But the man who was soon to become known as the country singer with the Midas touch had left her with a gift far more precious than gold.

On the radio, Jace strummed a final guitar chord. And as the last soulful note drifted away, a lone tear trailed down Erin's cheek in memory of that long-ago stolen night when heaven had been just a sin away.

CHAPTER ONE

Girls' Night Out
Five years earlier

"YOU ARE, WITHOUT A doubt, the most pitiful girl in this entire county," RaeAnn Cutter proclaimed as she and Erin pulled out of the parking lot of the Whiskey River Mercantile. A month's worth of groceries was piled into the back of the white Dodge pickup; when you lived sixty miles from the nearest market, it was important to buy in bulk. "I swear, if you're not careful, you're going to end up an old maid."

"That's a bit of an exaggeration," Erin said mildly, wondering why it was that whenever a woman got married, she suddenly wanted all of her friends to be in the same boat, "since I'm only twenty-one.

"And aside from the fact that two women of the nineties shouldn't think they need men to complete their lives, just because I turned down Kenny Nash's invitation to the rodeo concert tonight doesn't necessarily destine me to spinsterhood."

"That's a matter of opinion. And if you want to

talk about nineties women, while I realize some poor misguided souls are still sticking to that worn-out old line about a woman without a man being like a fish without a bicycle, in my book, males are pretty much the fudge frosting on the devil's food cake of life.''

"You're supposed to think that," Erin said. "You're still technically in the honeymoon stage."

"That's true enough," RaeAnn agreed with a slow smile that hinted at wifely pleasures. "But do you have any idea how valuable tickets to that concert are? The deejay on K-COLT said people from as far away as Phoenix and Albuquerque have been camping out in the parking lot of the fairgrounds for three days just to get into a lottery for a chance to buy them."

"All the more reason Kenny should take someone who might actually be seriously interested in him."

"Nobody's asking you to walk down the aisle with the guy, Erin." RaeAnn shook her head in frustration, causing the wild red curls—spiral permed by Patti Greene down at The Shear Delight beauty salon—to bounce like lively springs. "He was only asking you out on a date." She pulled a cellophane pack from her bag and ignoring her friend's frown, shook out a cigarette and lit it with a silver lighter studded with turquoise.

"Wouldn't it be worth suffering a few hours with the guy for a chance to see Alan Jackson up close and personal?'' RaeAnn persisted. "The man just happens to have the best Wrangler buns in the business. It's no wonder he's a country superstar.''

"And here I thought it was his singing that made him famous.''

"Well, there is that," RaeAnn allowed. "But you can't deny that his drop-dead-gorgeous looks contribute to his success.''

"I'm not certain you're supposed to be talking that way, given the fact that you and Jack only returned from Hawaii last week.''

"You have a lot to learn about being married, sweetie." RaeAnn drew in on the cigarette and let out a deep breath in a cloud of blue smoke. "Just because a girl has sworn to forsake others, doesn't stop her from looking. Or fantasizing. Why, I doubt if there's a female alive who hasn't fantasized about doing the Chattahoochee with that blond hunk in a hat.''

Erin laughed, enjoying herself for the first time in a very long while. She knew that she tended toward seriousness, which was one of the many reasons why she enjoyed having the outrageous RaeAnn as a friend. They complemented each other, she'd often thought. Erin provided some grounding for her quixotic best friend, while RaeAnn was always encouraging her to spread her wings.

"I missed you while you were gone," Erin said.

"Well, I'd like to say I missed you, too, but

since it would be a flat-out lie, I won't." RaeAnn put her boots up on the dashboard. "Remember how we used to talk about having a double wedding?"

"Of course. But I couldn't exactly grab some strange man off the street just so we could live out a childhood daydream."

"You wouldn't have had to work real hard to grab Kenny. The way he was looking at you in the market reminded me of a guy who's been locked away in solitary confinement livin' on bread and water and has just been given a side of beef. Why, if you'd have been a rib-eye steak, honey, you'd have been a goner."

"That's one more reason I turned him down," Erin said, serious again. "It wouldn't have been fair to get his hopes up."

"I suppose you have a point," RaeAnn admitted reluctantly. "But even if you didn't want to go with Kenny, you really should get out more. It's the last night of the fair, Erin. Why don't you just come with Jack and me?"

Her best friend had been making that offer for the past five days. And for the past five days, Erin had been inventing reasons to refuse. "Three's a crowd."

"Hell, Jack wouldn't mind. And even if he did, he'd never dare let on. Not if he wanted to get lucky afterward, anyway."

"It does sound like fun," Erin admitted, "but with Dad just home from the hospital—"

"Oh, pooh." RaeAnn cut her off with a wave of a hand tipped in Coral Sunset nail polish. "Your father was discharged from that Phoenix hospital nearly a month ago. And you know as well as I do that the Mary Poppins clone you forced the insurance company to pay to visit the ranch three days a week is more than capable of sitting with him."

"Dad's not a helpless baby to be handed off to some caretaker. You can't just hire someone to 'sit with him.' Besides, Julia Martin's not a nanny. She's a registered nurse. And, speaking of nurses—" Erin waved away some cigarette smoke "—I really wish you'd quit smoking. If I *am* doomed to spinsterhood, I sure don't want you dying and leaving me to face it alone."

"You know I wouldn't do that." Nevertheless, RaeAnn jabbed out the barely smoked cigarette into the truck's ashtray. "We're blood sisters, remember?"

"How could I forget?" The faint thin scar at the tip of her index finger was a constant reminder of that long-ago Indian-summer afternoon when the two best friends had sat on the bank of Whiskey River, nicked their fingers with a razor blade, then touched them together, mingling their blood. "I don't know what I would have done these past months without you," Erin confessed as she braked at the town's only stoplight.

It had, without question, been the worst year of her life—even worse than when she'd lost her mother in a car accident. But, of course, back then, Erin had barely passed her fourth birthday and hadn't entirely grasped the concept of death. Fortunately her father, though never one for soft words and openly tender emotions, had filled the void her mother's too-early death had left in Erin's life—and her heart. Only later would she understand how difficult it must have been for her father to put aside his own feelings of loss to concentrate on hers.

John Montgomery had always provided the foundation for her life. He was her rock, her very own Marlboro man, looking as if he'd stepped right out of all those advertisements in *Western Horseman* magazine. Unfortunately, the similarity between the Arizona rancher and the billboard cowboy ultimately proved all too true-to-life. Like the male model who'd posed for all those ads, her father had recently lost a lung to cancer. Fortunately, unlike the original Marlboro man, he was still alive.

A stream of pedestrians on their way to the fairgrounds passed in front of the truck. Most of them Erin knew; a few, undoubtedly from neighboring counties, she didn't. She was idly deciding what to cook for dinner when her attention was suddenly captured by a man crossing just inches in front of her bumper.

He was tall. Six feet five at the very least, she guessed, which made him stand head and shoulders above the crowd. And unlike that of so many big men, his body, clad in a black T-shirt, black leather vest and faded blue jeans, appeared not to have an ounce of excess flesh. He walked with a cocky, loose-hipped stride she supposed drew women like hummingbirds to sugar.

As if sensing her gaze on him, he turned his head. And in the suspended moment when their eyes met through the windshield, desire struck like a bolt of lightning from a clear blue summer sky— unbidden, and unwelcome.

Erin knew she was staring, but she couldn't help herself. A power far stronger than herself held her in its thrall. The stranger's eyes, beneath the bat-tered black Stetson, were as brown as Bambi's, but nowhere near as innocent. His nose canted a bit to the left, as if it had been broken at some time. For a reason that she'd have to think about later, when she didn't feel on the verge of overload, Erin knew that his full, sculpted mouth could bring a woman mind-numbing pleasure.

As if he possessed the ability to read her mind, those lips curved into a quick, wicked grin. Devils danced in eyes as dark and every bit as sinfully rich as chocolate while they took in her suddenly flushed face.

The traffic light, strung from wires across the street, changed from red to green. And still neither of them moved. They stayed right where they were, Erin taking note of the stranger, him staring right back at her. Behind the truck, a horn honked impatiently. Like a dog shaking off water, Erin pulled herself out of the strange, trance-like state and glanced up into her rearview mirror to see a fifty-something cowboy who didn't bother to conceal his irritation.

She looked back at the stranger again, just in time to witness his self-satisfied grin. He touched his fingers to the brim of his hat, then winked at her. It was a bold, wicked wink that suggested he knew the effect the brief encounter had had on her and was enjoying his masculine power immensely. Then he continued sauntering toward the curb.

"Heavens," RaeAnn said, fanning herself dramatically, "has it suddenly gotten hot in this truck or am I imagining it?"

The horn behind her sounded again. Longer. Louder. As she shifted into gear, Erin belatedly realized RaeAnn had been talking to her.

"I'm sorry. What did you say?"

"I was referring to that drop-dead-gorgeous cowboy."

"What cowboy?" Erin asked innocently.

"The one who just about melted the windshield. And you know what they say about getting right back up on a horse after you've fallen off."

Erin knew where RaeAnn was taking the conversation and attempted to head her off. "I don't want to talk about Ryan."

"Does it hurt that much?" The sympathy in her friend's voice was echoed in her whiskey-brown eyes.

"No. My heart is intact. It's my pride that's taken a bit of a beating."

"I still can't believe Ryan the Rattler took that slut Amanda to the Denim and Diamonds, where everyone in town could see them together before the two of you had even officially broken up," RaeAnn agreed.

"I appreciate the loyalty, but Amanda Dean isn't exactly a slut."

"Are you kidding?" RaeAnn lifted an eyebrow. "Honey, that girl has been ridden by more cowboys than all the bucking broncs at the rodeo this week combined. In fact, I hear there's talk of naming this year's national bull-riding competition in Vegas 'The Amanda Dean Roughriders Convention.'"

Feeling her lips twitch, Erin fought yet another smile. "You're terrible."

"And right," RaeAnn said with a wicked grin of her own. "Don't forget that. I wonder if it bothers Ryan to be plowing in some very deep furrows."

"I'd assume Amanda's money would soothe any pain," Erin retorted dryly.

"You've got a point. Personally, I still think we ought to geld that horny bastard."

RaeAnn had first come up with the suggestion while downing margaritas at the Denim and Diamonds as if Congress were going to put a prohibition on tequila at midnight. Erin had worried that her friend might actually try to follow through on the threat—especially after Ryan had made the mistake of walking into the honky-tonk with the brunette barrel racer draped over him like an anaconda.

The bouncer—who'd gone to high school with both RaeAnn and Erin—had been forced to kick them out when RaeAnn had started pulling out fistfuls of Amanda's frizzy perm in the ladies' room. But Erin couldn't deny enjoying the unmasked fear on Ryan's face when RaeAnn had thrown Arnold Schwarzenegger's "I'll be back" line over her shoulder at him as the bouncer had half dragged, half carried her out the front door.

"The only regret I have concerning Ryan is that I was foolish enough to go out with him in the first place," Erin said. "And although the idea of gelding him might be appealing, I'm sure it must be against the law. And Ryan is not worth going to jail for."

"That might not prove such a hardship," RaeAnn replied. "The sheriff may not be Alan Jackson, but the guy definitely has a rugged, been-there, done-that sex appeal."

Erin couldn't argue with that appraisal. There were very few women in Whiskey River who hadn't sat up and taken notice of the former Dallas homicide detective. "Trace Callahan's also married."

"Which definitely puts him off-limits," RaeAnn agreed. She might have been more generous with her favors than Erin before her marriage, but her sense of honor was as unbending as the two-hundred-year-old ponderosa pine trees surrounding the town. "More's the pity." She sighed. "What this place needs is some new male blood."

When RaeAnn's words caused the stranger's bold-as-brass grin to come instantly to mind, Erin decided that in that regard, at least, RaeAnn was right.

CHAPTER TWO

The Hand of Fate

JACE HONEYCUTT STOOD outside the Mogollon County Fairgrounds looking up at the marquee announcing the final day's events. There he was, sandwiched in between Alan Jackson and the Daredevil Demolition Derby. Oh, they might have spelled his name wrong—with an *s* instead of a *c*, and leaving one of the *t*'s off Honeycutt—but it still looked damn good, in his opinion. He pulled out the little Kodak camera he'd bought when he'd first gone on the road and took a picture for his mama, who he knew would put it in one of her prized scrapbooks, as she had all the others.

"Hey, cowboy," a sultry, accented voice called out to him. "Want me to take your picture next to that sign?"

Jace flashed a grin over his shoulder at the woman who worked the midway, billed as The Magnificent Maya. He didn't know if Maya was really a psychic, as she claimed, but no one could deny that "The Magnificent" was right on the money. The gal had a body like a Las Vegas showgirl, dark eyes that flashed with passion and tilted up at the corners like a cat's, and lips that looked as if they'd be more potent than moonshine. Not that he'd ever find out. Since she was married to her barker, the sexy psychic was definitely off-limits.

"Thanks." He handed her the compact camera, tilted his black Stetson back with his thumb, and smiled into the lens. "My mother thanks you."

When she didn't respond, but just kept looking up at him with that sly, knowing smile on her ruby-red lips, Jace asked, "What? Do you see something in my future?" He'd known enough "seers" back home in the hills to believe that some people were given powers that the rest of the world's population lacked.

"I may."

He hooked his thumbs into his front pockets. "You going to tell me?"

"Oh, no." She skimmed a lazy hand through lush clouds of black hair. "It doesn't work that way. But believe me, Jace Honeycutt, before tonight is over, you'll have discovered your destiny."

With that pronouncement hanging between them, she turned and walked away. Jace allowed himself a moment's pleasure as he watched her lush hips swivel in the full gypsy skirt. Then, with a long sigh, he decided to take a stroll through the midway before tonight's performance.

THE MOGOLLON COUNTY Fair was, hands down, the most important annual event to occur in the mountain community. It had even come to replace the now defunct Rattlesnake Roundup as the high point of the year. It was part Disneyland, part carnival, along with some tractor pulls, a rodeo and a concert—an all-around good time.

Country music rode on air scented with popcorn and barbecue, competing with the screams from riders on the Tilt-A-Whirl spinning overhead.

By the time Erin paid her admission fee and had her hand stamped by a redheaded woman who was doing her best to look like Reba McEntire, she was already glad RaeAnn had insisted that she come. It was difficult to worry when everyone around you was having such a great time.

The marquee announced the day's performers. Unsurprisingly, Alan Jackson held the top spot, the lit-up letters of his name twice as large as the others.

"Oh, look!" RaeAnn grabbed Erin's arm and pointed her in the direction of a black-and-red-striped tent emblazoned with gold lamé stars. "A fortune teller."

"The Magnificent Maya sees all," the barker, sensing a paying customer, assured them. "The Magnificent Maya knows all."

"Right," Erin replied with good-natured skepticism. "Cross The Magnificent Maya's palm with silver and she will tell me the secret of the universe.''

"Come on, Erin," RaeAnn coaxed. "It'll be fun. And maybe she can even see into your romantic future, now that you've shed Ryan the Rattler.''

"The Magnificent Maya is most adept at romantic situations,'' the man said.

Having expected nothing less, Erin found herself enjoying the conversation. "Now why could I have guessed you were going to say that?''

"Perhaps you, too, are psychic," he suggested. "Madame Maya can advise you on how to open yourself to your inner voice, and your most deeply hidden emotions." He raised his voice to a decibel designed to draw in more customers. "She predicted, just this morning, that I would meet not one, but two very special women this night. And here the sun has not yet set, and already her prediction has come true.''

He really was full of it, Erin thought.

"This one's taken," Jack Cutter, who'd remained silent but openly skeptical during the pitch, said. He put his arm around his bride's shoulder and spoke to her. "Randy Ferguson's competing in the chainsaw competition," he reminded RaeAnn. "I told him we'd try to drop by.''

"And we will," RaeAnn promised. "Why don't you run along, sweetie, and I'll catch up with you as soon as Erin gets her fortune read?''

He looked inclined to argue, but then she went up on the pointy toes of her red boots, framed his darkly tanned rancher's face between her palms and treated him to a long kiss. It lasted so long, Erin turned her eyes away and pretended vast interest in the announcement over the loudspeakers that the Daredevil Demolition Derby would begin in forty-five minutes, and if you wanted to be close enough to hear that metal crunching, you'd better hustle yourselves to the arena at the west end of the fairgrounds, just beyond the 4-H stock building.

When her drifting gaze skimmed over a tall man walking toward the livestock barn, Erin felt another strange jolt, like the one she'd experienced while driving back to the ranch from the mercantile.

It couldn't be him, she assured herself. Mogollon County was rife with tall, whipcord-lean men who looked good in jeans.

"Lord, I do love being married," RaeAnn declared, when the soulful kiss finally ended and Jack had left, following the high-pitched drone of chain saws. "We have to find you a husband," she said again, "so I can stop feeling guilty for having so much fun."

"Perhaps The Magnificent Maya can help," the barker suggested with a wink at Erin. His eyes were as bold as brass, but unlike her stranger's, didn't stir so much as a single chord inside her.

Erin handed over the ten-dollar "donation," entered the tent and found herself in a scene straight out of one of the old black-and-white B movies that showed up on cable late at night. Madame Maya was stunning, in a flashy, theatrical way; and at least two decades younger than Erin had expected.

"Enter." The gypsy waved a hand laden with woven gold rings toward two folding chairs covered in red velvet and fringed with gold tassels. "You come seeking answers."

"Well, we're sure as hell not here for shish kebabs," RaeAnn replied.

The woman didn't respond. Indeed, she didn't acknowledge RaeAnn's presence at all. Instead, she looked straight at Erin. "You've recently suffered a painful loss."

"Very few people manage to get through life scot-free," Erin said mildly as she sat down at the small round satin-draped table across from the fortune teller. "And I'm sorry to disillusion you, Madame Maya, but your radar's a little out of whack. My loss, such as it was, wasn't all that painful."

"The loss of the man, no," the woman said. "The loss of your pride was something else altogether."

All right. So, it was a fairly good guess. However, Erin seriously doubted if there was a woman alive who hadn't experienced a failed romance.

"He was not worthy of you," The Magnificent

Maya intoned in a way that had Erin expecting the table between them to begin floating at any time.

Ignoring Erin's obvious skepticism, the gypsy reached across the table and took hold of her hand. The woman's fingernails were as red as fresh blood and as long as talons; they skimmed over Erin's upturned palm, pointing out supposed truths in the mounts at the base of her thumb and fingers, all named for ancient mythological gods and goddesses.

"You have a warm and affectionate heart." The crimson-tipped nail skimmed from the Mount of Jupiter to Mercury. "You are a woman who will be much loved in your lifetime."

Since Erin doubted that Madame Maya would gain many return customers by telling them that they had cold hearts that would never know love, she didn't bother to respond.

"You will know ecstasy." The touch traced a faint cross-hatching. "And from that ecstasy will be born a joy beyond anything you could have imagined—along with a pain that, for a time, may seem a thousand times worse than what you've recently suffered due to that unfaithful rattlesnake of a rancher's son. However, if you listen to your heart, if you leave it open, true love will ultimately prevail."

Erin had heard RaeAnn's sharp intake of breath at the description of Ryan that only the two of them had shared. Refusing to look at her friend, she tugged her hand free.

"Well," she said brightly, "that was very interesting. Thank you, Madame Maya. I certainly got my money's worth."

"There is more," the gypsy said. "You will meet a man—"

"Of course I will," Erin said, playing along. "A tall dark stranger, who'll take me on a sea cruise."

"He is tall. And dark. But by the time the sun rises over the mountains, he will no longer be a stranger. This man is your destiny."

With that proclamation, the fortune teller declared the session ended.

Declining the invitation to join RaeAnn and Jack at the souped-up chainsaw competition, Erin decided to check out the baking pavilion. She assured herself that the fact that the exhibit hall just happened to be adjacent to the livestock barn, where she'd last seen her stranger, had nothing to do with her decision.

CHAPTER THREE

You Walked In

IT COULDN'T BE HER. While not impossible, the odds made it unlikely. Yet, when he'd responded to that faint, uneasy prickling sensation at the back of his neck, Jace had turned around just in time to see the woman going into The Magnificent Maya's tent. A woman who, at least from the back, reminded him of the one he'd seen while crossing the street earlier today.

Corny as it might sound, their eyes had literally *met*, not across a crowded room, but through the windshield of her truck. Although he couldn't remember what color the truck was, he remembered her eyes echoing the stunningly blue sky overhead. In that suspended moment, he'd felt as if his boots were literally bolted to the asphalt street. And, when she'd finally responded to the jackass who'd kept leaning on his horn in the truck behind her, Jace had experienced the weirdest urge to go running after her.

Her hair had been pale gold, and viewing it now, rippling down her slender back as sleek and shiny as a palomino's tail, he imagined filling his hands with the glittering strands; fantasized them draped over his bare chest, his thighs....

Hell. Jace discovered the hard way that hunger had claws. It wasn't all that surprising since the last time he'd tangled the sheets with a willing woman had been in Tulsa, which was, Jace figured, doing some quick mathematics, nearly two months ago. He decided that if he didn't want to spend the rest of the tour using up all the cold water in the bus's holding tanks, he was definitely going to have to see about getting laid.

After the concert tonight, he decided. Then tomorrow he could move on to Las Vegas with his mind and his body back under control.

ERIN HAD ALMOST reached the pavilion where the Bake-Off was being held when she saw her nemesis. Although she'd never considered herself a coward, her first thought was to run away. But then, remembering that no Montgomery had ever run from battle—not in America, or their native Scotland—she forced herself to face this one now.

"Hello, Ryan." She slanted a cool glance at the woman who appeared to have a death grip on his arm. "Amanda."

"Hi, Erin," Ryan replied. As his gaze shifted nervously back and forth between his former girl-friend and his current one, Erin wondered why it was that she'd never noticed how close-set his eyes were. How squinty, actually. "What a surprise to see you here."

"Oh?" Erin lifted an eyebrow. "I don't know why. Whiskey River is a small town. It only stands to reason that we'd run into each other from time to time."

"Oh, but Ryan's not going to be in Whiskey River all that much longer," Amanda volunteered.

"Really." Realizing that she wasn't even slightly interested, that whatever feelings she'd thought she had for this man were stone-cold dead, Erin turned to leave. But it appeared Amanda wasn't finished with rubbing it in.

"We're moving to Phoenix." Her smile reminded Erin of a smug barn cat who'd just caught a particularly plump mouse. "Daddy bought another car dealership. Cadillacs," she added significantly. "And he wants Ryan to manage it for him. After we're married, of course." Her strident, girlish laugh grated on Erin's last nerve; it almost amused her to think of Ryan sentenced to spending the rest of his life listening to it.

"Well, isn't that lovely." Her own smile was as fake as Amanda's. "I hope you'll both be very happy."

Surprisingly, Ryan was looking more and more uncomfortable. "I meant to call you and tell you myself, Erin—"

"Oh, gracious." She waved his apology away

with a flick of her wrist. "There was no need for you to do that, Ryan. After all—"

"There you are!" It was Erin's turn to be cut off. She turned a little to the left and could scarcely believe her eyes as she saw her handsome stranger approaching in a long-legged, ground-eating stride. "I was afraid I'd lost you, darlin'." He looped an arm around her shoulder as if he had every right to put it there, pulled her against him, and kissed her.

When the expert kiss ended, the stranger glanced over at the openly shocked couple, as if noticing them for the first time. "I'm sorry," he said. "I know it's going to sound downright silly, but I tend to get a little crazy if I'm away from my sweetheart for too long." Then he smiled down at her with his bold mouth and devilish eyes. "Erin tells me I'm too possessive." As if to bolster that claim, he trailed a finger around her still-tingling lips. "But you know how it is when you're in love."

"Love?" The croak came out of Ryan's throat as if he were choking. "Is this true, Erin? Are you and this—" he skimmed an unbelieving glance over the man "—cowboy really in love?"

"Of course we are," the stranger answered for her—which was just as well, Erin decided, since she appeared to have lost the capacity for speech. "And, for the record, I'm not a cowboy." He thrust the hand that wasn't still holding on to Erin toward the other man. "I'm Jace Honeycutt."

"Alan Jackson's opening act?" Amanda asked, her eyes widening.

"That's me."

"We saw your name on the marquee." Her fingers tightened on Ryan's upper arm. "Remember, Ryan, we were discussing how it was a shame that we couldn't get tickets—"

"The shows sell out pretty fast," Jace agreed. "I couldn't even get Erin a decent seat. Which is why I'm afraid she's going to have to settle for watching from the side of the stage."

"What?" Erin finally found her voice.

"I know." His expression turned as apologetic as a dog who'd gotten caught burying a bone in the azaleas. "I promised you a front-row seat, but believe me, darlin', I'm going to do my level best to make it up to you. Beginning right after the show."

Desperately struggling to make sense out of any of this, Erin wondered if perhaps she'd gotten hit on the head after having had her palm read. Perhaps one of The Magnificent Maya's tent poles had crashed down on her. Or maybe one of the bulls scheduled for the rodeo-riding competition had broken out of the corral and stomped on her.

She remembered an announcement for a demolition derby. Perhaps one of the cars had run her down.

Obviously something had happened to cause her to hallucinate, because there was no way any of this—a gorgeous cowboy singer kissing her, Ryan looking like an oil rig about ready to blow, Amanda seething red-hot with jealousy—could possibly be really happening to her.

If she just kept her wits about her and didn't panic, Erin was certain she'd wake up in the hospital any time now, with a kindhearted doctor dressed in a white coat standing beside her bed, explaining that she'd had herself a little accident, but assuring her that she'd be just fine. And back to her old self in no time.

The only problem with that scenario, Erin considered as she recalled in vivid, wonderful detail Jace's devastating kiss, was that she didn't want to be back to her old self any time soon. What she wanted, she realized as she stared up into Jace's devilishly warm eyes, was for him to kiss her again. And again. All over.

"Well, it's been a real pleasure meetin' you," she heard Jace saying to the couple who were looking a little shell-shocked themselves. Erin found herself wishing this weren't a hallucination; how she'd love to see the two of them this buffaloed in real life! "But I guess we'd better get going. It's nearly time for me to warm up for the show, and nobody helps me do that better than this little gal."

He skimmed his hand down her blond hair again in a way that reminded her of a cowboy patting the mane of his favorite cutting horse. Since none of this was real, Erin decided not to get snippy about the proprietary caress. Then he lowered the arm that had been around her shoulder down to her waist, where she could have sworn she felt the imprint of each of his long fingers burning through her blouse, and began shepherding her away. Strangely comfortable in her dazed state, Erin followed obligingly.

"That was wonderful," she said with a long, heartfelt sigh.

"Yeah." He grinned down at her. "I thought so, too. Want to do it again?"

"Oh." He thought she was talking about the kiss. Color flooded into her cheeks, making them feel as if they were on fire. She would have been embarrassed at such a display of emotions—if this was real. Which, of course, it wasn't. "Actually, I was referring to the way you destroyed those two." She laughed. "Amanda reminded me of the Wicked Witch of the West after Dorothy poured water on her."

Jace wondered if she had any idea what effect her smiling eyes, her rich, vibrant laughter had on him, then decided she did. All women knew the power they held over men. He'd always found that to be a part of their many charms.

"'I'm melting. I'm melting,'" he said the famous movie line.

Erin's laughter drifted off. The faint cloud of confusion that he thought he'd seen in her eyes darkened with an unmistakable feminine desire. "Me, too," she admitted.

It was little more than a whisper, but despite the noise of chain saws, car engines and the calliope from the carousel across the midway, Jace had no problem hearing her.

"Well, that sure as heck makes two of us." He tangled a hand in her hair and imagined he could feel the flame of silk burning his palm. "What would you suggest we do about it?"

Shy by nature, Erin had never been one for public demonstrations. But as her eyes met his, then drifted slowly down to those impossibly full, outrageously sexy lips, she reminded herself yet again that this was only a dream—a glorious, sexy dream she could only hope she'd remember when she woke up from whatever sleep or coma she was in.

Her hand felt unnaturally heavy as she lifted it to his tanned cheek. The stubble of his beard felt like sandpaper against her palm. Since he was, after all, only a product of her imagination, Erin allowed herself to wonder what it would feel like against her bare breasts.

"Perhaps, you should kiss me again."

Jace smiled as he gathered her into his arms. "Now *that*," he agreed, "is a dandy suggestion."

CHAPTER FOUR

What the Heart Wants

THE MOMENT HE TOUCHED his mouth to hers, Jace forgot everything he'd ever known about finesse. Control deserted him, scorched away by a blast of heat, engulfed by hunger. During the time since he'd left the Kentucky hills, more than one woman had praised him for his skilled seduction techniques, his practiced touch that left them limp and shuddering, yet still eager for more.

In the early days, during his teenage years when he'd been playing the back-road honky-tonks, Jace had gained a reputation for bedding more than his share of women, most of them a great deal older than he. Never one to look back, Jace didn't regret those days of drinking, fighting and womanizing; his numerous bed-partners had taught him all the ways in which to please a woman, and in return, he'd treated them not like groupies, but like queens. After all, despite the superficiality of his relationship with these women, they deserved the best he could give. He felt the same way about his audience—they deserved to get their money's worth—both on the stage and in bed.

But then his star had begun to rise—not with the cometlike burst he'd fantasized about while strumming his used guitar on the front porch of his family's cabin back in the hills, but it was a constant, steady climb nevertheless. As he'd gained some recognition, Jace had come to the realization that while his music was still a challenge, sex had become too easy. He discovered what others in his seemingly enviable position had already learned: that it was difficult to value anything that was available in such abundance.

He'd already cut back on his drinking when the daily hangovers had made it too damn difficult to climb back into the band's bus and drive on to the next town. He gave up fighting after a broken hand had kept him from playing the guitar for eight weeks. Since in both instances his career had benefited, Jace had also been willing to sacrifice his numerous bed partners.

That had been two years ago, and during the intervening months, although he still indulged in a little slap and tickle while on the road, he'd cut back considerably. From time to time, when the hunger got too hot and the lady in question was equally averse to strings, Jace would take the tumble, then drive away in the morning, leaving them both well satisfied.

As a songwriter, Jace was used to distilling complex emotions into uncomplicated basics. And the simple truth was that he'd begun to leave the thinking to the logical part of his brain. It was safer and less problematic that way.

But now, as he felt this woman's avid, erotic lips open to the probing of his tongue, as the diamond-hard tips of her breasts pressed against his chest, as ragged little moans were escaping from somewhere deep inside her sweet, curvy little body, Jace flat-out forgot to think.

Oh, heavens! The moment his sulky, dangerous mouth claimed hers, Erin realized that she'd been wrong. Jace Honeycutt was definitely no hallucination. And this hot, fevered kiss couldn't possibly be the product of her imagination. It was all too real—and, she thought, as she twined her arms around his neck and clung, too glorious.

Tongues tangled, teeth scraped. His hands skimmed up and down her sides, leaving trails of fire while, unaware that she was making a public display of herself, Erin sank into the heated kiss. Her body arched against his, straining as if to take him in. All the way in.

"Good Lord, darlin'." When he was on the verge of dragging her off to the nearest bed—or even to the ground—and ravishing her, Jace realized that he was suddenly standing on the edge of a very dangerous and rocky precipice.

He'd wanted other women before, more than he could count. Other women had made him hot, caused him to burn. In fact, there had been a divorced cocktail waitress in Jackson Hole, Wyoming, who'd kept him in her bed for three days straight during a late-summer blizzard and had damn near killed him. At the time, Jace would have been hard-pressed to think of a better way to go.

But not even during those long snowy days and nights had he needed any woman like he needed Erin at this moment. No woman had ever made him tremble as he was doing now. And never, in all his twenty-six years, had any female—no matter how delectably sweet—ever had him on the verge of begging.

He buried his mouth in her fragrant hair and forced his hands, which he'd dragged back up to her waist, to put the rest of her a little away from him. "If we're not careful, we're going to either get ourselves kicked out of here or win a blue ribbon for the most public display of lovemaking at a county fair."

"I know." As she stared, bewildered, up at him, Jace watched desire and confusion war in her remarkably blue eyes. "I've never behaved that way in my entire life," she admitted breathlessly.

Innocence was written in bold script across her flushed face—the kind of face that inspired men like himself to pen love songs. Jace sensed that she was not anything like the other women he'd enjoyed dallying with over the years; told himself that if he were a gentleman, he'd pat her pretty pink cheek and send her on her way with a sexy memory she could someday share with her grand-children.

But no one had ever called Jace Honeycutt a gentleman. And when the little voice of his con-science reminded him that to take what she was offering would be unconscionable, Jace ignored it.

He ran the back of his hand in a slow, sensual sweep up her face. Though he would have thought it impossible, her eyes, the dazzling hue of the vast Arizona sky overhead, widened even more. When she unconsciously licked the succulent pink lips he could still taste, Jace had to bite back his groan.

"Should I apologize?" he asked.

"Oh, no." She dragged a trembling hand through her sleek slide of golden hair. "I liked it. A lot, actually," she said with a nervous little laugh.

"Me, too." He caught her hand on its second sweep through her hair. "And I'd like to spend some time doing a lot more of it. But it really is time for me to be warming up."

He lifted her hand and kissed her fingertips one by one. It was admittedly one of his practiced se-duction techniques, taught to him by a long-ago lover. But when the fingertips beneath his lips turned to flame, and Erin's body literally shud-dered, Jace felt the heat curl in his own loins and wondered which of them was being seduced.

"What would you say to spending some time

with me after the concert? I hear there's a rodeo dance we could try out." A high-pitched shriek of pleasure had him glancing toward a booth where a freckle-faced teenage boy had just won a purple toy poodle for his girlfriend by shooting some fake ducks. "And I used to be a pretty good shot, if you're in the market for a stuffed animal."

Although she'd never considered herself a risk taker, Erin was suddenly in the mood for any-thing—and everything—Jace Honeycutt might suggest.

"I'd like that," she agreed, the warmth in her voice and her eyes letting him know exactly how much.

"I CAN'T BELIEVE THIS!" RaeAnn said, as she stood at the edge of the stage, watching Jace's per-formance. "I flat-out cannot believe that little ole me actually met Alan Jackson face-to-face." She grinned over at Erin. "I owe you big time, girl-friend."

"Just remember," Jack all but growled in good-natured complaint as he pulled his wife close against him, "you'll be going home with me."

"Well, of course I will, darlin'." She reached around and squeezed her husband's jeans-clad rear end. "There was never any doubt about that. Why, as cute as he is, not even Alan can hold a candle to my sweetie."

They were at it again—billing and cooing like

lovebirds. But this time Erin barely noticed—because her attention was riveted on Jace Honeycutt.

Even if the taste of his kiss weren't still lingering on her lips, Erin knew that his deep, rich vocal style would have grabbed her by the heart and taken her right along for the ride. A glance around at the women in the audience revealed that they were no less besotted than she.

Although she knew that just listening to the radio didn't make her an expert on country music, Erin did have the impression that Jace seemed to have figured out what a lot of other singers hadn't—that along with hard work and a great song, the best road to success was being comfortable with who you were; not trying to copy someone else. Unlike so many other popular country stars, he stayed away from the more contemporary styles, selecting instead a down-home, genuine sound that sparkled with bluegrass roots.

In fact, he set the crowd to roaring its approval when, right before a particular song about his beloved mountain home, he ripped open his black leather vest and revealed the message printed on the black T-shirt beneath: Twang Is Good.

Jace was a big man, and his deep voice reflected that. As he sang his way through a mix of songs that ranged from weepy, tearjerker ballads to lighter ditties that set boots to scootin' in the standing-room-only audience, there were times when his voice resonated so powerfully it nearly drowned out the fiddle players and steel-guitar licks.

He might currently be singing warm-up, but judging by the way he held the crowd in the palm of his wide hand from the first somebody-done-somebody-wrong song, Erin knew she was watching a man on the verge of superstardom. At any other time, even the idea that such a man would be remotely interested in her would have sent her running in the opposite direction.

Jace Honeycutt was too bold, too confident, too male. But, as she listened to him sustain his last note in a way that had her and every other audience member holding their collective breath, Erin realized that if there had ever been a time to throw caution to the wind, this was it.

She knew Jace was on the move. There was no way he'd suddenly decide to give up chasing his dream for a woman whose roots went so deep into the rocky soil of this high mountain country that she couldn't have pulled them out, even if she'd wanted to.

Though Erin hadn't been about to admit it to RaeAnn earlier this afternoon, she'd worn herself to a frazzle with work and worry these past months since her father had first become ill. She deserved to kick up her heels just once.

When the crowd rose to its feet to applaud Jace's performance, Erin watched in amazement as a pair of lacy pink panties went flying through the air, landing on the stage at his feet. He looked down at the panties, then grinned.

"Well, now," he drawled deeply into the microphone, "since I have the feelin' that those were originally meant for Alan, I'm honored." Erin decided that Jace's wicked male grin was undoubtedly strumming more than a few internal female chords in the audience. It certainly was affecting her. "And I'll be sure to pass them along to the boss man." He bent, scooped up the scrap of lingerie, and walked off the stage to laughter and a thunderous roar of applause.

As he approached, Erin watched him toss the panties uncaringly toward one of the stagehands and wondered if he would have been so dismissive of the obvious female invitation if he hadn't already had her waiting in the wings.

The thought that he might consider her little more than another sex-crazed groupie, like the "buckle bunnies" who followed the rodeo stars, was not a pleasant one. So, as he took hold of her hand, lacing his fingers with hers in an easy, familiar way, Erin decided, with an uncharacteristic lack of regard for the consequences of her actions, to just not think about it.

CHAPTER FIVE

Angel Flying Too Close to the Ground

ERIN FELT LIKE A teenager on a first date as she strolled the midway hand in hand with Jace. As he'd promised, he won not just one, but an armful of stuffed animals at the shooting gallery, drawing a crowd of admiring spectators while doing so. Knowing that her memories of this special night would be all the souvenir she'd ever need, Erin gave the plush toys away to children who'd gathered with their parents to watch Jace shoot.

"It wasn't that hard," he said as they continued along the midway and joined the line to buy tickets for the Ferris wheel. "Back home, most boys get their first rifle by the time they're nine."

"Where's home?"

"Kentucky." Jace dug into his jeans, pulled out some bills, handed them through the little window in the booth, and then, as if on reconsideration, shoved a fistful more through. "Little place called Honeycutt Gap... I hope you like Ferris wheels," he said when he saw her staring in disbelief at the long string of tickets he'd bought.

"Who doesn't?" She didn't need to be told that he'd bought so many tickets to give them some time alone together, away from the crowds. Far, far away, she thought, as she looked up at the double Ferris wheel that was lit like a Christmas tree. Erin decided that this was probably not the time to mention her fear of heights. "It must make you proud, having a town named after your family."

He threw back his head and laughed as they advanced in line. "Honey, the only reason the place was named after us was because we were the only family in the state fool enough to settle there." His dark eyes danced with self-directed humor. "My granddaddy Honeycutt was a sharecropper, but the land in that hollow was so darn stingy about giving up crops, his share didn't amount to more than a hill of beans." His chuckle was deep and reminiscent. "Lucky we all liked beans."

The Ferris wheel came to a stop in front of them. Jace handed the tickets to the worker who unlocked the bar. The kid looked at the long string of tickets, then at Erin, and winked at Jace.

"Have fun," he drawled as he fastened the steel bar down after they'd settled into the seat.

With a grinding of gears that tweaked more than one of Erin's acrophobic nerves, the wheel began its slow ascent.

"There's something I've been meaning to ask you," she said, trying to keep her mind off the fact that they were moving higher and higher.

"Shoot."

"Why did you do that? Kiss me and pretend you were my boyfriend."

"Well, for starters, it should be obvious why I kissed you." He tugged playfully on the ends of her hair. "You're a gorgeous, sexy woman and I was attracted to you right off the bat."

"So, do you kiss every woman you're attracted to?"

"No. Just the gorgeous blond cowgirls who make the mistake of getting hooked up with...uh, jerks."

From his pause, she suspected "jerks" was not his first choice of descriptive term. "Was it that obvious? That he'd dumped me for Amanda?"

"Probably not, to most folks. But I'd been watching you anyway, and overheard the conversation. It didn't take a rocket scientist to figure out that the girl who looked as if she'd stuck a wet finger into a light socket was trying to yank your chain. So, having watched my sisters suffer through a few similar occasions, I decided to do what I could to turn the tables a bit."

"Well, you certainly did that." She was feeling pretty happy—until she made the fatal mistake of glancing down.

"Are you cold?" he asked when he felt her slight tremor.

"No."

"But you're shivering."

"Really, I'm fine," she insisted in a shaky voice that said otherwise. They were going up backwards and the Ferris wheel had picked up speed. The people on the ground began to look like toy action figures. As she fought the all-too-familiar vertigo, Erin felt beads of perspiration popping up beneath her bangs. "Really," she said again, when she realized that Jace was looking at her, hard and deep.

"Aw, hell." He took her clammy hands in both of his and began massaging warmth back into them. "You should have told me you were afraid of heights."

"You didn't ask. Besides, I really wanted to do this."

"Yeah. Like a guy who can't swim wants to go scuba diving with killer sharks." Her hands now temporarily warmed to his satisfaction, Jace slipped his fingers beneath her hair and cupped the back of her neck. "As it happens, my mama's afraid of heights."

"Oh?" They were headed back down at a speed that seemed anything but prudent. Having already been found out, Erin no longer attempted to hide her affliction. Instead, she closed her eyes tight and prayed they'd reach solid ground without the bolts giving way.

"Since Mama had never been out of Honeycutt Gap, they never knew it until one time when my daddy got voted union foreman and they took a trip to Hazard—that's a little town not far away—

for a meeting. Well, there was a fair going on there—a lot like this one, I suppose—and since neither of them had ever been on a Ferris wheel, they decided to give it a try. And that's when they discovered Mama's fear of high places.''

The car jerked to a stop. *Oh, Lord,* Erin prayed silently, *please, please, don't let us get stuck up here.*

''They're just letting another couple on,'' Jace assured her, drawing her a little closer and pressing a soothing kiss against her temple. ''We'll be back on solid ground pretty soon, if you want off.''

''In a way, I do,'' she murmured. Then she opened her eyes. ''And, in another way, I don't.''

He smiled at that—a slow, pleased smile that made her think that risking her life this way might just be worth it, after all. ''We could try my daddy's remedy,'' he suggested. ''To help you make up your mind.''

''Your daddy had a remedy for acrophobia?''

''Well, I wouldn't want to call it a miracle cure or anything. But he always swore it worked like a charm on Mama.''

''Since you put it that way,'' she said, assuring herself that it was the altitude that had her voice suddenly sounding so breathless, ''how can I not give it a try?''

''I knew you had spunk.'' Jace skimmed the back of his free hand up her cheek. ''Now, the first thing you have to do is shut out everything around you and look straight into my eyes.''

Well, that was certainly no hardship. Erin's breathing turned even more shallow as she felt herself being pulled into the warmth of those chocolate eyes.

''What next?''

Jace cupped her chin in his fingers, holding her gaze to his. ''Now, think of anything besides where you are.''

''All right.'' Erin thought how unfair it was that a man should have been blessed with such long, thick dark eyelashes. Figuring that his ego already had to be over the moon, she kept her thoughts to herself.

''Terrific.'' His fingers tightened ever so slightly on her jaw. ''All right... Now, here's where it gets a little tricky.'' His thumb toyed with her lips, coaxing them just the slightest bit apart. ''Whatever you do—whatever *I* do—just keep your eyes on mine. Don't close them. And don't pull away.'' He brushed a light caress in the hollow between her parted lips and chin. ''Okay?''

''Okay.'' She'd no sooner gotten the word out when her mouth was captured by his. His right hand was still gently cupping her chin and his left was tangled in her hair, holding her to the slow, devastating kiss. Adrift in rising pleasure, Erin dropped her head back against his arm and allowed her eyes to slowly drift shut.

"You're forgetting the rules." His lips skimmed up her face. "You're supposed to keep your eyes open. I don't think it'll work if we don't do it the prescribed way." His mouth returned to hers and she could feel it curve into a smile. "Come on, darlin'," he coaxed in that same deep baritone voice he'd used onstage—the voice that had excited every woman in the arena. "Let me see your gorgeous blue eyes."

Unable to resist, Erin slowly forced her eyes open. Everything around her—the bright red, white and blue lights of the midway, the silver moon rising in the sky, even his handsome face—all were the slightest bit blurry, as if she were viewing them through a soft-focus lens.

Jace rewarded her with another heart-stealing smile. "That's my girl." With his eyes still on hers, he framed her face between his palms and kissed her. With her eyes drowning in his, Erin kissed him back.

"Wonderful." Rather than hear his words, Erin felt them against her mouth, sizzling through her like sparklers. "You are, Erin, absolutely amazing."

As her entire universe became focused on his sweet ravishing of her mouth and his mesmerizing dark eyes, Erin believed him. Never, in her entire life, had any man kissed her the way Jace Honeycutt was kissing her. It crossed her mind that if the gently swinging seat they were riding back up to the top of the double wheel did come off its moorings and fall crashing to the ground, she'd die a happy woman.

"I told you," he said finally.

It could have been minutes, hours, a lifetime. But the dazzling, mind-stealing kiss finally ended. "Told me what?" she asked dazedly.

"That you can't beat those old folk remedies." He trailed a fingertip around her love-swollen lips. "We've gone all the way around two more times. And you never even noticed."

Amazingly, although he'd relinquished her mouth, Erin could still feel him—taste him—on her lips. "If your daddy had been able to bottle that kiss therapy, he would have made a fortune," she said.

"Probably, back in his time. But things are a lot different these days. The government insists on lots and lots of tests before taking a cure to market." As if unwilling to abandon her mouth quite yet, he brushed his lips lightly against hers.

"Since it would be for a good cause—curing a phobia and all—I suppose I could work on the research with you," she suggested.

"That'd certainly be generous of you, volunteering your time and your lips like that." He was playing with her hair, draping it over his hand, letting the pale silk strands sift through his fingers like sand. "I wonder how many tests it'll take before we begin raking in the money."

"I don't know." Her own hand seemed inordinately heavy as she lifted it to his cheek. "But I'd guess bunches and bunches."

"Well, now." He caught hold of her wrist, turned it and pressed his clever, seductive lips against the sensitive skin of her palm, his tongue igniting flames along what The Magnificent Maya had proclaimed to be her generous heart line. "It's a good thing I bought all those tickets."

She laughed. "A very good thing," she agreed as she lifted her mouth to his again.

It was the last either of them was to say for a very long time.

CHAPTER SIX

Time Marches On

"I NEVER REALIZED THAT scientific research could make a guy so hungry," Jace said as they left the Ferris wheel after using up the last of their tickets. "What would you say to a little barbecue?"

"I think that sounds wonderful." Anything to prolong the evening, Erin thought.

"Want to drop in and see The Alligator Man?" he asked as they passed the green-and-white-striped tent.

"I think I could probably survive without seeing that particular attraction," Erin replied.

"Your choice. And probably a wise one, since the guy undoubtedly wouldn't be worth the price of the ticket." His grin set his eyes to dancing again. "When I was about six, I went to a fair—the same one in Hazard where my daddy discovered his cure—with a bunch of cousins. My cousin Eldon—he was six years older than me—bought tickets for all of us to see The Tattooed Lady and her husband, The Alligator Man."

"That would certainly be a high point for me," Erin said dryly.

"Hey, entertainment bein' what it was in that part of the country, it worked for us." His grin widened. "Anyway, there were two red velvet curtains, and when the first one went up, The Tattooed Lady was standing there in a two-piece bathing suit, with the tattoo of a snake twined all around her."

"She sounds delightful," Erin commented.

"It got even better, because after she done her gig, the other curtain went up. And there, in this tank of water, wearing what appeared to be a wet suit covered with cornflakes sprayed with glittery green paint, was Lyle Honeycutt, my second cousin on my daddy's side."

"You're kidding!"

"My hand to God." Jace lifted his right hand in a pledge. "Lord, he was truly a sight to behold. My cousin Lurleen—she was five at the time—and I thought that was the absolutely neatest thing ever. We kept calling out to Lyle, and waving to beat the band. But the poor guy just kept swimming around in circles, faster and faster, as if he was trying to get away from us. Finally, some huge guy I now realize was a bouncer kicked us out before we blew the gig."

"What happened to Lyle?"

"Oh, he left with the carnival the next morning and traveled around the country with them for a few years. And, to prove that life really is stranger than fiction, he ended up actually marrying The Tattooed Lady for real. These days they run a nice little feed store back in Hazard with their three kids, none of whom have tattoos or green scales—as far as I can tell, anyway.''

Erin laughed again, feeling wonderfully carefree for the first time in months.

There was a meal being served up on paper plates from a large red-and-white-striped tent called The Barbecue Pit. Clouds of blue haze from the smoker filled the air with the mouthwatering aroma of cooking meat.

''This is nearly as good as my uncle Vernon's,'' Jace said as they worked their way through an enormous platter of barbecued ribs, crunchy green slaw and honey-baked beans.

Erin prepared herself for another story. ''Is he from Honeycutt Gap, too?''

''He lived nearby over a ridge or two, with his wife Mary Beth and her people, in Nesbitt Hollow. But they were still close enough to be hollerin' neighbors. He was my daddy's older brother.''

'' 'Was'?''

''He died when I was about fifteen.''

''I'm sorry.''

Jace shrugged his shoulders. ''Dying young's a way of life in the hills. That's also why my mama and daddy were determined that I get out.''

''Well, you've certainly succeeded there.'' Erin

glanced up at the lighted marquee that was visible from The Barbecue Pit.

"I'm getting there," he agreed, thinking that one of these days they'd spell his name right. "But I've still a long ways to go."

"You'll make it."

He smiled at the force of her assertion. "You sound awfully sure of that. You wouldn't happen to have a second or third cousin in the music business, would you?"

"No. But you're a wonderful musician, Jace."

"So are a lot of guys who don't get much further than singin' in the shower," he reminded her. "Or playing the lounge at their local Holiday Inn." Jace figured he'd rather go back to his previous job of waiting tables, or the one before that—sitting in the audience of a Nashville strip joint, catching the girls' costumes over the heads of customers to save on overhead.

"I suppose you have a point." Erin admittedly didn't know anything about Jace's line of work, but she suspected that along with talent, a great deal of timing and luck was involved. In that respect, she decided, the music business sounded a bit like ranching.

Her first thought was that, along with a fondness for family, it was another thing she and Jace had in common. Her second thought was that she was better off not thinking the first thought. There wasn't any future in it for her. Jace's life—and *his* future—was certainly not here in Whiskey River.

Since she didn't want to contemplate the idea of him leaving in the morning, she picked up the conversation where she'd left it. "I watched that audience. You had them eating out of the palm of your hand. And not just the women, but the men, too."

He had, and it had felt damn good. But not wanting to sound conceited, Jace merely laughed and said, "Lord, lady, you're good for the ego. Perhaps you ought to just come on the road with me."

Having watched the romantic messes so many singers got themselves tangled up in while on tour, Jace had always stuck to fun-loving ladies who knew the score. He'd never uttered that dangerous suggestion to any other woman, and he was stunned to hear it coming out of his mouth right now. And even more amazing was how right it sounded.

Erin was surprised to hear Jace's suggestion, to say the least. He couldn't mean it, she thought. Not really. It was probably what he said to all the girls he wanted to spend a stolen night with.

A vaguely uncomfortable silence settled over the table.

"So," Erin said, grasping for something, anything to talk about rather than what would happen tomorrow when Jace inevitably moved on, "was your father a sharecropper, too?"

"No. He never could have made a decent living that way. Not with nearly a dozen kids to feed."

"A dozen?"

"Technically, there were ten. We didn't get cable TV in the hills," he reminded her, "which meant people had to create their own diversions."

"Well—" she toyed with her plastic utensils "—that's still quite a large family."

"Honeycutts have always believed in big families. You should see our reunions."

"I can imagine." She couldn't help wondering if Jace planned to follow in his father's procreative footsteps. "Has anyone ever asked the Honeycutt women how they feel about such large families?"

"I imagine so. After all, they sure don't marry the Honeycutt men for their talent for making money. We've always prided ourselves on other, more personal attributes."

Judging from the twinkle in his eyes, Erin had a pretty good idea where this was going. "Like kissing," she guessed.

Jace wiped his hands on the stack of paper napkins, tipped his hat back with his thumb and grinned at her from beneath the black brim. "Among other things."

And she could well imagine what other things, Erin realized, as her flesh warmed and her head went light.

"Daddy was a coal miner," Jace said, answering her earlier question. "We were about as hard-

scrabble poor as people can be, but for some reason—perhaps because everyone around us was in
the same circumstances—we never noticed the
lack of money all that much. And, we may have
slept three to a bed, but so did all the other kids
we knew.'' He smiled back at the memory of how
one kid's nightmare was all it took to land the rest
of them on the floor. ''My dad always said we had
three rooms and running water. If you wanted to
run and get it, that is.''

Erin smiled at that, even though she couldn't
imagine living such a hand-to-mouth existence.
She might live a great distance from a city, and
there wasn't all that much money in ranching, but
the sprawling Montgomery house that had been
added on to over the years was warm and cozy and
she'd never lacked for basic amenities. ''What
about your mother? I assume she stayed home and
took care of all the little Honeycutts.''

''She might have wanted to, but it was a luxury
she couldn't afford. Mama cleaned the bathrooms
of the rich ladies whose husbands owned the
mines. She also took in ironing.'' She'd done it
late at night by lantern light and there were still
times when, right before he fell asleep, Jace could
recall the scent of the blue starch she used so
clearly it was almost as if he were back in the little
tin-roofed cabin where he'd been born. And where
his father had been born, and *his* father before him.

"Amazing. To think of her working so hard with all those children to tend to," Erin murmured. And she'd always considered the sunup-to-sundown ranching work to be tough. "How on earth did she manage?"

"I'm not sure. To tell the truth, I wasn't paying a whole lot of attention at the time." He thought back to how, whenever he could sneak away, he'd find himself a stump somewhere in the woods, where he could write and sing his songs to the squirrels and cardinals. "But she's Scots-Irish, stubborn as all get-out and, like the rest of her people, she's never been one to back away from a challenge. As for the kids, it's not quite as hard as it sounds, since the big kids can look after the young uns."

"Spoken like a man who never raised ten children," Erin said dryly.

"Good point," he allowed with one of those quick, boyish grins that made her heart leap.

"My parents were hardworking, salt-of-the-earth people who created an even dozen sons and daughters and buried two as young children," he revealed. As a rule, Jace didn't talk about his family much. Not because he was ashamed of them, but because usually, when he was with a woman, he stuck to pretty words designed to flatter. And seduce. But for some reason he couldn't quite figure out, he wanted to tell this woman about where he'd come from, and who he was.

"When I was growing up, Sunday mornings were spent in church, giving thanks for what little we had. Sunday evenings we'd all gather on the porch after supper and play our music."

"Where do you fit in the birth order?"

"Pretty much smack in the middle."

"Which would have made it more difficult to get attention. I suppose that might have something to do with your decision to become a performer."

"Yeah, the same thought's occurred to me." He smiled over warm memories of his childhood. It had been hard to know how poor you were when you were surrounded by so much love. "My folks couldn't really understand my burning desire to take my music beyond our world, but I've got to give them credit for humoring me when I stuck that old empty tin can on top of a carved stick and pretended it was a microphone."

Erin laughed at that idea and remembered pretending she was Annie Oakley.

"They also shared the tightfistedness that's the hallmark of hill people. I can't remember Mama ever owning a pretty bottle of perfume or a flow-ered hat. And my daddy's single extravagance was the can of Copenhagen he hoarded as if it were the Honeycutt crown jewels. Yet, after I graduated from high school and told them that I was headed off to sing myself onto the stage of the Grand Ole Opry, Daddy got out the Old Masters cigar box where he'd kept our rainy-day money, took the bus into Hazard and returned home with a used red double-cutaway Gibson electric guitar.''

"Just remember where you come from, boy," Carl Honeycutt had said gruffly as he'd shoved the guitar toward his son. Jace's father had always been uncomfortable with words and outward displays of affection. Yet, even as young and foolish as he'd been then, Jace had understood that no flowery words penned by any poet could have been underscored with more paternal love.

"That's a wonderful story," Erin murmured. "Even better than the one about Lyle, the alligator man. But surely they must have worried about you, going out on your own at such a young age." If she was ever fortunate enough to have a son, she'd certainly worry when the time came for him to seek his own way in the world. Of course, she hoped that any child of hers would want to do the same thing she had—settle down on the Flying M Ranch just as the four preceding generations of Montgomerys had done.

"Mama fought back a few tears." The memory still stunned him as it had that long-ago day. He'd never seen his mother cry. Not even when burying her babies. "Then she straightened the collar on my single white dress shirt—the same collar she'd starched so stiff the night before that I was afraid it'd cut my head right off my neck before the bus made it out of Kentucky.''

He ran a finger around the neck of his black T-shirt in a way that suggested he could still feel the starch. "Then she told me, in the way only a mama can, that I wasn't to be doing any drinkin', swearin', or foolin' around with fast women.''

"I suspect she may have been a bit late with that instruction.''

"You just might suspect right,'' he agreed with another one of those heart-melting smiles that seemed to come so naturally.

Erin wondered what had made his mother think this man could avoid romantic affairs. He was a walking, talking, singing, flirting female magnet. She also suspected that if Jace's father was anything like his sexy son, Mrs. Honeycutt had probably known very well the futility of her advice.

"I haven't been able to keep all my promises to my mother,'' Jace admitted. Hell, the truth was, he hadn't kept any, but not for lack of trying. "But I *have* done my best not to besmirch the Honeycutt name.''

"You've done much more than that. You've actually put it up in lights, Jace. Your family must be so proud.''

"Not long after I left home, Daddy died of the black lung from all those years working underground in the mines. But he lived long enough to hear the demo tape I sent him—the one cut while I was waiting tables days and singing nights at a joint just outside Nashville.''

Rachel Honeycutt had reported back during Jace's monthly phone call home that his father had proclaimed it ''Right fine.'' Which, Jace had known, was high praise indeed coming from the taciturn man.

Jace was distracted from his reminiscing by music drifting from the barn where the rodeo dance was being held. And as much as he was enjoying talking with Erin—just being with her—Jace decided the time had come to move things to the next stage.

''You know what I'd like to do now?''

''What?'' From the wicked gleam in his eyes, Erin had a very good idea. It was probably the same dangerous idea she'd been considering since that stunning, heart-stealing moment when he'd kissed her in front of Ryan and Amanda. No, even before then—from the instant their eyes had met through the windshield of her truck, and her reckless heart had taken a tumble.

''I want to dance with you.''

Actually, what he really wanted was to hold her in his arms. And that was just the beginning. But even with the night wearing on, Jace was enjoying himself too much to rush things. If all they were ever going to have together was memories, then he damn well wanted to make certain they were good ones.

Once again, Erin didn't hesitate. "That sounds wonderful."

CHAPTER SEVEN

This Night Can't Last Forever

HEAVEN. THAT WAS WHAT it was. As she swayed in Jace's arms, her fingers linked together behind his neck, all Erin could think about was how perfect it felt to be with this man in this way. The light touch of his hand on her back seemed to be burning through her blouse. The feel of his denim-clad hips brushing against hers as they moved slowly to a John Michael Montgomery song made her blood hum in her veins.

Even the sight of Ryan and Amanda couldn't puncture her bubble of pleasure. Indeed, as she watched them dancing together, with Amanda doing the leading, Erin wondered what she'd thought she'd ever seen in Ryan.

The pitiful truth was that it had been a long time since she'd been involved with anyone. And during the period when her father had been getting sicker and sicker, after a rough day at the hospital she'd been willing to settle for anyone's arms. Even if they'd been the wrong arms.

"That guy's not bad," Jace said, nodding his

head toward the hat-wearing cowboy singer who'd moved on to George Strait's "Round About Way." "But he's not Alan. Are you sure you didn't want to stay for the rest of the concert?"

When he brushed his lips against her hair, the faint stir of his breath against her temple felt like butterfly wings. She smiled up at him. "I can hear Alan Jackson on the radio any old time." Her fingers played with the sexy little chestnut curls at the nape of his neck. "But it's not every day I get a chance to spend time with the man who's going to set the country-music world on fire."

He laughed at that—a rich, bold sound that started low in his chest and vibrated against hers. "From your sweet lips to God's ears." When he leaned down and took a light nip at one of *her* ears, it was all Erin could do not to swoon right there on the spot.

"It'll happen," she insisted.

"Now you sound just like my mama. She's absolutely positive that I'm going to be even hotter than Waylon or Willie."

The warmth in Jace's baritone voice whenever he mentioned his mother told Erin a lot about him. She'd heard it said that if you wanted to know how a man would treat the woman in his life, you should check out how he treated his mother.

Not that she was really the woman in Jace Honeycutt's life, she reminded her foolish romantic heart. Just the woman for tonight. That thought had her feeling both anticipation and a touch of sadness at the same time.

"Well, I, for one, think you ought to listen to your mama because she sounds like a very wise woman."

"She's the best," he agreed easily as he skimmed a hand down her back to just below her waist and drew her even closer.

Erin watched an elderly couple dance together— the smooth way they moved as one, attesting to many decades of rodeo dances in each other's arms. Although they might not be dancing as close as Erin and Jace, the warm, wonderful way the man was looking down at the woman, and the loving smile she gave back to him, caused Erin's heart to clench just a little. That was what she wanted. The "forever after" kind of love that would have her husband still loving her—and wanting her— after a lifetime together.

The way Jace was nuzzling at her neck distracted her from her thoughts, and had her vibrating inside like a tuning fork. The male scent of him—warm skin and leather—stimulated her senses. As he pressed her against him, the feel of his arousal started her pulse to hum.

"What would you say to getting ourselves a breath of fresh air?" Jace's voice sounded as ragged as a bald tire running on a pitted gravel road— which was more than she could say for herself. Erin wasn't sure she could even speak at all.

"Clear our heads," he added. The hard-edged masculine intensity in his eyes had her foolish heart fluttering like a wild bird in her breast. "I don't know about yours, but my blood could use a little cooling down right about now."

Reveling in the glorious, fuzzy warm feeling, Erin wasn't all that eager to clear her head. As for cooling her blood… Why on earth would she want to do that when it felt so delicious just the way it was? Hot and thick, like warm honey.

Erin was trying to come up with an answer when the romantic ballad came to an end and the band suddenly launched into a rollicking version of "That's My Story," with the lead singer coaxing dancers to line up to do The Cadillac Ranch Romp.

The sensual mood was shattered. But watching the frustration rise in his dark eyes—a frustration that equaled her own—Erin knew that the night was far from over.

"Real cowboys don't line-dance." They said it together, as if their minds, having been linked together in those erotic thoughts, were still in sync. They laughed, just a little. But their moods didn't lighten.

The long fingers that had created such hot licks on his guitar strings earlier, linked with hers again. Erin offered not a single objection as Jace led her off the dance floor and out of the big red barn.

"I want to be alone with you. Somewhere quiet," he said as they returned to the crowded midway that was anything but quiet, "and private, where we can talk."

Erin suspected it wasn't talking Jace was interested in. But then again, if she were to be perfectly honest, neither was she. A little voice in the far reaches of her mind tried to counsel caution, attempted to point out that for all their talking, this man was still a stranger—a stranger whose life was already worlds away from hers. All they had in common was unbridled lust. But for the life of her, Erin couldn't see why that was so bad.

She mentally ran through a list of places in town where they might be allowed a modicum of privacy. Unfortunately, she couldn't come up with a single one. The Denim and Diamonds was definitely out; on a Saturday night the restaurant and Western dance club would undoubtedly be more crowded than the fair.

The only other restaurant in Whiskey River was The Branding Iron Café, and although its owner, Iris Johnson, was a nice enough woman, she couldn't exactly be counted on to keep a secret. In a community the size of Whiskey River, gossip was the coin of the realm, and since everyone eventually showed up at The Branding Iron, Iris had taken it upon herself to be the unofficial town crier.

"I know a quiet place out by the river," Erin suggested. "I go there whenever I want to be alone. I like to think of it as my own secret dreaming place." She'd never taken anyone there, not even RaeAnn. Even so, Erin didn't find it at all strange that she'd be offering to share it with Jace now.

His slow, pleased smile hinted of sensual pleasures yet to come. "Sounds great."

Since he'd arrived in Whiskey River on the band's bus, there was no choice but to take Erin's truck. And since she knew the way, they also agreed that she'd drive.

Although she climbed in and out of the cab every day of the week without any trouble, Erin enjoyed the way he lifted her up onto the bench seat as if she weighed no more than a pillowcaseful of feathers.

She used the moment it took him to walk around the front of the truck to attempt to collect her scattered senses. But it wasn't any use—because if her behavior thus far tonight was any indication, she'd already lost her mind the first time Jace had kissed her.

A light laugh escaped her lips as he climbed up beside her. He paused in the act of putting on his seat belt. "Something funny?"

"I was just thinking that I never realized insanity could be so much fun."

"Neither did I—until tonight. And it must be contagious, sweetheart, because I've definitely gone plumb crazy." With his eyes on hers, he lightly traced the shape of her mouth with a fingertip. "Crazy about you." When her lips parted ever so slightly beneath his gentle caress, he bent his head and kissed her—a slow, lazy mating of lips that caused her temperature to spike, like a fever in her blood.

Twining her hands around his neck, Erin sank into the glorious kiss that filled her mouth with his taste and promised more. So much more.

She was so sweet. Like fruit that had been left to ripen beneath a benevolent summer sun. Because he wanted her badly enough to take her in one greedy gulp, Jace resisted the urge to press her down onto the seat and ravish her in a wild whirlwind of passion.

"You realize, don't you, that you've got me about as hot and out of control as some hormone-driven eighteen-year-old?"

"And here I thought you'd already dedicated yourself to your music when you were eighteen."

Her teasing tone made him laugh. "I might have been dedicated, darlin', but I was aiming for the Grand Ole Opry, not the monastery. If celibacy had been part of the deal, I'd still be strumming that old red guitar on my porch back in Honeycutt Gap."

Erin didn't want to think about how many women he'd slept with since he'd left home. The fact that she hated every one of them was disconcerting enough.

"But you're different." He took hold of her

hand and laced their fingers together. "Tonight's different."

Erin felt exactly the same way. And, although she suspected RaeAnn would call her a fool, she decided to believe him.

She started the truck and pulled out of the parking lot. And while she had not a single qualm about what she was about to do, Erin's nerves tangled into a jumble, creating a sudden need to fill the silence between them.

The words tumbled out of her mouth as she told him all about the Flying M Ranch; how it had been in her family for so many generations, and how it would continue to be a family business when she eventually took it over. She left out the part about her father's illness because she didn't want his sympathy—or worse yet, his pity—to intrude on this magical night.

Nor did she tell him about how she'd had to drop out of Northern Arizona University to come home and take care of her ailing father. Needless to say, her plans for a veterinary career had gone straight down the drain, right along with her college degree.

Erin didn't want to dwell on negatives tonight. Tonight was a once-in-a-lifetime gift, and she was going to take it, enjoy it, be thankful for it, and not make the mistake of asking for more.

"Nice little town," Jace said as they drove down the darkened main street.

"We like it." That was an understatement. Erin couldn't imagine living anywhere else. And she certainly couldn't imagine living the nomadic existence that Jace had chosen for himself.

"How many people live here?"

"About 350, including those scattered about on the ranches." They were passing The Branding Iron. When it looked as if every booth was filled, Erin knew she'd made the right decision not to take Jace there. "But we get a lot of tourists in the summer—city folk from Tucson and Phoenix escaping the desert heat."

"The place looks vaguely familiar."

"That's probably because Hollywood films a lot of movies here. Clint Eastwood, John Wayne, Gene Autry and Kevin Costner have all ridden down this very street," she told him with no small measure of civic pride. "So did Doc Holliday and Wyatt Earp. There are even rumors that the Sundance Kid hid out here for a time on his way back to Hole-in-the-Wall from South America. But for some reason no one's ever quite figured out, the make-believe movie cowboys have a bigger display in the historical museum."

He laughed at that. "A sign of the times, I suppose."

"I suppose so." She sighed and wondered how hopelessly old-fashioned she must appear to Jace. Granted, from what he'd told her, he'd grown up in a place even more rustic and remote than Whiskey River. But there was a polish to him, a veneer of self-confidence that revealed he'd left Honeycutt Gap, Kentucky, far behind.

"It must be exciting," she said, "traveling all around like you do."

"It was in the beginning. And when I'm on-stage, and the audience is in the groove with me, it's gotta be the best feeling in the world." He glanced at her, his dark eyes skimming over her from the top of her head down to the pointed toes of her teal-colored dress boots. "Make that *one* of the best."

His smile was a wicked, sexy slash of white, and the way his fingers, which were resting on her denim-clad thigh, tightened ever so slightly, Erin had not a single doubt as to what Jace would consider the *very* best feeling to be. "But I can't deny that the actual moving from city to city can get old pretty fast. We're finishing up a tour of forty states and tomorrow we'll hit forty-one when we play a gig at the bull-riding finals in Las Vegas. Then L.A. Then it's off to Europe for two months."

"That's a long time to be away from home," she murmured.

"It's toughest on the married guys, especially the ones with kids."

"I can imagine." Erin tried to remember a time when her father hadn't been there for her, and she came up blank.

Watching her, Jace knew this sweet woman was

different from the ones he met on the tour—country-music groupies who considered a roll in the hay a souvenir, like a T-shirt or a program. Because he damn well didn't want a fine lady like Erin to start smelling orange blossoms, Jace decided the time had come to be brutally honest. Then, if she changed her mind, he'd just have her drive him back to the bus. No harm done.

"That's why I've made the decision not to get married until I'm famous enough that I can cut back on the touring and concentrate on family, because my daddy always told me that whatever a man chooses to do in life, his family should come first."

Erin's own father had told her much the same thing. "I think that's probably wise."

Her easy tone told him that she was okay with that. Though she seemed awfully innocent, Jace decided that if she was still willing to play the game now that she knew the rules, he wasn't going to say another thing to change her mind.

Her female scent—of soap, powder, cologne and a shampoo that had her pale hair smelling like strawberries—seemed to bloom in the close interior of the truck cab. The dashboard clock glowed in the surrounding darkness, reminding him that the bus would be leaving in a few hours. And while the other guys had lost track of time in a friendly bar or friendlier bed before, Jace had never failed to be onboard when the band hit the road again.

Those who didn't make it on time were required
to put a hefty fine into an old pickle jar, the pro-
ceeds going to pay for a blowout party at the end
of the tour.

Las Vegas wasn't all that far away, Jace decided,
as Erin turned off the highway onto an unmarked
National Forest Service road. He could enjoy tonight, enjoy her, then catch a ride on the Greyhound out of Whiskey River in the morning and
still make tomorrow night's gig with plenty of time
to spare.

Just the anticipation of making love to this
sweet-smelling cowgirl caused an erotic swelling
in Jace's loins. Oh yeah, he told himself. Tonight
was going to be more than worth whatever he'd
end up putting into that jar.

CHAPTER EIGHT

If Tomorrow Never Comes

HER NERVOUS CONVERSATION finally ran down, like a seven-day clock on the eighth day. But by the time Erin parked the truck along the bank of Whiskey River and cut the engine, the surrounding silence had her even more anxious.

She twisted the key again and turned on the radio—at first, welcoming the familiar country sound of K-COLT, until she realized that every single tune was a love song. It was almost as if the middle-of-the-night deejay sitting alone in a studio somewhere knew exactly what she was planning to do.

Not that tonight was about love, Erin reminded herself firmly. Only a foolish, overly romantic woman would believe in love at first sight. And having been brought up to be a practical, pragmatic rancher, Erin thought of herself as neither.

His fingers, which had been playing idly in her hair, cupped her neck; in response, hers tightened on the steering wheel. When she turned her head and saw the hot, hungry way Jace was looking at her, she realized for the first time in her life that she was, indeed, an overly romantic woman. Erin had never considered herself a greedy person. Yet, heaven help her, she was suddenly wanting more than just this one stolen night with Jace. As impossible as it was, she wanted a lifetime.

"You're awfully quiet all of a sudden." His deep, rich voice enveloped her, filled her, made her ache for so many unmentionable things she didn't dare admit to.

"I was just listening to the music," she lied, "and thinking what a lovely night it is."

"Absolutely lovely," he agreed, not taking his eyes from hers. He touched a palm to her cheek; rubbed his calloused thumb across her lips. "I think, perhaps, that there's something I should say right about now."

She didn't—couldn't—answer.

"Whatever happens tonight, sweetheart, is up to you. I'm not going to lie and say I don't want you, because I do. I think I've wanted you since that first moment when you stopped for that red light and I suddenly knew exactly what it felt like to be hit by lightning."

So she hadn't been imagining that strange, connected feeling when their eyes had met through the windshield! The idea renewed Erin's courage, and her resolve. "I felt the same way," she admitted softly.

He smiled at that, and skimmed his hand back

up her cheek, causing her blood to heat beneath her already warm face. "I'm glad. But the thing is, sweetheart, wanting and doing something about it are two very different things."

He was talking to her as if she were a child—not a twenty-one-year-old woman who, if circumstances had been different, would have a college degree and be on her way to vet school.

Erin tilted her chin. "Well, I know that."

He didn't answer immediately. He just sat there, his fingers playing with the ends of her hair, looking at her in a deep, serious way that had Erin fearing he could see all the way into her rebellious, needy heart.

Something wasn't quite right, here. Jace had always been a man to trust his instincts and at the moment they were telling him that he was missing something important about all this.

"I can't promise anything," he said finally.

Her tangled nerves eased, but were replaced by a rising irritation. If Jace wanted to make love to her, Erin thought, why didn't he just do it? Why was he insisting on talking it to death?

"I don't believe I asked you for any promises." She tossed her head, her eyes flashing like blue lasers in the slanting silver moonlight. "Whiskey River might not be as big and bustling as Nashville, but I'm certainly not some country bumpkin incapable of knowing her own mind. I know what

I want. And, I thought I knew what you wanted. But I guess I was wrong.''

Embarrassed enough to be on the verge of furious, she reached out again to start the engine. But he was faster, catching hold of her hand. ''No. You didn't guess wrong.'' He lifted her hand to his lips, kissing each fingertip as he had earlier—one at a time.

A weakening warmth started to flow through her, like a river born from a secret underground spring she'd never known was lurking inside her. Erin was grateful she was sitting down, because she didn't think her legs would have been capable of supporting her. When he'd finished with her fingers he pressed his mouth against the sensitive skin at the center of her palm. It was at that hot, sizzling moment that Erin realized a body could, indeed, melt.

''I do want you. I just wanted to make certain we were on the same page, darlin'.''

Erin decided, for discretion's sake, not to mention that if he was referring to experience, not only were they not on the same page, she doubted they were even in the same book. She was at the primer stage, while from what she'd witnessed thus far, Jace was definitely at the graduate level.

''So,'' he murmured, his words slightly muffled as he continued creating sensual havoc in her by nibbling at the soft, fleshy place between the base of her thumb and her palm, "now that we have that settled, how about another dance?"

"You want to dance with me?" Erin figured that might prove the challenge of a lifetime since she felt about as capable of standing on her own two feet as the Raggedy Ann doll Santa had brought her when she was four.

"Among other things—" he opened the passenger door and slid out, pulling her right along with him "—which we'll get to in good time. But I've always believed in pacing myself." He reached in and turned the radio up, just a little, so they could hear it over the sound of the river.

Although he was a good head taller than her, Erin was surprised, yet again, at how well they fit together as they swayed to a classic love ballad. His body was hard and firm against hers, which seemed to have turned to putty, molding itself against his solid frame.

"I knew it the first time I saw you," he murmured.

"Knew what?"

"That we'd fit together so perfectly," he said, once again seeming to possess the power to read her mind. He was resting his chin on the top of her head and his warm breath stirred her hair—and a whole lot more.

When she rose, just a bit, onto the toes of her boots, her breasts rubbed against the rocklike wall of his chest, stimulating her nipples to an exquisite point just this side of pain. And, apparently, if the deep growl echoing from his throat was any indication, she wasn't the only one stimulated.

His hands moved from her waist to her back, then lower, lifting her body even higher, pressing her against him so tightly that it would have been impossible for even the faintest breeze to slip between them. "And you know what else?"

When he began to do a little rubbing of his own, Erin was amazed they didn't spontaneously combust. "What?" she managed as flames began licking at that sensitive flesh between her thighs.

"I have the feeling that everything else between us is going to fit just as perfect."

Her knees literally buckled as he cupped her intimately, his palm holding her heat, his roughened fingertips making a scraping sound against the crisp dark denim of her jeans.

Jace was holding her up with one wide hand, while the other had somehow managed to get between them and was opening her blouse, the buttons no challenge to his practiced touch. And all the while, he was kissing her—hotly, deeply, possessively.

"Lord, you are sweet," he whispered into her mouth, sharing her breath as he pushed the cotton blouse aside and freed her from her bra with one deft stroke of his wicked fingers. "Like a ripe, sun-warmed peach." This time he lifted her right off her feet—high enough to allow him to take her breast into his mouth and began licking, biting, sucking, driving her higher and higher with just his lips and teeth and tongue.

"Jace…please…" The way he was holding Erin caused her back to arch in a way that pressed her pelvis against his. She could feel his stony length straining against the placket of his jeans. And she wanted it. "Let me…" Her hands reached for the metal fly-buttons on his jeans that looked so sexy on a man, but were proving horrendously difficult to open. "I want to touch you."

"I want that, too, sweetheart." Relinquishing her swollen breasts for now, he laid her onto the truck seat. "But I also want this to last. And the way I feel right now, one touch of those gorgeous fingers—" he took one of her fingers into his mouth and sucked on it, creating a corresponding tug deep in her womb "—and I'd probably explode right on the spot."

He was still outside the truck, bending over her, his mouth on hers again while his hands returned to her waist. The hand-tooled leather belt proved no problem. Then he turned to her zipper. As his tongue delved deeply into the moist recesses of her mouth, Jace slowly, painstakingly lowered it, tooth by metal tooth. Although her head felt as if it were somewhere high above them in the night-darkened clouds, Erin was coherent enough to think that the sound of that zipper going down was the sexiest thing she'd ever heard.

Thankfully her jeans were cowboy cut, which allowed them to slide easily over her boots. The boots were the next to go, along with her socks. Somehow, her blouse and bra disappeared. Then he caressed her with achingly slow hands, exquisitely and at length. Time passed. The moon rose higher.

On some distant level, Erin realized that it was foolish, being out here all alone in the middle of the forest with a stranger. Yet for some reason, she wasn't concerned. And, as the clouds parted, bathing her secret dreaming spot in silver light, Erin looked up into Jace's face hovering over hers, and knew why. He wasn't really a stranger at all. He was the man she'd been dreaming of forever; the man she'd been waiting for all of her life.

The desire she viewed in his midnight eyes echoed her own. But there was something else there, as well—something she couldn't quite decipher.

But then he was undressing quickly and the puzzle fled her mind. After he'd put on protection, he slipped his hand beneath the elastic band of her panties and delved into her moist heat. Erin arched her back, straining against the erotic touch, every nerve ending in her body poised for that moment when he would finally put an end to this aching need.

She was trembling. Amazingly, so was he. He ripped away the flimsy panties, covered her body with his, looked deep into her eyes and said in a rough voice that rumbled through her, "Now."

"Thank God," she whispered, her relief so powerful she nearly wept. Her skin was burning from the inside out, her blood was molten; she'd feared that she'd literally burst into flames before she had a chance to feel him inside her.

He surged into her, filling her with his heat and strength. Erin clung to him, wrapped herself around him, swallowed his rough moans as he was swallowing hers. And although she wouldn't have believed it possible, her body flamed even hotter as he dragged her into the inferno.

"Look at me, sweetheart. I want to watch you burn for me."

She feared that if she were to open her eyes, Jace would be able to read her secret—that she loved him; truly, madly, deeply. But, unable to resist, she forced her heavy lids open and found herself looking straight into his eyes. The hot passion she saw there, along with the wet stroke of the rough pad of his thumb against her ultrasensitive clitoris, was all it took to scorch away the last of her restraint.

She came first, crying out—screaming, actually—as she'd never done in her life. And while the unrestrained sound of passion echoed around them in the still mountain air, Erin drank in the magnificent sight of Jace, every muscle tensed, his head thrown back, his body gleaming like molten copper in the moonlight, and knew that the primitively masculine image would remain imprinted on her mind for the rest of her life.

And then his own shout was ringing out over the treetops, scattering a few skittish birds from their night perches. Erin felt his body's violent shudder, and then, with one last mighty groan, he collapsed on top of her.

CHAPTER NINE

How a Cowgirl Says Goodbye

ERIN HAD NO IDEA how long they lay there, but on some distant level it occurred to her that though he should be crushing her, nothing in her life had ever felt as right as his cooling body atop hers.

Reveling in the shared closeness, she finally allowed her eyes to drift shut again and idly combed her fingers through his damp hair. No wonder RaeAnn was constantly touting the perks of marriage, she mused.

Thankfully, there was no way he could have known she was a virgin, she decided, thinking back on their heated lovemaking. She might have been a bit reserved in the beginning, her fingers might have fumbled a little, and her touch perhaps hadn't been as sure as that of his other women, but he'd undoubtedly put that down to her obvious nervousness.

"I'm crushing you." When she would have held him tight against her, Jace somehow managed to roll over onto his side, taking her with him without the two of them falling off the narrow bench seat onto the floor.

"No, you weren't."

He laughed at that—a husky sound that wrapped around her, through her. "Liar." He nuzzled her neck. "You were magnificent."

Those three little words, which she feared he tossed around freely at such times, still pleased her immensely. "You're not so bad yourself, cowboy," she said.

He ran a hand down her bare back, from her shoulders to her bottom. "You deserve better."

She snuggled against him. "If you had been any better, there'd be nothing left of me but ashes."

He chuckled and pressed her tighter against him. Amazingly, he was becoming aroused all over again. "I was talking about the ambience. You should be lying on satin sheets instead of these seat covers."

"I imagine satin would be terribly slippery."

"Probably. But I wish now that I'd insisted on driving to Flagstaff or Payson—"

"No." She cut him off with a finger to his mouth—that full, sexy mouth she could still taste. "We would have lost over an hour, each way."

"Good point." He nipped at her fingertip in a playful way that affected her almost as deeply as his passionate kisses. "But I want you again, darlin'. And there's got to be a better answer than this."

"There's a sleeping bag in the back of the truck," she offered, feeling that old familiar shyness returning. "I keep it there for emergencies."

"In my book, this definitely qualifies as an emergency." As if to prove his claim, he took her hand and dragged it down to the male flesh that swelled anew at her touch. The feel of him, bold and strong and hot, was enough to stir smoldering embers inside her.

Stopping now and again to exchange slow, deep kisses, they moved to the back of the truck, and to Erin's amazement, the second time was even better than the first.

She was still lying in his arms when the first silvery pink light of day began to shimmer over the treetops.

"It's morning." He touched his lips to her hair, inhaled her shampoo and knew that he'd never eat another strawberry again without thinking of her.

"I know." She'd always been a lark, finding pleasure in greeting each new day. But this was different, because today the rising sun was an enemy. Erin sighed. "You missed the bus."

"Yep." He smiled down into her worried face. "And it was definitely worth it."

"Will you get in trouble?" Last night, such a thought hadn't occurred to her. Then again, Erin realized, last night she hadn't been thinking, period.

"Naw." As he smoothed the faint worry-lines

on her forehead with a fingertip, Jace felt the tug of an unfamiliar emotion he couldn't quite place. "It won't be any problem catching up with the guys in Vegas." He cupped her bare shoulders with his palms; her flesh was cool from the night air. "You're shivering." Before she could assure him that her slight trembling had more to do with his touch than the temperature, he'd retrieved his T-shirt from where it had landed on a nearby juniper branch and tugged it over her head.

The cotton shirt swam on her, covering her from shoulders to knees. And it smelled like him. Erin wished she could keep it forever—as proof that she hadn't imagined this magical night.

The forest began to wake in earnest. A bright blue Steller's jay skimmed through the trees to land on a nearby limb that hung over the river. The bird's crested head bobbed as he scolded them noisily.

"He's looking for a handout," Erin murmured.

"Then he's out of luck, because the only thing I've got is a pack of Big Red gum, which doesn't make for much of a breakfast." He smoothed his hands over her shoulders again, then down her arms, linking their fingers together. "How's the food at that café we passed on the way out of town?"

"Actually, it's quite good. Iris is famous for her breakfasts."

"Terrific. Breakfast for two coming right up."

He bent his head and kissed her—a hard, quick kiss that ended far too soon—then began gathering up their scattered clothing.

"Are you asking me out for breakfast?"

He paused in the act of turning her jeans right side out. His expression was as serious as she'd ever seen it, his dark eyes a little sad—and, she thought, regretful. "I may not be interested in marriage, or 'forever afters,' but I'm not the kind of jerk who disappears right after having sex, Erin."

It was the first time he'd said her name. Erin hadn't realized that until she heard it said so seriously in that deep, unforgettable baritone. Last night he'd called her "darlin'" or "sweetheart"—and even once, though she wasn't foolish enough to think he really meant it, "love." But never had he used her given name. And for some reason she'd have to consider later, after he was gone and she could think clearly again, just hearing it affected her more strongly than any endearment offered in the midst of passion.

Later, after they had shared a very public breakfast at The Branding Iron, she waited with him for the Greyhound to Las Vegas. Before boarding the bus, he gave her another long, breath-stealing kiss and asked her one more time to come to Vegas with him. And although it was the hardest thing she'd ever done, Erin declined. Not wanting to complicate matters further, she didn't explain that there was no way she could leave her father or the ranch right now.

But she did say she'd love it if he called her from the road, and yes, she'd enjoy hearing all about his European tour. The idea that he was even considering some sort of continuing relationship filled her with joy.

And although she wept when the bus finally turned the corner, taking him away from Whiskey River and from her, by the time she was back home at the Flying M, Erin was already looking forward to the future because, incredibly, it appeared that her magical, stolen night with Jace Honeycutt had changed her life.

CHAPTER TEN

Where Do I Go to Start All Over?
Five years later

RACHEL HONEYCUTT WAS standing at the oversize double stainless-steel sink snapping green beans. She'd picked them fresh this morning, from the garden out back, and was intending to serve them with a roast chicken and potatoes. Not that Jace would notice, she thought with a frustrated sigh. From the way her son had been acting, she could probably put scraps from the compost heap in front of him and he'd assure her that it tasted just fine, just the way he liked it.

She watched as he walked—*stomped* was more like it—from the five-car garage that was bigger than the cabin she'd raised her babies in, toward the house.

"Dinner'll be ready in about half an hour," she said as he came in through the kitchen door, "if that's okay with you."

She took the muffled grunt as an assent.

"You all done packing?"

There was another grunt as he went to the enormous double-door refrigerator and pulled out a can of beer. Rachel, who'd been "temperance" all her life, raised an eyebrow, but since Jace hadn't shown any signs of a drinking problem since that memorable night five years ago when he'd shown up in Honeycutt Gap drunk as a skunk, she didn't say anything.

"You gonna see that little gal while you're in Arizona?"

He'd taken a long swallow of beer and nearly choked at her words. Trust his mama never to forget a damn thing. Jace waited until he was certain he had control over his voice—and his damn knee-jerk emotions—before answering. "What gal?"

"The one you keep writing all those songs about."

His fingers tightened on the metal can and he felt a muscle jerk in his cheek, but he did his best to hide his reaction. "You've lost me, Mama."

She turned from the sink and wiped her hands on her apron. "You might be able to fool all those reporters who are always asking if your songs are about a real woman," she said. "You may even, from time to time, be able to fool yourself, son. But I know better. I also know that you were planning to take some time off the road after that Japanese tour. Yet here you are, barely home and heading right off again...to Arizona."

"This isn't a tour," he argued. His eyes were still shuttered, his voice still guarded. "Randy

Travis came down with laryngitis. Since he's a friend, I offered to fill in for him for this one night."

"That's your story and you're stickin' to it," Rachel said knowingly. "But for your information, Jace, I just happened to overhear you call Randy and ask him to let you take that show in Whiskey River."

"Hell." Jace threw himself into a kitchen chair and glared out the window at the swimming pool surrounded by those white statues of naked people that were just too damn pretentious for his taste. "When does a guy stop being his mother's kid, anyway?"

"Never. It's natural for a mother to be concerned about her son all her life. And, since I'm not planning to die anytime soon, you may as well get used to it." Despite the serious nature of the conversation, she smiled. "Unless you want to hear about all those hours I spent suffering in labor just to bring you into the world."

"I believe the phrase goes, 'Just to bring such an ungrateful son into the world,'" Jace said dryly. He'd certainly heard it on more than one occasion, but always in a teasing way.

"I do believe you're right," Rachel agreed. "And just wait until you have your own children and you'll discover the value of guilt."

Stretching out his legs, he sprawled in the chair,

studying his beer as if it held the secrets of the universe. "To tell you the truth, I don't really know why I'm going to Whiskey River, Mama. I just know that I don't have any damn choice if I want to get on with my life."

"Some people might say you've been getting along real well."

"Some people might only be looking at the trappings."

"True." She sat down in a chair across the table from him. The table, which had been hand carved by his granddaddy Virgil, was just about the only thing Jace had kept from the old hardscrabble days. "Are you going to warn her that you're coming?"

"She didn't give me any warning when she dumped me for that other guy."

"But you *are* planning on seeing her?"

Jace shrugged, her interrogation making him feel a lot like the time when he was ten years old and had accidentally left the gate open and let his old dog Ferlin into the garden. The damn hound had dug up a winter's worth of greens in a single afternoon and Jace had gotten an earful from his mama and daddy that he'd never forgotten.

"I'm sending her a ticket to the show. If she comes, fine. If not..." He shrugged again, not quite willing to admit that he didn't really have a backup plan—unless driving out to the damn Flying M Ranch and dragging Erin back here to Nashville with him—where she belonged—could be considered a plan.

"What if she's married?"

Jace didn't even want to consider that possibility. The truth was, he still couldn't figure out what the hell had happened between them. He'd known when he'd gotten on the Greyhound bus that morning that whatever they'd shared the night before— at the time he hadn't been prepared to call it "love"—had been damn special.

She'd certainly sounded like her warm, passionate self when he'd phoned her from Las Vegas where a record-company scout had caught his act and actually signed him to a contract. As often as he analyzed it, Jace knew he hadn't imagined her excitement and pleasure. And it was then that he'd realized how different he felt, having someone besides his mother who truly cared about what happened to him. At that moment, Jace had accepted that somehow, when he hadn't been looking, he'd fallen in love with Erin Montgomery.

But a little later, when he'd called her from Dublin, he'd thought he'd caught something different in her voice, a hesitation that hadn't been there before. At the time, he'd put it down to the rotten phone connection and hadn't worried about it. During the two-month-long tour, whenever he'd managed to call her, Jace had heard a distancing that had nothing to do with the fact that he was an ocean away.

Meanwhile the record company, eager to get him out in the marketplace as soon as possible, had arranged to have him cut an album in various studios during his travels, and while it wasn't the way Jace would have chosen to work, he hadn't been in any position to be picky. By the time he'd returned to the States, "Cinderella Cowgirl" was climbing the *Billboard* hits chart—and Erin had told him that she couldn't see him again.

He'd tried to latch on to something that could have changed between them. All right, he'd been away, but she'd seemed to accept the traveling as part of the business. So what the hell had happened between that night on the banks of the Whiskey River and his return to Nashville? "Is there someone else?" he'd demanded to know.

She'd paused before answering his question. An agonizingly uncomfortable silence had hovered on the long-distance line between Tennessee and Arizona. "Yes," she'd said finally. "It *is* someone else, in a way. And I'm sorry, Jace, but—"

He hadn't let her finish. Not wanting to hear some half-baked excuse about how she'd been lonely, and had decided that settling down with an Arizona cowboy was a safer bet than taking on a man with a dream. Little did she know it was a dream that, during their time apart, had expanded to include her and a passel of kids.

"Jace?" His mother's quiet voice shattered his reverie. Which was just as well, since it was, hands down, the most rotten memory of his life. "I asked you a question. What are you going to do if she's married?"

He shrugged. "I guess I'll just walk away." He wasn't certain that was what he'd do, but knew it was what his mother wanted to hear.

"Good." She patted his hand, which had unconsciously clenched into a fist. "Because I'd hate to think that I'd raised a son who'd covet another man's wife."

He flexed his tight fingers and turned his hand, lacing their fingers together. "I'm a man, Mama, with a man's feelings and a man's needs. I can't promise that I won't covet Erin—" Jace thought it a measure of personal growth that he'd managed to say her name out loud without choking "—but I'll try my damnedest not to do anything about it."

His mother smiled at him, with her lips and her eyes. "That's all I can ask, son."

Jace was wondering if his father had realized what a special woman he'd married, when the kitchen door burst open and his younger brother John came barreling in. "Well, I've done it. But I still think you're crazy."

Jace had hired John to be his personal manager

when it became apparent that his sudden success was about to change his life. Having witnessed so many of the hazards of the music business, he'd known he'd need someone he could trust unequivocally. And that was his brother—even if the guy did have lousy taste, Jace thought, not for the first time since he'd walked in the front door of the house John had chosen for him while he'd been touring in Japan.

"What did they say?" Jace had had John tell the record company that he wasn't going to tour all fifty states for this new album. Following a "less is more" philosophy, he would cut back, making each concert a major event. Besides, the truth was, he was already sick of spending fifty weeks a year on the road.

"Half of the guys in those fancy executive offices think the same thing I do—that you're flat-out nuts. The others think you're playing hard to get, trying to renegotiate your contract for higher royalties."

It figured. "Did you remind them about the HBO concert special?"

"Yeah." John threw his bulk into one of the wooden chairs, earning a frown from his mother when he tipped it precariously onto the back legs. "That's the only thing that kept them from cutting their throats. Or yours."

"They wouldn't cut Jace's," Rachel declared. "Since it's making them all that money."

"Good point, Mama," Jace said with a grin. "How would you like to be my new manager? I believe it's time to get someone who can look at the big picture."

"I'm looking at the big picture," John grumbled. "It's just that from my point of view, it's not looking all that great."

"It'll work. Trust me," Jace said. "The songs will be a lot better if I have enough down time to concentrate on writing them."

Unlike a lot of touring singers, he'd made a personal vow to write his own songs. The decision hadn't been difficult during that heady, initial period when he'd first realized that he'd fallen in love with Erin—or during that equally dark time after she'd dumped him. In those days, words of anger and pain had literally poured out of him, creating a dark, edgy album that had surprised critics, who'd at first thought he was going solely after the female audience who tuned in to the radio to hear love songs.

"That's what you keep saying," John said, obviously still skeptical, but willing to defer to Jace's judgment. "But I gotta tell you, there are an awful lot of suits at the record company who don't agree, so the stuff better be great. Oh, and by the way, I called that Realtor in Colorado. She'll be expecting you the day after your Arizona gig.''

"Good." Jace nodded, satisfied. Although men might not possess the same biological clock as women, now that he'd turned thirty-one and had garnered the fame he'd chased in his younger years, he found himself experiencing an almost overwhelming urge to settle down, get married and have kids.

When he'd professed interest in buying a ranch somewhere far from Music City, where he could get back in touch with the "real world," members of his band had jokingly accused him of nest building. Which, Jace admitted to himself, he probably was. The idea brought his thoughts circling back, as they always did, to Erin Montgomery.

He went through a checklist with his brother of all the things he wanted taken care of while he was gone. "And put this monstrosity of a house up for sale, too." Whether he ended up buying the Colorado ranch or not, he wasn't about to stay in this place.

"I don't know why you don't like it," John grumbled. "It's the third-biggest house in Nashville."

"Contrary to what you learned in the ninth-grade locker room, bigger isn't always better," Jace countered. "It reminds me of a whorehouse." His living room had gilt on seemingly every surface where it would stick and his master bedroom was done in nightmare shades of red and black.

"I guess that's not so surprising," John admitted. "The previous owner was a former evangelical TV minister who ended up in prison for 'initiating' the young female parishioners in the inner sanctum of his church."

Jeez! And the guys at the record company thought *he* was crazy. As he went upstairs to finish packing, Jace decided that the real world was looking better and better.

CHAPTER ELEVEN

What If I Said

"SO, WHAT ARE YOU going to do?" RaeAnn asked as she sat in the kitchen of the Montgomery ranch, staring at the single ticket in the middle of the table.

"I really don't have much choice," Erin said. The curt note accompanying the ticket had informed her that she could either come to see Jace after his show at the fairgrounds, or he'd be coming out to the ranch to see her. "I'm going to have to go."

"Well, I realize that no one's asked me," Julia Martin Montgomery said as she rolled out pie dough on the counter, "but I think it's about time you and C.J.'s father had a serious talk about the future." The nurse who'd at first visited the ranch to keep a professional eye on Erin's father after his successful surgery, had stayed on to become his wife. Erin had been delighted when, after all those years of being a widower, her father had married again. And lately, the couple had professed a desire to buy a motor home and see the country. Finances, always tight, had precluded such an adventure.

"The boy's got a right to know his father," John Montgomery seconded his wife.

"I know." Erin sighed again. "It's just so difficult."

"It's not difficult at all," RaeAnn argued. "For heaven's sake, Erin, those of us who know the situation can tell that Jace has been writing all those songs about you, which means that he was wild about you back then."

"And furious at me now," Erin said glumly. The dark album entitled *Promises in the Wind* hadn't left any doubt as to how he'd felt when she'd refused to see him after the European tour.

"What happened is in the past. And granted, it can't be changed, but even though some could argue that you may have used poor judgment, that's no reason why you and Jace can't have a second chance," Julia said sensibly.

"And whatever happens, at least C.J. won't be the only kid in kindergarten next year who doesn't know who his father is," her father added, returning to the argument he'd been making since the FedEx man had brought the concert ticket to the ranch.

"I'm going to tell him," Erin assured them all. She'd come to realize, even before receiving Jace's note, that she owed both him and C.J. the truth. "After the concert."

RaeAnn stood. ''Now that we've got that settled, let's go into town and get you a dynamite new dress—one that'll knock his socks off and make him forget what he was angry about.''

Erin opened her mouth to argue that she didn't need a new dress just to tell Jace he was a father. But some deep-seated feminine instinct she thought she'd put away when she'd made the decision to have her child alone, stirred in her.

Was it so wrong of her to want him to find her attractive—to look at her the way he had that long-ago, unforgettable night? Short of finding a time machine in Whiskey River that would transport her back to that fateful morning five years ago, when she'd rejected Jace's offer to take her to Las Vegas with him, Erin decided that a new dress might be exactly what she needed.

THIS TIME THEY'D SPELLED his name right. This time he was at the top of the marquee, above the demolition derby and the little wranglers' goat-roping competition. This time the audience had come to see him. And this time Jace was more nervous than he'd ever been before in his life.

Fortunately, he managed to click onto autopilot the moment he stepped onstage to the screams of his fans. Somehow he made it through the entire show without screwing up once, even though afterward, he couldn't recall having sung a single note.

THE DRESSING ROOM, which was really just an eight-by-ten Airstream trailer parked behind the rodeo grounds, had finally emptied, leaving him alone, wondering if she was going to come—and what the hell he was going to do if she didn't.

A hesitant knock answered that nagging question. "Come on in. It's open." Deciding not to make it easy on her, he didn't bother to open the door himself.

As she paused in the doorway, backlit by the setting sun, Jace realized that his memory hadn't failed him. Five years ago she'd been lovely. But she'd been a girl, only a few years out of her teens. The woman who looked as if she was prepared to bolt at any moment had matured into the most stunning female he'd ever seen.

"Hello, Jace." Her voice, which hadn't changed, slipped beneath his skin. The scent he'd not been able to get out of his mind engulfed him. And Jace knew he was sunk.

"Erin." He pushed himself out of the chair and took the few steps toward her. "It's good of you to come."

His voice was distant. His chocolate-dark eyes were not. Erin decided to focus on them. "I didn't have all that much choice," she reminded him as she forced herself to enter the trailer and shut the door behind her.

"We always have choices."

He was close, too close. She could smell the

musky scent of sweat from his energetic performance, feel the warmth radiating from his body. It could have been that night five years ago, were it not for the anger surrounding him—anger she had to admit he was entitled to. If he was furious with her now, she worried, how was he going to react when he learned she'd kept the existence of his son from him for all these years?

Without warning, his hand fisted in her hair and he pulled her against him, as close as they'd been when they'd danced together by the river that night. The air became so charged, Erin could practically hear the electricity crackling around them.

"One question." His harsh voice might have frightened her if it hadn't stirred so many feminine chords. "Are you married?"

He'd pulled her head back, forcing her to look a long, long way up at him. Her breath tumbled out from between lips that had gone painfully dry. "No."

"Thank God." She was his. That settled, at least in his own mind, Jace dragged her up and plundered. Everything he ever knew about seduction was washed away by a tidal wave of hunger. All his lovemaking skills—his slow hands, tender kisses, murmured words—were swept away by stark need. He didn't give a damn about control, didn't care about making her float. The desire to take, to possess, to conquer, threatened to overwhelm him. Erin Montgomery belonged to him;

and finally, after all the waiting, after the hurting, he was going to have her—and keep her.

Bypassing the preliminaries, he crushed the delicate fabric of her dress in his fist and yanked it up to her waist. Ignoring her gasp, he ripped away the tiny scrap of lace and silk with hands that were anything but gentle.

But having been dragged instantly, mindlessly into passion, Erin didn't want "gentle." When Jace plunged his fingers into her, finding her already hot and moist and ready for him, she wanted him. All of him. Now. As greedy as he was and every bit as mad, she tore at his clothes, ripping his shirt and sending buttons flying before tugging at his zipper. All the while, her lips were devouring—his mouth, his face, his throat.

Fighting for breath, he pushed her up against the wall and captured her mouth in a forceful kiss that had her clutching at him for balance.

"Put your legs around my waist." The words were rough, raw.

It had been so long. Too long, Erin thought, as she locked her ankles behind his back and returned his kisses, tangling her tongue with his, sucking on it, drawing him even deeper.

Her instant compliance, along with the friction of her lower body moving against his, ripped a growl from his throat. His hands were beneath her, lifting her to him. "Tell me you want me." He was pressing against her, a breath away from the core of her heat, her need.

"Can't you tell?" she moaned. "Can't you taste how much?" She clamped her mouth over his. Hard. "Can't you feel?" Practically sobbing from five years of pent-up need, she was desperate to feel him inside her.

"I want to hear the words." His mouth ate into hers, his teeth savaged her bottom lip. Even as her body reached to take him in, he kept his distance, tormenting her, torturing them both. "Say it, Erin. Say, 'I want you, Jace.'"

"I...want...you," she panted in a shallow, painful breath. Her fingernails dug into the hard ridge of his shoulders as she writhed against him, scraping her back against the wall, but only distantly aware of the discomfort. "Dammit, Jace," she cried out, willing to beg if necessary. "I want you. It's always been you. Only you."

It was what he'd been waiting to hear for five long years. The admission, ripped from her on a ragged cry of need, was all it took to send him over the edge. Jace entered her in one powerful thrust, burying himself all the way to the hilt in her glorious warm sheath.

Erin's breath strangled in her throat as he forcefully claimed her. Her body yielded willingly, welcomed him wonderfully. Engulfed by wave after wave of titanic sensation, all she could do was to cling to him for dear life and sob out his name, over and over, as he raced toward his own explosive release.

She climaxed again with him, her mouth buried in his neck, her arms and legs still wrapped around him, little convulsions rippling inside her body.

Their passion spent, at least for the time being, they slid to the floor in a tangle of arms and legs. "That," Jace said with a deep breath, "was almost worth waiting for."

"Yes." She pressed her lips against his damp chest and reveled in the taste she'd never been able to get out of her mind. "Absolutely."

"I said *almost*." He cupped her chin in his fingers and lifted her gaze to his. "We need to talk."

"Yes. That's one reason I came here tonight."

"But not the only reason."

"No." Since this was a night for truth, Erin knew she had to be open with him about everything, including the fact that she'd imagined making love with him when she'd bought this outrageously expensive dress she doubted he'd even noticed. "I wanted to make love with you, Jace." She touched a hand to his cheek and understood how badly she'd hurt him when she felt the muscle clench beneath her fingertips. "I've dreamed of this moment for years. And I haven't thought of anything else since you sent me that ticket."

"You've got a pretty funny way of showing me that you wanted me," he countered, unable to eliminate the grievance from his tone. Although the hot sex they'd just shared had done a lot to ease his body, his heart and his pride were demanding a hell of a lot more.

"I know." She sighed. "It's complicated." When she would have pulled away, he wrapped his arms around her and held her even tighter, unwilling to let her escape again, even to cross the room.

"So's life." He closed his eyes, inhaled the familiar strawberry scent and decided that explanations could wait. "We've got a lot of catching up to do." He ran his hand down her bare leg; was rewarded by her slight tremor. "I want you to spend the night with me."

"I want that, too." Although she hadn't had any idea how her meeting with Jace would go, she'd already told her father and Julia not to expect her home.

"But not here." He looked around the cramped trailer with overt disdain. "One of these days we're going to have to try out a bed for a change, just to see how we like it."

The knowledge that he was considering a future with her made Erin's romantic heart flutter. The fear that once he heard what she'd come here tonight to tell him might destroy what little truce they'd managed to establish, terrified her.

"I don't care where you love me, Jace." Her voice trembled as she fought back tears. She pressed her hand against his chest, bare of the shirt she'd practically ripped off him. "So long as you do."

He took hold of her hand. Although her body was still warm and lush, her hand had turned to ice. He rubbed it between his own. "That's all I've ever wanted to do."

Erin could only hope that he'd feel the same way tomorrow, after he'd learned her secret.

Willing to put off the moment of truth for as long as possible, Erin instantly accepted his invitation to dinner. But when he stopped the rental car at the Whiskey River airfield, she realized that little about the evening was turning out as she'd planned.

"Where are we going?"

"I booked a room at a resort in Phoenix. According to the concierge, it's supposed to have all the amenities—golf, tennis, a spa for milady, a five-star restaurant. Not that we'll be taking advantage of much of that." He leaned between the bucket seats and kissed her—lightly, but with meaning. "But I've been assured that the beds are terrific. And the Jacuzzi tub is big enough for two."

She'd known Jace was rich. How could he not be, with all his success? But still, flying off to another town for dinner was something she'd only ever seen in the movies. When they reached the sleek red-and-white plane, she received another surprise.

"You're going to fly this yourself?"

"I was planning to, unless you're afraid to go up with me."

She was afraid, but not of this. "No." She forced her concern to a distant corner of her mind. "Not if you promise to use your daddy's cure if I get afraid of heights again."

"Absolutely."

CHAPTER TWELVE

Don't Love Make a Diamond Shine!

AS IT TURNED OUT, she so enjoyed streaking into the blazing Arizona sunset, Erin forgot all about her fear of heights. A limousine was waiting at Sky Harbor International Airport to take them to the resort-hotel, where they were immediately escorted to a luxurious suite.

Erin stared in wonder at all the preparations—at least five-dozen red roses arranged in tall crystal vases, a bottle of champagne nestled in a silver bucket of ice, chocolate-dipped strawberries. And that was just in the living room.

"Satin sheets?" she murmured as she gazed down at the king-size bed.

"It took me five years," he said. "But I'm finally going to make love to you the way I've always wanted to."

The evening passed in a gilt-edged romantic blur. Erin was certain that the French champagne must have been exquisite. And the midnight dinner, as well. The view of the city lights was undoubtedly magnificent, if she'd been paying any attention—which she hadn't—because every atom in her body was concentrated on Jace.

She didn't keep track of how many times they made love that night, but somewhere, just before dawn, they'd agreed that both the bed and the tub lived up to the concierge's promise.

But in the back of her mind, Erin had known she was living on borrowed time. And finally, she couldn't put it off any longer.

"I have something to show you," she said, taking the snapshot out of her wallet. It was a photograph of C.J., taken astride Ginger, the sweet-tempered mare her father had bought for him.

He didn't have to ask. Jace took one look at the face that could have been his own at that age and closed his eyes rather than let her witness his pain.

"Why?" The single word was edged with barely restrained fury. "Why the hell didn't you tell me that I had a son?"

Erin sank down onto the sofa and twisted her fingers together. "It's a bit complicated to explain."

He opened his eyes and looked right at her, his hot, accusing gaze a contrast to his icy tone. "Why don't you try?"

"When you called from Las Vegas, I had no way of knowing."

"I'll buy that. How about Dublin?"

"I suspected I was pregnant, but I wasn't certain."

"So when did you know? By London? Zurich? Rome?"

"I found out between London and Zurich." She still recalled the day she'd sat there, staring at the test strip, feeling strangely thrilled by the idea of a life stirring inside her.

"I called you from Switzerland—three times. And I'm sure I'd remember you mentioning that you were pregnant with my child."

"How could I have known you'd even believe it was your child?" she retorted. "After all, you'd used a condom both times, and—"

"I would have believed you."

She knew immediately that it was the truth. "I had no way of knowing that for sure," she stressed. "Not every man would have accepted my word without proof."

"But you hadn't had sex with any other man. Only me."

"How did you know that?" She remembered being certain she'd fooled him. "After all, I'd spent years riding horses. There was no physical barrier—"

"You were a virgin, Erin. I suspected it that night and by the time the band left Las Vegas, all the little pieces that had been nagging at me fell into place—just about the time I realized I'd fallen in love with you."

Those words, which she would have given anything to hear five years ago, spoken now in such a matter-of-fact way, stole the breath from her lungs. She slumped back against the cushions and put a hand over her eyes. "You didn't say anything."

"No, I didn't. Which, I suppose, makes us both guilty of keeping secrets."

"I really was going to tell you when you came back to the States." It was vital that he understood that she hadn't meant to keep his son from him. "But I had no idea you'd be so accepting, so I wanted to wait until we could have the conversation face-to-face."

Jace reluctantly decided that made sense, but it also didn't explain the intervening years—nor what she'd told him that morning he'd called from Nashville, dying to talk to her. To be with her. To love her.

"I seem to recall suggesting that I come to Arizona. But you told me that there was another man."

"You asked if there was someone else," she corrected faintly, daring to look at him again. "I told you there was."

"Don't split hairs with me, Erin!" He was on his feet and had begun to pace. The sight of his hands curled into huge fists at his sides was not encouraging. "You knew how I'd take it, dammit! You knew I'd think that you'd gone back to that jerk at the fair."

"I suppose I did." At the time, she hadn't admitted it—even to herself. "But there really were extenuating circumstances." She went on to haltingly explain about her father; and how she hadn't felt free to leave him so soon after his life-threatening surgery, how there was no way of knowing that the cancer wouldn't show up in his other lung.

"I would have understood that. And we could have worked something out. I wouldn't have minded you staying at the ranch, Erin. So long as we were married, I could still be with you when I wasn't on the road."

"That's just the point. You were on the road."

"You knew that when you slept with me, when you got pregnant with my child," he reminded her. "If I'd asked you to marry me when I called with the news of the contract, what would you have said?"

"Yes," she answered promptly, "without hesitation."

His curse was ripe and harsh. He turned away, his hands jammed into the jeans he'd pulled on for breakfast, and glared out the windows at the verdant green golf course and gardens beyond. In the morning sun, the ripples in the swimming pool glistened like sapphires.

He spun back toward her, a muscle in his dark cheek jerking dangerously. "Would you have accepted if I'd asked from Zurich?"

She paused, then nodded.

"I still don't get it, dammit. What the hell

changed between Zurich and when I got back to Nashville?''

"You became famous." Her tone was so soft he had to strain to hear it.

"What?" Frustrated and unable to believe he'd heard her correctly, Jace raked a hand through his hair.

"I said, you'd gotten famous. 'Cinderella Cowgirl' didn't just change your life, Jace. It changed mine, too." And C.J.'s, she thought miserably.

"Most women would probably have been more willing to take on a rich-and-famous husband than a poor, struggling one."

She lifted her chin at that, showing a bit of the Montgomery spunk that had so attracted him that first night. "I'm not most women."

"No." Exhausted, he dragged a hand down his face. The lingering pleasure from their night of lovemaking had definitely disintegrated. "You're not." He threw his long body into the chair across from her.

"You have to understand," she said earnestly, leaning forward to place a supplicating hand on his leg. "I was a little frightened when I found out I was pregnant, but I figured we could deal with it, somehow. But then your album came out, and you were so white-hot, I realized how terrible it would be if the first thing people were to find out about your life was that you'd gotten a groupie pregnant while on tour.''

"I never thought of you as a groupie," he said firmly.

"I know. But I was afraid that's what other people would think. And I couldn't bear what they might say about you—and me."

"I've never worried about what people said about me."

"That's admirable. But I did. And I couldn't stand the idea of seeing our baby being called a bastard on the covers of all the tabloids."

He thought about that for a long, silent moment that had her nerves tangling and her hopes beginning to stir anew.

"What about now?" he asked.

"Now?"

"There will still be people who'll think the same thing, say the same thing."

"I know." She'd thought about nothing else for days.

"And?"

"And I don't care." Realizing that since she was the one who'd torn them apart it was up to her to make the move, she left the sofa and settled on his lap. Encouraged when he didn't dump her off onto the Navajo rug, she twined her hands around his neck and looked straight into his midnight eyes. "I love you, Jace. I've always loved you. And if you'd only give me another chance, I'll spend the rest of my life trying to make this up to you."

"While that's an attractive scenario, I think I'll pass."

She went ice cold—head, hands, and heart. "Oh." She bit her lip and struggled not to cry.

"Because you don't have to make anything up to me, Erin. Not if you just say you'll be my wife. And live with me—hopefully on the Flying M if you think your dad would be willing to sell it to me—and have my babies."

Erin gasped with joy. And, although she had not a single qualm about marrying this man she'd given her heart to so long ago, there was still one little thing…

"How many babies?" she asked cautiously.

He rubbed his chin as if thinking her question over. "Well, since I've never considered myself in competition with my daddy, I figure three, counting the one we've already got, might be a nice round number. If that's okay with you."

"Yes, yes, and yes!" Erin began to weep, her tears born not of sorrow, but happiness. The kiss they exchanged might not have been as hot as some others they'd shared, but it was world's sweeter, because it promised so much.

He took from his pocket the diamond ring he'd bought years ago with his signing bonus and slipped it onto her finger. Before Erin had time to properly admire it, he scooped her into his arms and carried her toward the bedroom.

"What's my son's name?"

"Carl John." She watched recognition dawn in his love-filled eyes and knew that they were going to be okay. "After your daddy and mine. But we call him C.J."

"C.J." Jace tried the name out several times, enjoying the sound of it. "Lord, I've got a son named C.J. Wait until my mama hears about this."

"You'll have to call her."

"I will—" he was standing beside the bed "—later." His wicked grin was the same one she'd been dreaming about for five long and lonely years.

Erin bounced when he dropped her unceremoniously onto the mattress, then rose up on her knees and held her arms out to him. She was still laughing as Jace showed her what a good husband he would be.

A Lark in the Dark
Heather MacAllister

To G. with thanks.

CHAPTER ONE

"WHAT DO YOU MEAN, he didn't make the payment?" Annie Denton clutched the telephone and concentrated on what Jennifer, her stepdaughter—technically ex-stepdaughter—was saying.

"I got a letter from the University of Texas telling me that I'd lost my dormitory reservation because a deposit hadn't been received by the deadline. So I called Daddy—"

"Not that the scum bothered to return her call," lamented Jennifer's mother, who'd been audibly sniffling on the extension phone. "We finally had to go through the lawyers."

"Mom." Jennifer's voice held a patience Annie definitely didn't share.

"I'll be quiet," Deena said, though she still sniffled.

"So is he going to send the check or not?" Annie asked.

"Not!" Deena wailed.

"It's too late anyway." Jennifer sounded remarkably calm, or maybe it was the contrast with her mother, whose maternal despair practically vibrated the phone in Annie's hand. "Even if I could find a place to stay, I'd have to live on the tuition money for the spring semester. And, you know, I wasn't all that thrilled about going to college anyhow.''

That was a lie, and Annie knew it.

Judging by the howl from Deena, she knew it, too. ''Ronald was supposed to pay! That was the agreement!''

Having been married to Ronald herself, Annie was well aware of—and wholeheartedly supported—the agreement. But the Ronald she'd divorced last year wasn't the Ronald she'd married. However, the Ronald she'd married was the Ronald Deena had divorced.

''It'll be okay,'' Jennifer said. ''I'll get a job, save money and go to college some day. Or maybe I don't need college. Uncle Nick never went to college.''

The seductive image of Deena's brother flashed through Annie's mind and she winced. He personified the allure of the irresponsible. Had she made no impression on her stepdaughter at all? '''You want fries with that?' is not a career mantra, Jennifer.'' The financial situation must be desperate if Jennifer planned to model her life after that of her uncle, the human tumbleweed.

Annie herself had nearly succumbed to Nick's appeal, once. Without trying, she could still hear his voice, still lose herself in his heated gaze…still crave his touch.

She was not proud of this. It was as though she went into a trance every time she thought of the man, which was why she didn't let herself think about him.

So stop thinking about him. She sucked her breath between her teeth. Right now, she had to help Jennifer stick to her goal of a college education and not emulate her uncle's nomadic life-style.

Annie couldn't say much more about careers and education without insulting Deena, who had never had a career, but worked as a clerk at Sew and Sew, a fabric shop. Annie didn't want Jennifer growing up unequipped to support herself like her mother. And she didn't think that was what Jennifer wanted, either.

Deena's sobs had quieted, but Annie guessed it was because she'd muffled the phone.

"Jennifer, you remember those frozen strawberry daiquiris I showed you how to make?"

"The ones Uncle Nick said were women's drinks?"

Annie smiled through gritted teeth. "And we're women, aren't we? Go make your mother a blenderful right now."

"Okay."

Annie waited until she heard Jennifer click off her extension. "Deena, what did the lawyer say?"

A sniffle, followed by a long shaky breath, sounded in the receiver. "I'm trying not to overreact, Annie. But I'm just so…so damn mad. Did you hear that? I said 'damn.'''

"I'm proud of you."

"I mean, just a month ago, we were all together here in Richardson and watched her graduate and talk about college. And the whole time, he *knew* he hadn't made that payment. He *knew* she wouldn't be going."

"What did the lawyer say?" Annie repeated.

"The same thing he said every month when the child-support check didn't arrive—that Mr. Haggarty's financial situation was in flux and they'd petitioned the court for an adjustment."

"But he *paid* child support!" Annie should know—she'd lent Ronald money for that very purpose.

"Not…not since he married Lynn."

"That was in October." If she hadn't already been sitting on a kitchen stool, Annie's knees would have given way. Ronald had come to her before Christmas and like a sap, she'd fallen for the old father-asking-for-money-so-his-kids-won't-do-without line. She was too embarrassed to admit that to Deena.

Very faintly in the background, she heard the sound of a blender crushing ice and briefly envied Ronald's first wife.

"I'd give you the money if I could, but I—"

"That's not why I called," Deena interrupted. "The lawyer says HI-Com isn't doing well and

Ronald doesn't have any liquid assets. You work with him—is that true?''

''We've been struggling because Texafone is offering lowball deals to grab accounts, but that isn't anything we haven't weathered before.'' But this time felt different, and Annie couldn't figure out why.

She'd started working for Haggarty Industrial Communications in Houston right out of school, and considered its founder, Ronald Haggarty, her mentor. Only after his divorce did their relationship become something more. During their marriage, they worked together to build HI-Com into an extremely successful business. Annie became, and still served as, vice president.

''We *can't* be doing as bad as all that,'' she said with more conviction in her voice.

''Then what has he done with his money?'' Deena asked.

''Good question. I'll try to find out.'' But that wouldn't solve the immediate problem—Jennifer and college.

''Thanks, Annie. I really only wanted to know if it's worth bringing in my lawyer. If Ronald is actually broke, then I won't waste what little money I've got.''

The more Annie considered the situation, the angrier she became. In fact, she now felt Deena was showing remarkable restraint. ''Wait a minute…what about your brother?'' Annie couldn't bring herself to say his name. That way, it was easier to ignore the pull—and even after all these years, there was still a pull. "Could you borrow from him?"

"Nick? He's still here. I guess I could ask...." Deena didn't sound hopeful and Annie wasn't surprised.

Nick Mandola traveled constantly and his main residence appeared to be a post-office box. He'd laid claim to a corner of Deena's attic to store a couple of trunks and as far as Annie could tell, those trunks comprised his entire worldly goods. Jennifer and her brother, Kevin, naturally adored him. Why not? Their uncle Nick was fun and exciting, and was never around long enough to bore them—just long enough to stir things up and take off again, without a thought to those he left behind.

"Don't bother. If Nick hasn't offered to help, he isn't going to." Annie was aware that she sounded more derogatory than was wise.

Sure enough, Deena began defending her younger brother. "The kids aren't his responsibility."

"And heaven forbid, Nick should take on any responsibility," Annie muttered in spite of herself.

There was a short silence. "They aren't your responsibility, either," Deena reminded gently.

Ouch. "I'm sorry. I deserved that. I just want this for Jennifer."

"So do I," Deena said. "But if it doesn't happen, it doesn't happen. Look at Nick. He's turned out okay."

If you considered a man who would attempt to seduce a woman two nights before her wedding to someone else "okay," then...

Blotting out the memory of Nick's dark eyes filled with fake sincerity, Annie decided she'd better get off the telephone before she said anything else about Deena's brother. "Tell Jennifer not to worry. We'll think of something."

But Annie had no idea what. She'd already been concerned enough about the dismal quarterly reports to ask questions, but she hadn't done any real digging.

Maybe now was the time.

Unfortunately, real digging meant reading Ronald's personal business diary, a journal he'd started in order to make it easier for biographers to explain the brilliance of his business maneuvers to future generations—assuming he didn't write the story of his success himself.

Annie traced the beginning of the decline of her marriage to Ronald to the night he began writing in that diary, which he kept beside the bed. Recounting his business triumphs fed his ego, which swelled to the point where she felt crowded.

Lynn, his current wife, proved to be an all-you-can-eat buffet for Ronald and his ego.

Annie hoped the three of them were very happy.

She, herself, was wildly happy.

Okay, maybe not exactly happy yet, but definitely better off without Ronald. Sitting at the kitchen bar, she gazed around her tiny post-divorce apartment, clogged with her share of the furniture. She'd traded her half of the house for HI-Com stock.

Okay, maybe she wasn't *exactly* better off, but she did have money in the bank—or she had until she'd lent it to Ronald to pay child support, which, according to Deena, he hadn't.

Okay, no liquid assets. But she had stock…stock in a company that was inexplicably failing; stock whose value had started a freefall right after the divorce.

The brutal truth was that she was no better off than if she'd gone away with Nick Mandola all those years ago.

No!

Yes.

Closing her eyes, she slumped on the barstool and groaned. "Annie, you are a gullible mess."

She'd been swindled by Ronald and she wasn't sure exactly how.

But of course she knew *how*, if not the precise details. She'd followed the rules, both legal and moral, and Ronald hadn't. She always followed the rules. Ronald only did when following rules was profitable.

She should have seen his treachery coming, but she hadn't. And the worst of it was that Ronald was getting away with whatever he was doing because she was good old predictable Annie.

Faithful Annie.

Loyal Annie.

Mad-as-hell Annie.

Even worse was the fact that as vice president of HI-Com, she had to attend the Wireless Communications Businessman of the Year banquet tomorrow night. Ronald was a nominee. Since HI-Com's meteoric rise, Ronald had been a nominee for the past five years straight, but he'd never won.

His failure to take home the glass winner's trophy had become a professional embarrassment to him and, on a personal level, he felt his memoirs would lack a triumphant high point.

With HI-Com's luster dulling, Annie had been surprised by the nomination this year, but not by the fact that Ronald had never won; Ronald's "stick-it-to-'em" business dealings caused resentment among his colleagues.

She slid off the barstool and walked into the bedroom where her expensive new dinner dress hung from the closet door.

Short, tight and shiny, the dress was supposed to compensate for her lack of an escort. The plan was to look so sexy that every man at the banquet would think Ronald was crazy for letting her get away.

Thoughtfully, she fingered the material. Ronald

always insisted on hosting a party after the banquet and rented a suite at the hotel for the night. This year was no different, so presumably he and Lynn would be spending the night in the suite, which meant their house would be empty. All night.

Plenty of time for her to search it.

Annie dropped the edge of the dress. That was breaking and entering, even if she had once lived there. Definitely illegal. Besides, how was she supposed to get in and out without Ronald realizing that someone had been searching his house?

Now, wait a minute. There were ways. In fact, there were people who made a living—probably a good one—breaking into places and spying on other people.

She should probably hire one of them.

No, there wasn't time, and she wouldn't know what to tell them to look for, anyway.

Finding out what Ronald had done with his money was something she was going to have to do by herself.

It was amazing how much better she felt once she'd actively decided to do something about getting Deena's child support and Jennifer's college money back.

Speaking of money... Annie took down the dress and put it into the plastic garment bag. Her classic black cocktail suit was more professional anyway, and she could use the money she would have spent on this dress to buy whatever equipment she needed.

Annie smiled. Ronald wasn't going to get away with this. She was no longer Annie Denton, pathetic divorcée.

She was Annie Denton, spy.

CHAPTER TWO

SHE WAS ANNIE DENTON, pathetic spy.

After sitting through dinner—fortunately not at the same table as Ronald and Lynn—Annie had had the pleasure of seeing Ronald lose out on the Wireless Communications Businessman of the Year award one more time. Then she had slipped away just as the dancing had begun.

She'd raced home, changed clothes, grabbed the knapsack she'd filled with spy tools the helpful man at Spy Supply had rented her, and now crouched in the bushes by the front door of the house she'd once shared with Ronald Haggarty. She would have preferred to be crouched by the back door, but the fence gate was locked and even more exposed than the front door. Annie decided she was only up for picking one lock per break-in.

It was nearly midnight. There was a full moon and not a cloud in the sky. The world's brightest streetlight blazed upon a front door of the purest, gleaming white. It was so bright out, she could read the *Private Investigating for Dummies* book she'd bought without using a flashlight.

Annie had worn black, head to toe. She should

have worn white to blend in. On the other hand, anyone seeing her would probably assume she was just a giant Houston cockroach, especially if she scurried away really, really fast.

She opened the book and flipped to the section on "Getting into Places That Are Locked."

Warning: This is otherwise known as "breaking and entering," generally frowned upon by police. Tip 1: Make sure object is actually locked. Tip 2: For every lock, there is a key. Always try to enter without breaking.

As if Ronald would give her a key. Swatting at the mosquitoes, Annie closed the book and removed the lockpick gun that she'd practiced with on her own bathroom door. She didn't quite have the hang of it and would have to remember to call Maintenance for a new lock on Monday.

She took a few deep breaths. Okay, she could do this. Annie had verified that the door was locked, and she knew the alarm wasn't on because Ronald always complained that Lynn's poodle kept setting it off. So now all she had to do was point this thing at the lock and pull the trigger.

More deep breaths. Peering out between the leaves of the prickly holly bushes, Annie waited until the street was clear of traffic, then slowly emerged from the bushes. Positioning the lockpick gun, she pulled the trigger.

In the quiet darkness the clicking sound seemed much louder than when she'd practiced in her bathroom. Startled, Annie dropped the gun and took a step backward. Her foot came down on something soft—something that yowled, then streaked into the night followed by the echoes of Annie's scream.

She leaped back into the bushes, where she was welcomed enthusiastically by the mosquitoes. Only the thought of Jennifer doomed to a career inhaling grease-laden air kept Annie from fleeing.

When the minutes passed and no sirens wailed, Annie thought she'd stopped shaking enough to have another try at the lock.

Reaching out from the bushes, she retrieved the gun, only to discover that the pick had broken when she'd dropped it. She had another pick with her, but it was curved. But maybe Ronald's lock was crooked, just like he was.

She spent more endless minutes sweating in the humid air as she attempted to fit the new pick in the gun. Ready at last, she shot the lock again, but managed to break that pick, too.

Back to the bushes. She was a failure.

What now? "Picking locks is harder than it looks, huh?" sympathized the unhelpful book. "Sure you can't get a key?"

Well, actually... Annie dug out her key ring where she still had her old house key. She could try sneaking into Lynn's office at HI-Com—which was Annie's former office next to Ronald's—and steal the new key out of her purse, leaving the old key in its place.

Annie was rather taken with the poetic justice of it all. She imagined Lynn's frustration the next time she tried to unlock the door. She and Ronald would never realize that Annie had switched keys because Annie just didn't *do* that sort of thing. No, predictably, Annie trod the straight and narrow.

Except tonight she'd strayed, though not with any great success. She almost wished they could see her right now. *That* would teach them not to underestimate her. They'd *never* believe that Annie would try to break into...

She stared at the key in her hand, gleaming in the moonlight. As if in a dream, she calmly walked out of the bushes, put the key into the lock and opened the door.

Incensed, she slipped inside. *They hadn't even bothered to change the locks!* Somehow, that made everything worse.

Never mind. She would use their complacency to her advantage and ferret out Ronald's secrets. He'd never know what she'd done until she was ready for him to know.

She was no longer Annie Goody Two-Shoes. She was Annie Denton, woman of unexpected depths.

Annie set her backpack by the door and got out a penlight and the book.

So now you're inside. Congratulations! Whatever you do, don't move!

Annie froze.

You have two objectives: accomplish whatever it was that made it necessary for you to be where you shouldn't be, and do it undetected. Do not move anything without being able to put it back exactly as you found it—this rule also applies to our national parks and forests.

Though Annie was not in the mood for "Dummies" book humor, the advice was sound. Speaking of sound... A quickly crescendoing canine growl vibrated from beneath the dining-room table.

"Uh...it's okay, Poopsie. We've, ah, met before, actually. You might remember me? Ronald's second wife?" Annie frantically dug in the backpack for the meat she'd brought for the poodle. "Here's a present. I bet Lynn never feeds you filet." It was left over from tonight's dinner, since she'd been too nervous to eat.

Annie also withdrew the Russian military surplus night-vision scope she'd rented. The thing was heavy, but she didn't want to have to turn on lights.

Feeling like a spy and—okay—liking the feeling a little, Annie peered through the eyepiece in the general direction of the growling Poopsie.

A green lump glowed beneath the green dining-room table. In fact, everything was green. Annie supposed the scope was useful if you were checking for enemy troop movements—little green men, she thought hysterically—but for navigating around a house in the suburbs, it was more trouble than it was worth.

She drew the curtains and turned on the dining-room lights, dimming them immediately.

Poopsie barked.

"Calm down. I've got your bribe right here." What kind of woman would name a dog Poopsie? It was a symptom of Ronald's besottedness that he actually once commented that the name fit the dog. But when Poopsie slunk out from under the table, Annie saw that unfortunately, the name was appropriate.

She felt a pang, then realized this was no longer her rug, so no longer her responsibility. Peeling open the plastic bag, Annie let Poopsie get a good whiff, then ran for the utility room. With Poopsie scrambling after her, she tossed the meat inside and shut the door.

That took care of that problem.

With the dog out of the way, Annie finally relaxed enough to look around the house. So what decorating atrocities had Lynn committed?

The dining-room furniture was new, since Annie had taken possession of the old reproduction Queen Anne set she'd been so proud of. She also had the china hutch. The entire set took up most of the room in her apartment, but she could serve eight with style—twelve when she added the leaf and opened a closet. A couple of the stuffed chairs, a lamp and coffee table were about the only other pieces she could accommodate.

She was surprised to see that Lynn had merely filled in the gaps with her furniture, which was mostly glass and metal and struck an off-key note in Annie's elegant—if she did say so herself—decor. Obviously, Ronald and Lynn hadn't been blowing money on interior designers.

Annie wandered from room to room, avoiding the master bedroom, seeing bits and pieces of her life with Ronald interspersed with pieces from his life with Lynn. The sight gave her a very unsettled, sad and angry feeling, so she decided to quit snooping around and start looking for information on HI-Com. She headed for the home office to see what she could discover there.

She pulled the shade and turned on the desk light. Everything looked nearly the same as when this had been *her* office with Ronald, except that her laptop computer wasn't there.

Without knowing exactly what to look for, Annie opened the file drawers. It wouldn't be so simple as finding a file labeled Set of Cooked Books now, would it?

No.

The problem with not being devious yourself

was that it made it harder to think like a devious person. Sighing, Annie began a spot check of any file she didn't recognize. What she really needed to see was Ronald's check register. She had the bank file halfway out of the drawer when she heard a scratching noise.

Though it was probably just Poopsie's nails on the vinyl utility-room floor, Annie quickly turned off the light and crept to the doorway, then down the hall.

Someone was at the front door.

Annie's heart started pounding so hard she couldn't hear anything else. What were Ronald and Lynn doing back?

Where could she hide?

Forcing herself to move, Annie headed toward the kitchen, obviously the least-used room in the house.

She caught a glimpse of the front door swinging open just as she hid in the pantry.

Her backpack was by the front door. She'd left the dining-room light on dim. Great. They'd know someone had been in the house. Or maybe they'd think they'd left the light on by accident. Maybe they wouldn't notice the backpack.

She cracked the door open to hear them talking.

There was no talking. Wait a minute. Right now, Ronald should be in full rant over not winning the award. Lynn should be soothing him.

Annie armed herself with a can of something, held her breath and pushed her ear against the slit.

In the room next door, Poopsie growled.

Quiet footfalls stealthily roamed the house.

Oh, great. An intruder. *Private Investigating for Dummies* didn't cover encounters with other intruders.

And wasn't this her typical luck? The *one* time she tried something daring and out of character, look what happened.

But maybe this wasn't a specialized intruder like she was, but just an ordinary robber. The awards banquet had been publicized, so Annie wasn't the only person who could have figured out that Ronald and Lynn wouldn't be at home tonight.

That was it. A clever robber was going to cart off their valuables while Ronald threw his annual I-don't-care-that-I-didn't-win party.

Well, good luck. According to the lawyers, he and Lynn didn't have any valuables. But there were the usual electronic goodies the robber might like to pawn. Annie would be safe if she just stayed in the pantry, since canned goods probably weren't high on the list of pawnable items. These guys were quick. They'd be gone within minutes.

But though she continued to listen, Annie didn't hear the sounds of heavy objects being carted off. Was he going for the jewelry? If Lynn had any, she wisely hadn't been wearing it around the office.

Annie nudged the pantry door open a little more with her foot, then froze as a beam of amber light pierced the darkness.

Fabulous—a hungry thief.

But the light bobbed away. Annie got to her feet and peered out the opening. The robber was going down the hallway to the bedrooms.

The light veered to the left. The master bedroom was on the right.

Annie waited, but the light didn't reappear.

Only the office and guest bedroom were on the left. When he realized his mistake, the robber would go into the master bedroom, so right now would be an excellent time to escape. Annie eased out of the pantry and cut through the dining room to the front door.

And heard the sound of a file cabinet drawer opening.

What kind of robber was this?

A robber just like she was, that's what. Someone else was wondering about Ronald's business practices. And that someone else would find and take the evidence she needed to get Ronald to pay back the child support, Jennifer's college money, and the money he'd borrowed from Annie.

She looked between the front curtains, hoping to see a car, but there wasn't one. Obviously, parking the getaway vehicle away from the place being burgled was common knowledge.

Every ounce of common sense in her was

screaming for her to leave and leave fast. That would be the rule for this situation, but Annie wasn't following rules tonight. She was tired of following rules. She'd followed the rules and ended up broke and divorced, so what was the point?

Quietly unplugging one of Lynn's ugly metal lamps, Annie took off the shade. Holding the lamp base like a weapon, she crept down the hallway, trailing the cord after her.

The glow toward the left meant the robber was still in the office.

Telling herself she was just going to look and see who it was, Annie approached the room.

Hugging the wall, trying to breathe quietly, she inched toward the doorway and looked in. A tiny light on the desk illuminated the open drawer of the file cabinet, but the office was empty.

So where was—

A hand covered her mouth as someone grabbed her from behind and jerked her backward.

The hard-muscled body told Annie it was a man—a man with arms of steel and thighs of…some other metal.

Metal! The lamp!

She swung it behind her as hard as she could, though she couldn't get much momentum since her upper arms were pinioned against her sides. At the same time, she threw her weight against the man.

He staggered, and his grip over her mouth slipped enough for her to bite his hand.

He inhaled sharply and jerked his hand away before letting loose with an impressive string of curses, some of which weren't in English, all of them whispered furiously.

No whispering for Annie. She screamed as she'd never screamed before—screamed her throat raw as she tried to run and got tangled up in the lamp cord.

"Hey! Don't!" He grabbed her turtleneck. "I'm not going to hurt you!"

Annie screamed again and kicked his legs for good measure.

"*Shut up,* damn it! Somebody's going to hear you!"

"That's the whole point!" Annie was inhaling for another scream when it registered that there was something familiar about the voice. Groping for the hall light switch, she found it and flipped it on.

"*Nick?*" There, holding his hand and glowering at her from beneath lowered eyebrows, was Deena's little brother.

CHAPTER THREE

STILL-GORGEOUS BROTHER, Annie mentally corrected, remembering the hard feel of his body when he'd held her against him.

She'd felt his confident strength, the kind that came from not having to prove anything—because it had already been proved.

And he's certainly proved he can tempt you, hasn't he?

Maybe he'd forgotten. She intended to act like she had.

They stared at each other for a charged moment as Annie willed her runaway heart to slow.

Nick gestured to the wall switch with his eyes. "Turn off the light."

Still shaking, Annie did so. "What are you doing here?"

"Same thing as you, I imagine—trying to find out where Ronnie stashed his cash." He moved passed her, a huge shadow in the near darkness.

"Did I... Does your hand hurt?"

"Yes."

"I'm sorry."

"Forget it."

Picking up the lamp, she followed him. "If it's bleeding, then—"

"Be quiet, Annie." He stole across the living room to the windows and parted the curtains slightly.

Annie had never seen anyone sneak like that before. No wonder she hadn't heard him leave the office. But he'd probably had lots of practice leaving bedrooms in the night. Nick wasn't the sort to commit.

He searched the street in front of the house, his dark eyes moving back and forth. The streetlamp cast a bluish beam of light across his face, shading his jaw and emphasizing his chiseled cheekbones.

Though she'd seen him at Jennifer's graduation just a month ago, Annie had spent the time avoiding eye contact with him, and hadn't really studied him. Now she did.

His hair wasn't cut in the businessman-short style she normally preferred, but curled around his forehead, temples and ears and along the back of his neck, reminding Annie of a Roman statue. She'd thought his hair was longer because he'd avoided regular haircuts—unlike a responsible person—but now that she'd spent some time inspecting him, it was obvious that she was looking at the work of a really good hairdresser. Her fingers idly touched the too-dry ends of her own shoulder-length hair. Maybe she'd ask him whom he used.

Deena's little brother had grown up in the past

seven years. Maturity had settled well on his features, given him a potent air of masculinity. Not that he hadn't always been attractive—and known it—but there had been nothing substantive behind the good looks.

Annie very much suspected that now there was. Something substantive and intriguing.

"Do you hear any sirens?" he asked her, speaking barely above a whisper—a low, rumbling sound that vibrated through her.

"Do you think somebody called the police?" Her voice was husky from screaming.

"Is this the sort of neighborhood where people call the police if they hear screaming in the middle of the night?"

"It used to be." Annie thought of something. "But why would the police put on their sirens? That would alert burglars to the fact that they were on their way."

"Perhaps there's a rule about running the sirens. You'd want them to follow the rules, wouldn't you, Annie?" He glanced down at her, his gaze holding hers for a fraction of a second before sweeping downward over her body, then quickly returning to the window.

Awareness spritzed through her. She'd just been checked out—and found wanting. Who was Nick Mandola to find *her* lacking? Besides, any quality Nick valued wasn't one she wanted.

"Do you see anything?" she asked, conscious of the stiffness in her voice.

"No." He opened the curtains a bit wider. "It looks like your caterwauling didn't attract any attention." Letting the curtain drop, he turned to her.

Now what? She could feel him staring at her, though with his back to the dim light coming from the dining room, she could no longer see his eyes.

Annie swallowed. Was she imagining the electric tension in the silence? Somebody should say something. She was the responsible party here; it was up to her to take the lead and set the tone for the situation in which they found themselves.

"I didn't expect to see you here," she said. Not brilliant but, okay, it was a start.

"I know." He spoke quietly, just loud enough to take the whisper out of his voice. "You were lucky."

The nerve. "To have the wits scared out of me? I think not."

"You were lucky it was me and not some crazed killer."

"Oh? And how did you know that *I* wasn't a crazed killer?"

He pointed to *Private Investigating for Dummies* on top of her backpack by the front door.

"Well... I—I don't do this often."

"I'm glad to hear it. You aren't very good."

"Excuse me, I was hiding and you never even knew I was there."

"The kitchen, right? Or were you in the laundry room with the dog?"

Sure, *now* he could figure out where she'd been, but she'd bet he'd had a few nervous moments himself.

He took the lamp she still held and trailed the cord across the carpet. "Hear that?"

She nodded.

"So did I." He set the lamp on a table. Not the right one, but Annie could move it later.

Bending down, he picked up her backpack. "What have you got in here?"

"My equipment."

Nick snorted derisively and moved into the dining room where he emptied her backpack onto the table.

"Watch it, you'll chip the glass."

"And you care?"

"I'm here to find out what's going on, not to engage in wanton destruction."

"For a minute there, I thought you were about to say 'wanton *behavior.*'"

Same old sophomoric Nick. She relaxed a little. "You wish."

"Yes, I do. A little wantonness would be good for you." He looked right at her as he spoke and this time Annie could see his eyes.

She wished she couldn't.

There was nothing sophomoric about the way he was looking at her. No, this was the look of a mature man who knew what he wanted and how to get it. But Nick had always been able to look sincerely interested when he wished to. It was part of his charm—charm to which she was immune.

At least, now she was.

Before she could think of a suitably scathing remark, he turned back to the stuff from her backpack.

"Piece of junk" was his opinion of the broken lockpick gun, which he tossed into the backpack.

Annie winced at the sound it made on the table. Maybe the canvas material would protect it. "I got inside, didn't I?"

"A miracle."

A key, but Annie wasn't going to admit it. "Well, what were you going to use?"

He held her gaze for a long moment, reached into the multipocketed vest he wore, withdrew a flat, leather packet and handed it to her. Annie untied the packet. Inside were more than a dozen slim metal tools. Even Spy Supply Shop hadn't had lockpicking kits as elaborate as this one.

These were not the tools of an amateur, onetime burglar. She hardly knew what to say. Her thumb traced the squiggly end of one of the picks.

"That's a rake," Nick said, and pointed. "Next to it is a ball rake and a double-ball rake. These are feeler picks. Those are tension wrenches, like the one you used to turn the lock cylinder after you aligned the pins with your gun."

Annie hadn't aligned anything and was very much afraid she'd loaded the gun with the tension wrench instead of one of the picks. That would explain the difficulty she'd had in making the gun work—and why it had broken. "You seem to know a lot about picking locks."

"Yes." He took the set back, secured it and stowed it in a pocket in one smooth movement that told Annie he'd done the same thing many times before. "It comes in handy when I'm researching a location."

Yeah, right. "You're a *travel* writer—or so you've been telling everybody."

"I am." He glanced at her. "Among other things."

She would *not* ask him what other things, though it was clear he wanted her to.

"Hey, nice." He picked up a tiny camera used for photographing documents. "This set you back a few bucks."

"I rented it."

"'Rented'?" He shook his head. "You left a paper trail wider than the Dallas-Fort Worth turnpike. Always pay cash."

"I didn't have the cash," Annie said through gritted teeth. "That's why I'm here."

Nick set the camera to one side. "Where was your lawyer during the settlement negotiations?"

Annie's face heated. It was none of his business. "The same place Deena's was," she snapped.

He gave her a long look from under raised eyebrows.

Annie felt like scum. "I'm sorry. That was a nasty remark."

"Don't apologize. I'm beginning to think you're an interesting woman, after all." A corner of his mouth tilted upward in a suggestive smile.

Interesting to Nick? What was happening to her?

He picked up the night-vision scope, turned it over, then looked at her through it. "Cold-war surplus. This is probably twenty-five years old."

She pushed it away. "It was too much trouble."

"Not when all you've got is starlight," he murmured, and returned the scope to the backpack.

Oh, honestly. He was so transparent. He'd probably gotten involved in murky doings in some backwater country and felt all grown-up now.

Was she supposed to be impressed?

Had lots of women been?

"And what were you planning to do with this?" He held up what looked like a smoke detector.

"Surveillance. It's a camera and microphone. If I don't find what I need tonight, then I'm planting that here."

"And then sit in your car about a block away, eavesdropping night after night, hoping they'll incriminate themselves?"

She hadn't thought that far ahead, but pretended she had. "If that's what it takes to catch Ronald, then yes."

"Where are you going to put it? In the bedroom?"

"I already caught Ronald there, thank you very much." Caught him with Lynn after he'd done everything but rent a billboard announcing the affair. Everyone but Annie had known. To her mortification, she felt her cheeks burn at the memory.

Surprisingly gentle fingers nudged her chin up until Annie was forced to meet Nick's gaze. She glared at him.

"I'm sorry," he said. His index finger swept softly along her jaw before he dropped his hand and turned away.

Annie swallowed, her skin tingling from Nick's touch. She didn't want her skin—or anything else—tingling from Nick's touch. She brushed her fingertips against her sensitized jaw. Really, she didn't.

NICK FLIPPED THROUGH the "Dummies" book without reading.

Annie. After all the years he'd stayed away and all the miles he'd put between them, after all the recklessly dangerous situations he'd put himself in, thinking he could scare the memory of her out of him, she was here, standing next to him.

And she still had the power to affect him as no other woman ever had.

Her skin was as soft as he remembered, and her resolve—just as hard.

He'd been young and so certain that the strength of his feelings would be enough to offer her, enough to show her she belonged with him and not with his former brother-in-law.

But when she'd looked at him with contempt at Jennifer's graduation, Nick had known that Annie hadn't and wouldn't ever forgive him. Things were still only black-and-white with her.

And yet…she was here in a gray situation.

Had she changed? *Could* she change?

Were her feelings for him gone, or locked away?

Nick snapped the book shut and returned it to her backpack.

Before the night was over, he intended to find out.

"YOU CAN STOP SNEERING at my equipment and go home now. I've got everything under control."

Slowly, Nick zipped up her backpack and turned. "I'm not going anywhere."

"That's a switch." She reached for her backpack.

"Neither am I going to let you keep taking verbal potshots at me because you're embarrassed."

"I'm not embarrassed," Annie retorted quickly and dragged her pack from the table.

"Yes, you are. You've avoided me for the last seven years." He moved away from the table.

"Avoided you?" Annie managed a credible

laugh as she backstepped. "Our paths never crossed, that's all."

"And you made sure they didn't."

"It wasn't hard. I rarely travel in Outer Mongolia."

"I'm in Richardson a couple of times a year." He took another step toward her.

Annie positioned the backpack between them. "And just because I don't happen to be there at the same time, you think I'm avoiding you?"

His lips curved upward. "Either that, or you're afraid."

She clutched the backpack. "Of you?"

"Of yourself."

"Oh...oh, that is so...so typical," Annie spluttered. "You think a woman can't be near you without wanting to rip off her clothes and beg you to—" Her throat closed and she finished the sentence by gesturing with her hand.

He smiled wryly. "I wish women would act on these impulses."

"I'm sure many have." Now she sounded prissy. What business of hers was it what Nick had done and whom he'd done it with?

"Maybe I was wrong." His voice eddied around her. Annie meant to stand her ground, but the sheer forcefulness of him made her yield another small step backward. "You're not afraid, you're jealous."

"*Jealous?* Of being in your collection of one-night stands?'' Why was she wasting time talking to him, anyway? There were a lot of files to go through. Annie tried to step around him, but he blocked her path.

"I was right the first time. You *are* afraid." He stepped forward, again forcing Annie to retreat. "Afraid to admit you made a mistake? Afraid to admit you have regrets?"

She felt the wall at her back. "Because I didn't run away with you? I was engaged to Ronald. It was two days before my wedding."

"Was that the only reason you didn't come with me?"

It seemed like a darned good reason to Annie— no matter how her marriage had ultimately turned out. But conventions and rules had never mattered to Nick. "I—I didn't even know you."

"You knew all you needed to know."

She knew that he was exciting, impulsive, and fun. She was staid, responsible, and serious. "Maybe that's why I didn't come with you."

He blinked—the only sign that her words might have had any effect on him. "You didn't come with me because you were scared. It was easier to stay with the safe and the comfortable than to take a chance and go with me."

"You weren't offering anything!" she retorted. That wasn't what she'd wanted to say at all—nor the way she'd wanted to say it.

She tried to move away, but he planted a hand

on either side of her shoulders, standing close enough for her to feel the heat of his body. "I was offering everything."

Had he been?

She remembered that day seven years ago all too clearly. She and Ronald had driven from Houston to Richardson to pick up Jennifer and Kevin, who were coming to their wedding. Nick had been there, visiting Deena and the kids. It had been the first time Annie had met her future stepchildren's uncle, though she'd heard a lot about him.

Even now, she could remember how his dark eyes had studied her in frank admiration—so frank, in fact, that she'd glanced at Ronald to see if he'd noticed. But Ronald's attention had been on an anxious Deena.

The plan had been for Annie to take the kids to Six Flags Over Texas while Ronald and Deena met with their lawyers; Annie had willingly signed a prenuptial agreement securing Jennifer and Kevin's inheritance, and there were a few other details to be discussed before the wedding.

Nick had come along with Annie and the children to the amusement park.

She found it incredible to remember that they'd only spent a day together. It had been a magical day, a day when Annie had fallen under Nick's spell. He'd made her feel alive in a way that Ronald never had.

Throughout that day she'd listened as he'd entertained Jennifer and Kevin—and her—with descriptions of faraway lands, until she could smell the leather of a Moroccan souk, feel the dankness of old underground Edinburgh, and taste the saltiness of Greek olives.

And always, always, Nick's eyes had sought hers, sending increasingly intimate messages she should have ignored.

She wasn't proud of the fact that much later, when Nick had kissed her—his lips warm and seductive—she'd kissed him back. More than once. The potent effect of his mouth had drugged her so that she'd listened in a fog as he'd asked her to come away with him, to travel to foreign lands and experience the life he could show her.

She was even less proud that she—a woman about to be married in thirty-six hours—had listened. The fact that she was another man's fiancée had been of no concern to Nick. And truthfully, when Annie had been lost in his mind-numbing kisses and bold caresses, it had been of no concern to her, either.

So close to her now, Nick's mouth softened and he dipped his head. "Are you remembering how it was between us?"

So help her, she was.

"Regrets, Annie?"

He'd been leaving at dawn the next morning. "Meet me at the coffee shop," he'd said.

"No," she managed.

"Never?"

"I was *engaged*."

"But you're not married or engaged now, are you?"

She could barely move her head enough to shake it.

"Good." He stared at her for several moments longer, his gaze roaming her face and lingering on her lips.

He was about to kiss her. She could feel it. He stood only inches away. He'd tilted his head. In spite of herself, she had leaned slightly away from the wall toward him.

But instead of kissing her, he lifted his hand and brushed his thumb, slowly and softly, down the length of her cheek. Then, with a little smile, he pushed away from the wall and strode toward the office.

Annie stared after him, annoyed that her hands were trembling and her heart was pounding. Why, *why* did he still affect her? If she'd gone with him all those years ago, he would have dumped her after a few weeks, leaving her with nothing but lovely memories and a broken heart.

Instead…she'd been dumped after a few *years* and left with ugly memories and a bruised heart.

The backpack slid down to her knees. This was not a thought she wanted to have at this precise moment. She'd made the right choice. She'd gone for stability, prosperity, responsibility, and other grown-up, multisyllabic concepts. All Nick had offered was the instant gratification of single syllables: fun, trips, and sex.

Annie waited for the wave of revulsion to wash over her. There wasn't even a ripple. Standing against the dining-room wall of her ex-husband's house, she tried to remember why single-syllable things were bad. The fact that she couldn't probably meant she was having a premature midlife crisis. Trust her to have a crisis when it was most inconvenient.

Midlife was the time when women cut their hair, pierced something or got a tattoo—or both—and ran off with their tennis coaches. Or personal trainers. Or their ex-husband's ex-wife's brother, especially if he looked like Nick.

Annie swallowed air, then had to pound her chest.

She'd tweaked his pride once, and he was going to take advantage now, if she'd let him. Nick thought she was ripe for the plucking—that was it.

Well, she hadn't been ripe then, and she wasn't now. She tossed her head, briefly considered a haircut, and strode down the hall after him.

CHAPTER FOUR

ANNIE FOUND NICK rifling through a file drawer. Allowing herself just fractions of a second to admire the strong lines of his solid neck and broad shoulders, she cleared her throat. "Do you know what you're looking for?"

"I figure that a guy who's been up for Grand Emperor of the cell-phone biz as many times as Ronnie has is too smart to let his personal funds tank," he answered, as though nothing had happened between them just moments ago. Probably because nothing had. "He's got to have an offshore account." He glanced up at her. "What are you looking for?"

Annie would be crisply professional. The consummate burglar. She would not be plucked. "Another set of books. HI-Com can't be doing as bad as he says."

"So we're both convinced there's money somewhere."

"If there's not, then I want to know where it went."

They were having a normal—for the circumstances—conversation. Annie was proud of herself.

Without warning, Nick shined his light—a piercing amber beam—right in her face. "If you find the money, what will you do?"

"Hey!" She shielded her eyes. "What kind of light is that?"

"A high-powered LED. Answer the question."

Annie didn't like his tone, but she answered anyway. "I'm going to make sure Jennifer enrolls in college, even if she has to live in a motel until a dorm room opens up." And he'd better not argue with her.

He immediately lowered the light. "That's the right answer."

"That's the only answer." She'd expected him to argue about the necessity of a college education. At least he'd gained some sense in the past seven years. "What was with the light in my eyes?"

"I wanted to see your face so I'd know if you were lying."

Annie dropped her backpack and took out her own penlight. She'd thought it very high-tech, until she'd seen Nick's. "People can't squint and lie at the same time?"

"Sure they can, but I'll know it."

Really? Annie walked over to the file drawer, pointed her light at his face and pressed the button. "So what are *your* plans?"

He didn't squint, but her light wasn't as bright as his. "Lawyers give me hives. I thought I'd negotiate one-on-one with old Ronnie, and I needed something to negotiate with."

"You mean blackmail."

He gave her a half smile. "That's the idea."

Annie turned the concept over in her mind. "I like it." She tilted her penlight to the files and began reading labels. Pulling a correspondence file, she said, "You help me, and I'll help you. Deena and the kids win."

For a moment, Nick didn't move. "You *are* more interesting." He reached for the file drawer and echoed her words. "I like it."

Annie tried not to feel pleased. To change the subject, she gestured to his hand. The tiny light she'd seen on the desk earlier was now wrapped around his finger. "Nifty little gadget you've got there."

"Yeah." He wiggled his fingers, sending the amber light dancing around the room. "Lets my hands roam free."

Various images involving Nick's roaming hands flickered through Annie's mind.

The darkness was creating a false intimacy, that was the problem. "Cute as a ring light is, can we turn on the desk lamp? I pulled the shade earlier."

Nick moved away to do as she asked, and she drew a deep breath. *Think pure thoughts,* she instructed herself.

Nick leaned against the file cabinet and watched her. "You know, I've always admired the way you helped raise Jennifer and Kevin, and that you kept in contact with them after the divorce.''

"They were my stepchildren." She looked up at him. "I divorced their father, but I couldn't divorce them. I'm grateful that Deena understood."

"'Understood'? She had me tracked down in Africa when she found out you and Ronald were divorcing. I thought somebody had died. Then I had to convince her that, no, I didn't think Ronald was doing this to get back at her for wanting more child support."

Annie laughed. "That sounds like Deena."

"Yeah." He smiled. "You've been a good friend to her."

A friend? Annie hadn't ever thought of herself as Deena's friend. "I like Deena," she said slowly, just realizing it was true.

"You two aren't much alike," he observed.

"I know." Annie would never have let herself be like Deena—a housewife with no marketable skills. Deena had dropped out of school to marry Ronald. She'd been exactly what he'd wanted her to be—a stay-at-home wife and mother while he concentrated on building HI-Com.

And then he got bored with her. He'd changed and she'd stayed the same. Annie had always wondered why Deena hadn't seen the breakup coming. But then, Annie hadn't seen it in her own marriage, had she?

She glanced at Nick to find him still watching

her, apparently waiting for her to comment. "I suppose I thought Deena got a raw deal. She followed all Ronald's rules, then he changed them."

"Friendship out of guilt?"

"Not guilt in the way you mean." Annie withdrew the bank-statement file from the drawer and tossed it on the desk. "I did *not* break up her marriage to Ronald."

He raised an eyebrow. "Not intentionally."

"What do you mean?"

He propped his jaw on his fist, openly allowing his gaze to drift over her. "I mean, you just are."

Yuck. New Age stuff. "I 'just am' what?"

"You're smart and quick, loyal and kind."

"I sound like a Labrador retriever."

"You take injustice personally, and you aren't afraid to fight for what you believe is right."

"A patriotic Labrador retriever."

"You have compassion in your eyes and romance in your soul," he continued, his voice dropping in both volume and pitch.

It was the voice of seduction—passion honed by time and experience. Nothing New Age about it. Annie felt goose bumps on her arms in spite of herself.

"You have a timeless allure."

"Nick—"

He stepped forward and wrapped an arm around her waist, pulling her close to his body. The unexpectedness of the gesture effectively stopped her words. He placed his finger against her parted lips. Then, instead of immediately dropping his hand, he slowly and sensuously traced the outline of her mouth, sensitizing every nerve more effectively than a kiss.

She should have protested, but that would have required moving her lips.

He bent to speak in her ear. "And when you make love, you pour your entire being into the experience. What man wouldn't want that?" he whispered. She could feel his warm breath caress her cheek. "What man wouldn't want you?"

He was speaking hypothetically and yet, the expression in his eyes, the dim light, the palpable timbre of his voice as it wrapped itself around her, the tingling in her lips, the solidity of him against her... For a moment, she believed.

Then she remembered. "Ronald obviously didn't." She pulled away from him and slammed shut the file drawer.

Nick straightened, his expression unchanged. It unnerved her and she suspected he knew it. "I wasn't finished with that drawer," he protested lightly.

Annie had already opened the one beneath it. "There wasn't anything new in there. Remember, I set up those files."

"And you don't think they've added anything in the past year?" He was right behind her reading over her shoulder.

Annie felt his breath on her cheek. She needed to find something else for him to do—something on the other side of the room.

"Wait a minute. I just remembered something." Shoving closed the file drawer, she bent and opened the one beneath it, in the process bumping against Nick. "Sorry."

"I'm not."

Ignore him. You're an unripe fruit clinging to the tree. "Ronald used to keep keys in here." She pulled the *K* file and triumphantly found three keys.

"He files his keys under *K?*" Nick asked in disbelief.

"Great hiding place, huh? It's so obvious, you never would have thought to look there."

"Hmm."

Annie dropped one of the keys back into the file. "That's the key to this file drawer." She handed the other two to Nick. "The big one should fit the desk drawer. He used to keep copies of HI-Com financial records in there when he brought them home."

Nick was already on the other side of the desk. "What's the little one open?"

"That's a spare to a locked box where he keeps his memoirs."

"His *memoirs?* What's he writing, *How to Lose Wives and Alienate People?*"

"No. He's overqualified."

Nick laughed as he unlocked the drawer. "All right, Annie! I like this side of you."

She sighed. "You encourage the worst in me."

"Relax. If that's your worst, then you're a saint." Sitting in the desk chair, Nick looked through the files. "Ever hear of Texafone?"

"Yes." Annie felt her blood pressure rise. "They're a start-up company with the usual low-ball offers to build a customer base. They've been particularly cutthroat."

"So...HI-Com is losing customers?"

Annie sat on the edge of the desk and started flipping through the correspondence file she'd withdrawn earlier. "We ignored them at first. Many times, new phone companies can't deliver what they've promised. If they stick around, then we either match their offers, or lose the smaller customers. The larger businesses know that any savings will be lost in the hassle of switching accounts and access codes. Still, this time, we've had to adjust a few contracts."

Nick was silent. She leaned over the desk to see what had captured his attention.

"There are more rewarding ways to strain your back," he murmured and pulled out a bulging hanging file labeled Texafone. "I'll be happy to demonstrate."

Annie straightened. "I didn't realize you found hauling your ego around so rewarding." She reached for the file as he laughed.

"You always have a way of lightening the load."

Ignoring him, Annie sat with her back to him and looked through the file. But she couldn't ignore him. Little prickles of awareness skipped down her spine. She found herself listening for the sound of his fingers sifting through the files. Every rustling sound she heard set her nerves tingling as though his hands were touching her, not the papers.

The desk creaked as Nick stretched across it toward her, his head dangerously close to her breast as he studied the file in front of her.

"See anything?" he asked.

Keeping her body still, she turned only her head to answer him. One false move, and there would be contact.

Still looking at the file, he said, "Ronnie's got copies of Texafone's correspondence."

Annie tried to focus on the papers in front of her. Nick was right. At first, she thought she was looking at correspondence between HI-Com and Texafone, but these letters had been written on Texafone stationery.

"It looks like he's done a bit of industrial spying on the side," Nick commented, sitting up and reaching around her to flip the pages.

In the process, his forearm brushed against her breast—purely by accident. Annie was prepared to give him the benefit of the doubt. But the action had sent pulses of sensation shooting through her entire body.

"What else is in that file?" He reached for a blue folder.

It was labeled Contracts. Annie should have been paying attention instead of obsessing over Nick's strange magnetism. His potent, manly magnetism. His *nearby,* potent, manly magnetism. The fact that he was so close she could touch him if she wanted, and make it look like an accident... "Stop that!"

"What?" a startled Nick asked at the same time she jerked toward him, surprised that she'd spoken aloud.

Her shoulder bumped into his wide, hard chest in inadvertent intimacy. Annie yelped and sprang back.

"Annie, settle down. Obviously, you don't have the nerves for snooping. What's the matter?"

You. She swallowed dryly. *I'm thinking too much. I should talk more and think less.* "I—I was allowing my thoughts to run away with...possibilities instead of carefully evaluating the facts in hand." That was better.

But maybe not. Nick's expression hardened. "You're afraid you'll find something in the file that will make Ronnie look bad, and you don't want me to see it."

"I don't?" This was so far from what Annie

was actually thinking that it took her a minute to follow his train of thought.

"You're still trying to protect him." Nick shook his head. "What kind of hold does this man have over you women?"

"No hold, I swear. Here." She thrust the entire file at him and hopped off the desk. "Have at it."

Nick snatched up the file with a deflating eagerness. So much for Annie's timeless allure. "Does this look familiar?" He handed her a stapled packet of papers.

Annie flipped through the paragraphs of legal babble. "It appears to be a copy of a Texafone commercial contract. Hey, they can't promise unlimited airtime for that price. They'll go broke!"

"Isn't that what you want?"

"They won't go broke fast enough." Annie slumped. "HI-Com can't match this—we've got too many customers. All Texafone has to do is wait us out."

"But don't people realize that they'll get sucked in and then the rates will skyrocket?"

She paged through the contract. "They won't skyrocket for a year—look at the dates." Angrily, she thrust the contract at him as he leaned over, and ended up punching him in the chest with it. The papers crumpled.

His hand closed over hers.

"I'm so sorry!" Annie could feel his heart beating.

"I've accepted the fact that being around you is painful." There was no smile. After a moment, Nick slid his hand to the contract and peeled it out of her clenched fingers.

Talk, Annie. She couldn't think of anything to say. Blindly grabbing the first thing her hand encountered—fortunately, an inanimate object—she stared until the words on the papers she picked up made sense.

It was the HI-Com correspondence file. And once the words sank in, Annie gasped.

"What now?" Nick asked.

"These are letters offering contract discounts to our existing customers. Ronald offered retroactive rebates and a year's extension!" This was far more than an adjustment, and Annie hadn't known anything about it. No wonder profits were down so sharply. "He can't do that!"

"It's his company."

"Not entirely. I own a substantial chunk of stock. I took it for my share of the house. And...and every time Ronald needed to borrow money, he'd trade me stock for it." Annie was struggling between anger and embarrassment. She was the vice president; how could Ronald justify not telling her about the scope of the contract discounts? And by keeping the files here, he made sure she wouldn't find out.

"Why did he need to borrow money?"

"For the—" Annie broke off when she remembered she was talking to Deena's brother. "He just did."

"Ann-ie..."

She couldn't look him in the eye. "We had a lot of equipment expenditures this year." And office redecorating Ronald had insisted was necessary.

"That's company money."

"Well...sometimes Ronald fronts money from his personal funds until the financing comes through. He gets impatient."

Nick made a tsking sound. "Mingling corporate and personal funds? Can he do that?"

"He does it anyway." Annie had argued with Ronald on countless occasions about that very thing. More often than not, it had been Annie against Ronald *and* Lynn. Lynn had figured out some legal tap dance and also had soon waltzed off with Annie's husband.

"And what happens if the financing doesn't come through?"

"It usually does. Sometimes it takes a while— Look, don't worry about it, okay?"

Nick slid off the desk. "I thought we were here *because* we're worried."

He sounded so calm and rational, and Annie didn't want "calm and rational." She wanted righteous anger. She wanted more "Ronald is scum" talk. Okay, she'd start. "We're here because Ronald is scum."

"We already know that. We're trying to find out new stuff," Nick replied in that patronizing way men have of talking to women whom they suspect are experiencing PMS.

"We're trying to find money," Annie said, smacking the files.

Nick moved her hand. "You said you usually wait out the upstarts."

"What?"

Nick pointed to the dates on the letters. "HI-Com didn't wait very long."

Annie stared. The first of the letters offering discounts was dated late last summer, which was something she should have caught herself. She paged through them and noticed when the text of the letters changed. "A rate increase for new customers? Now? Is he insane?"

"That theory has always appealed to me." Nick rummaged through her backpack and withdrew the copy camera she'd rented. "Shall we break this in?"

Annie nodded. She wanted proof of Ronald's astonishing offers. "Don't you have some more advanced giz-widget?"

Nick laughed lightly. "A scanner, but I'm feeling nostalgic at the moment." Deftly, he tilted the desk lamp over the letters and gestured for Annie to pick the ones she wanted photographed. Sitting, he propped his elbows on the desk.

As he photographed, Annie read more and more

of the correspondence. "It's like Ronald's deliberately trying to torpedo HI-Com. Why?" She was talking more to herself than to Nick.

"You tell me."

"I have no idea."

"Sure you do. You were married to him—you know what makes him tick."

"I didn't like what made him tick," Annie mumbled. "That's why we're divorced."

"Why? What did he want?"

"The usual—money and power, with the adulation of his peers thrown in for good measure, which is why bankrupting the company makes no sense."

"Unless it gets him what he wants."

"But how…" Ronald's business diary. All his plans, his goals and his methods were meticulously recorded there. She had to get a look at it.

Nick looked up. "You've got an interesting gleam in your eye."

Annie picked up the small key that fit Ronald's lockbox and dangled it in front of Nick's face. "Why don't we let Ronald himself tell us what he's up to?" She headed for the master bedroom.

"Hang on, Annie. Are you finished here?"

"For now."

"Then let's clean up and put away our toys."

"Can't we do that later?" Annie was impatient to read Ronald's diary.

"It has been my experience that covering your tracks as you go is best."

Annie tried to ignore this comment as she had his other oblique references to their nefarious doings, and she could practically hear Ronald's diary calling to her.

She turned in the doorway. Nick was carefully replacing the papers in the file, smoothing the crumpled contract. The desk lamp cast sharp shadows on his handsome face and picked out the rich glints in his dark hair.

Annie had kept a mental image of Nick Mandola for seven years and she was finally admitting to herself that the man who sat at the desk no longer matched that image. Now she wanted to know who he had become. After all, he was a huge influence on Jennifer and Kevin. A responsible ex-stepparent would be concerned, wouldn't she? And Annie was, and ever would be, responsible.

Trying to appear offhand, she returned to the cabinet and replaced the files Nick had sorted. "Have you, er, had much experience covering your tracks?"

"What?"

He knew what she meant; he just wanted the satisfaction of having her formulate the question. Maybe he hadn't changed so much, after all.

"You said that we had to finish here because *in your experience* it was best to cover your tracks as you went along," she repeated, hating herself for succumbing to his vague allusions to clandestine activities. "So go ahead and tell me all about it. You've been dying to all night."

SHE WAS RIGHT, AND HE wasn't proud of it. An inescapable fact of the past several years had been that Annie's opinion of him mattered. And from comments made by his niece and nephew, he knew that opinion wasn't high, which was why he'd given in to the temptation to let her know that his travel research was occasionally a mask for more covert activities. He *had* wanted to impress her. It was juvenile and she'd called him on it.

By itself, researching for travel guides was a respectable occupation, yet why she objected to it, he didn't know. To hear her talk, he was little better than a vagabond.

So he didn't have a house in the suburbs—why would he want one? He traveled most of the time—it was his job. And as for being irresponsible—that one still stung—wouldn't entering a relationship with false promises of commitment be more irresponsible than keeping it casual right from the start?

"Well?" she prompted. "Here's your chance to impress me."

Instead, he asked, "Why don't you like me, Annie?"

She looked startled, then uncomfortable.

"Come on, here's your chance to tell me off."

Nick sat back in the desk chair and crossed his arms.

"It's—it's nothing personal," she stammered. "You've chosen a way of life that—that I wouldn't have."

"And that makes it wrong?"

"It makes you an inappropriate role model for Jennifer and Kevin," she said primly.

"And you *are?*"

She flushed, but stood her ground. "I'm a responsible—"

"There's that word again."

"Because decent people *are* responsible. They deal with their problems instead of running away from them. They know that life isn't a never-ending vacation and that relationships, both business and personal, require hard work."

"Hey—*I'm* responsible. I'm employed. I meet deadlines. And you wouldn't believe the problems I've dealt with."

"Problems requiring a lockpick?"

"Sometimes, yes. I've had my passport confiscated a time or two, and a lockpick sure cuts through the red tape."

She made a disgusted sound. "That sounds like you…stir things up, then run away and let others clean up the mess."

He stared at her. "Where did *that* come from?"

"You're never around long enough in any one place to see what effects your actions have."

"What are you talking about?"

"I'm— Well, as *one* example, I'm talking about the time you told Kevin that learning was more important than grades."

"Isn't it?"

She inhaled through gritted teeth. "Yes, but you were talking to a ten-year-old boy. After that, he wouldn't do his homework because Uncle Nick said it wasn't important. Deena had to keep taking time off work to talk to Kevin's teachers. Since she's paid by the hour, that meant no pay. And because he had three zeros, Kevin missed a class field trip."

"I had no idea." In fact, he couldn't even remember uttering those words to Kevin. Deena had never mentioned the problem they had created. What else hadn't Deena mentioned?

"That's my point. By then, you were gone." Annie gestured with her hands. "When the going gets tough, you get going."

"T-shirt philosophy? I expected better of you, Annie."

"Why? You expected me to walk away from my engagement to Ronald as though it meant nothing. What kind of person would do that?"

A smart person, Nick thought. A woman with an ironclad sense of who she was. An adventurous woman. A woman who had a zest for life. The woman he'd thought Annie was. "Well, you didn't walk away. No harm done."

"No harm?" Her eyes were bright. "For you, maybe. You'd probably forgotten about me before the plane cleared the end of the runway. But I had to live with the guilt of what I'd done."

"Guilt over a few kisses?"

"I wasn't free to kiss anybody but Ronald. I'd given my word."

Nick understood. "Kissing me forced you to realize that you weren't in love with Ronald and you've resented it ever since, haven't you?"

She shook her head. "I—"

"You should have been grateful that I gave you an opportunity to keep from making a big mistake."

"I didn't make a mistake," she insisted. "My marriage may have failed, but at least I made the commitment and spent six years trying to make it work."

"What were you trying for—a medal? Annie, you shouldn't have married the guy in the first place."

"How can you say that?"

"He was my brother-in-law for fourteen years, that's how. He dumped my sister, but not until he'd done such a number on her that she thought she was a completely useless and ineffective human being." He gazed at her. "Which makes me wonder what he did to you, Annie."

"Nothing," she answered quickly. "My self-confidence is intact. My pride was bruised some, that's all.''

Nick didn't buy it for a minute. By the time Ronald had left her, Deena had been convinced that she deserved to be left, that everything was her fault. ''Why did you stick around HI-Com? Ronald's new wife works there, too, doesn't she?''

''Yes.'' Her clipped response told him Annie's pride hadn't healed as much as she wanted to believe.

''And you stayed? Didn't you think you could get a job anywhere else?''

''Lynn took my husband. I didn't want her to have the satisfaction of taking my job, too. Plus, remember the stock I own. The better the company does, the better off I am.''

''But the company isn't doing well.''

Her lips pressed together. ''I'm going to go look for Ronald's diary. Go ahead and finish up in here.'' And she was out the door.

''Okay, now who's running away?'' he called after her.

Silence.

Good, let her think.

Grinning, Nick was congratulating himself on making some real progress with Annie when a cry of utter anguish tore through the house.

CHAPTER FIVE

"Ohhh!" Annie snapped her teeth together and bit her tongue.

"What happened?" Nick ran into the room and threw a protective arm in front of her.

Annie pushed it down. "They didn't even change the bedspread!" she wailed.

There in front of her was the very bed—with the very same blue-and-white custom bedspread—in which she'd discovered Ronald and Lynn.

"It matches the curtains," Nick said.

Slowly, Annie turned and gazed at him with contempt. "That is such a typically male comment."

"No way. How many men would notice that the bedspread and curtains match?"

"Just—just stop it," Annie snapped.

"Stop what?"

"Stop being right."

His mouth opened and closed. "I don't understand. If you'd wanted the bedspread so much, then why didn't you take it?"

Of course he didn't understand. Annie hadn't expected him to. "I didn't want it! I *don't* want it!

And she shouldn't, either. How can she sleep in another woman's bed?''

"It's a piece of furniture!"

"It's not a piece of furniture—it's a bed!"

"But it's not your bed anymore, so what do you care?"

Why couldn't he just drop it? Right now, male logic was infuriating Annie. She stormed over to the bed, wanting to knife it to shreds. Instead, she grabbed a pillow. "Do you see that piping?" She thrust the pillow at Nick and jabbed a finger at the edging. "*I* sewed that piping! I made these pillow covers from scraps of fabric from the bedspread that *I* ordered for *our* bed. I sewed miles of piping."

"It looks nice," Nick offered, clearly at a loss.

Annie snatched the pillow away from him, clutching it to her chest. "I didn't go to all that trouble for 'nice'!"

Nick stepped back. "It looks great," he said cautiously. "No, better than great. Stupendous. I can safely say that I've never seen any bedspread as attractive and as well made and accented so charmingly with pillows as—"

"You've seen a lot of bedspreads, I'll bet."

"Enough to know a good one when I see one."

Annie rearranged the pillows the correct way—her way. Lynn obviously had no taste. "You've never taken the time to notice a bedspread in your life. Admit it."

"I sure will from now on," he muttered.

"You do that." Annie glared at him. "Notice the next time you're taking advantage of some poor woman in a foreign country who invites you to her home, leads you to the bedroom and waits for your reaction to the bedspread she wove from yarn she spun from sheep she spent untold, boring, hours tending—except for the brief moments when she walked through the fields to hunt for berries and bark to make her own dyes—never mind the scratches on her legs, or the bugs, or the hot sun beating on her face, giving her premature wrinkles—"

"Breathe, Annie."

"Not until you acknowledge that poor woman's bedspread!"

Nick stared at her, his hair pushed up in front from where he'd rubbed his temple. "But you didn't weave this yourself. You just chose the fabric."

"Uuugh!" She lunged for one of the pillows and began beating the bed with it. "How *could* he? If he'd wanted a divorce, then why didn't he just *say* so? Why did he have to make me the butt of *jokes* and *snickers* and *pity?*" The pillow flew out of her fingers, so she grabbed another one—a long neck-roll with which she'd struggled to sew around its curves. "I *trusted* him. And to set me up—everyone in the whole *office* knew what was going to happen and when. '*Lynn* and I have a lunch meeting, Annie, then we'll head over to the *Bellaire* Merchants Association. Pull their file for me, will you, babe?' *Babe!*" "Babe" deserved an extra swat with the pillow. "He knew I hated being called 'babe' at the office. It's demeaning and unprofessional."

Annie's arms were tiring, but she didn't care. Anger, hurt and betrayal bubbled to the surface as strong now as it had been that day. "And then I couldn't find the file. I asked everyone where it was before I figured out that he must have left it *here*. So like a good little vice president/wifey, I ran here to get it myself instead of sending a secretary, just the way he knew I would. And he and Lynn were *right here*, naked, in the bed with *my* bedspread!"

ABOUT THE TIME ANNIE started babbling about sewing pillows, Nick realized this was a situation where nothing he said would be right, so he'd better keep quiet. He'd known the story of Ronald's affair with Lynn because Deena had told him, but hearing Annie's anguished version twisted something inside him.

Ronald would pay. He'd tramped through the lives of at least two fine women and a couple of kids and no one had made him pay. Not Nick's sister, who'd reined in her lawyer to avoid a protracted legal battle, nor Annie, who had been a too-good-to-be-true stepmother.

By all accounts, she'd been a too-good-to-be-true ex-wife, as well. Nick watched her beat the bed with pillows, knowing it was therapeutic for her, and that she should have released her anger long ago.

The best he could offer now was a shoulder for the inevitable tears.

"I just stood there," Annie said, staring at nothing. "I didn't scream. I didn't cry. I remember thinking, *I have to work with her. I have to be professional.*" She looked at Nick. "She's in bed with my husband in my home and *I'm* worried about being professional. Isn't that pathetic?"

"No." Nick ventured a couple of steps toward her. "You'd received a shock and this was your mind's way of dealing with it."

Annie seemed to want to believe him, but her gaze was drawn back to the bed. "And you know what he said? He said, 'It took you long enough.'" Her face was flushed. "I was so stupid." She dropped the pillow and covered her face with her hands. "I didn't know. I didn't even suspect."

Nick simply stepped forward and opened his arms. Annie leaned into him, a deep keening escaping from within her.

"Shh, Annie," he whispered, rubbing circles over her back. "He's not worth it." He didn't know if she'd heard him or not.

Annie raised her arms until they were linked loosely around his waist. "I know he's not worth it,'' she sobbed into his shoulder. ''But I thought he was. How could I have been so wrong? I'd worked with him every day for years before I married him. We were together all the time.''

She pulled back and looked up at Nick, tear tracks on her cheeks. It was the same expression he'd seen on his sister's face.

''Do you think that was what happened?'' Annie asked. ''We were together too much and he got bored with me?''

Hating Ronald, Nick shook his head.

''I—I tried to stay interesting,'' she continued. ''I read books, I took classes, I exercised—''

''Annie, you don't have to tell me this,'' Nick interrupted. ''Ronald was the jerk here, not you.'' His former brother-in-law had pulled the same mind games on Annie that he'd subjected Deena to. Somehow, he'd convinced Annie that she was unattractive and undesirable. Nick would be willing to bet any amount of money that there hadn't been a man in Annie's life since the divorce.

She pushed away, wiped her cheeks, and ran a shaky hand through her hair. ''I know. I keep telling myself that. But—'' she gestured toward the bed ''—it's embarrassingly obvious that I still haven't... I mean, after all this time, you'd think I'd be over it.''

''Your problem is that you've been too nice. You've been the one paying emotionally. Ronald hasn't paid anything. Stop being so nice and civil, Annie. Be uncivil. Get him back.''

"I don't want him back."

"No, I'm talking revenge."

"I'm not a revenge-type person." Even as she spoke, Annie was straightening the bed, smoothing the bedspread and arranging the pillows.

Nick wanted to shake her—anything to get her to take some action and reclaim her pride. "But, Annie, Ronald broke the rules."

Her hands stilled.

Talk of rules would get her attention. He should have known. "And he got away with it. He's still breaking rules—otherwise we wouldn't be here. So, come on. Isn't it time to show Ronald what happens to people who break the rules?"

She gave a last pat to the pillows. "How?"

A slow grin spread across Nick's face. "That's my girl." Annie's answering smile, though tentative, was just what he wanted to see. "Part of the satisfaction of revenge comes from the plotting— and there are rules, here."

"Revenge has rules?"

"Yes. Revenge must be limited to the person who deserves it—innocents can't suffer."

"That makes sense."

"And poetic justice provides an extra twist of the knife. Any ideas?"

"Pepper in Lynn's underwear?"

That surprised a laugh out of Nick. "Where do you come up with this stuff?"

"Girl Scout camp."

"Uh, we're looking for something a little more effective and long-lasting."

"Have you ever had pepper in your underwear on a hot, sweaty day?" she asked seriously.

"No. But we can do better. Where's Ronnie's diary?"

"When we were married, he kept it in the nightstand." She pulled open the drawer, then shrieked, "Condoms!"

Nick peered over her shoulder. "Good brand."

Annie slammed the door shut.

"Well, Annie, they're married. You've got to assume they're having sex."

She stared speculatively at the drawer. "We could poke holes in them. Tiny, microscopic pinholes."

"Nope. Violates the innocents-shouldn't-suffer rule."

"Lynn isn't innocent."

"Do you really want some poor kid to have Ronald as a father and Lynn as a mother?"

"Good point. We'll have to read the diary, then." Annie got down on her hands and knees and looked under the bed. "Here we go." She pulled out a metal box and unlocked it.

"Are you sure that's it?" Nick asked.

Annie nodded and held up an innocuous-looking notebook.

"Why does he bother? I could break into that thing in two seconds."

"It's a fireproof, floodproof box." She sat on the floor. "It wouldn't do for Ronald's memoirs to be lost to posterity."

"He couldn't spring for a leather-bound journal?"

"Oh, no. That would look too contrived. He wants something that looks casual." She grimaced. "'Uncensored brilliance' is what he called it."

"And you stayed married to this guy how many years?"

"He didn't start keeping a journal until he read a biography of some big shot and thought it was boring." She started paging through the notebook.

"Bring it up here by the light," Nick suggested.

"I refuse to sit on that bed."

Nick blinked down at the hunched shoulders and the way she ducked her head. Ronald had really done a number on her, whether or not she'd admit it. Annie was a woman who needed to be healed and Nick Mandola had just the medicine for her.

The evening's priorities shifted. Yes, getting his niece's college money was important, but not as important as convincing Annie that she was both attractive and desirable.

Nick smiled. He always felt a keen sense of satisfaction when doing the right thing was in his own best interests.

"You know, you need to exorcise the memories you associate with that bed." He joined her on the floor and lowered his voice. "I could help."

She glanced up from the book, but didn't slap him or yell or pull away, which Nick took as a favorable sign, so he continued. "Take a long lunch some day when Ronnie's in a meeting and we'll break in here and create a fantastic new memory—and we won't make the bed afterward."

SHE SHOULDN'T BE listening to him. He was just talking, toying with her the way he had all evening. He didn't mean anything by it.

But Annie wanted him to mean something. He was probably just what she needed. Fun, games, and no strings—still words of one syllable.

"In fact—" he inched closer until their thighs were touching "—we'll lie right on the bedspread. And afterward, we'll wrap ourselves in it until the scent of our lovemaking permeates each and every thread."

"Stop," she whispered.

"Are you sure?"

She closed her eyes. "No." Her judgment was all skewed. She wanted to believe he was attracted to her—still. She wanted to believe that the instinct that had drawn her to him had been right all those years ago. Of course, she hadn't followed it then—

she'd known Ronald for years, and she'd known Nick for only a short time, although it had felt as if she'd known him for a lifetime.

Yet, in the end, it had been Ronald she hadn't known at all.

"Annie?"

She looked up at Nick.

"Annie, I...have to kiss you now."

"That isn't what you were going to say."

"No, but it's what I'm going to do." He spoke with a steady determination.

In a way, Annie was relieved that the push and pull of the evening was finally going to be resolved.

In another way, she was anxious. It had been such a long time.

He looked at her, and she could follow his eyes as they roamed the contours of her face. What did he see?

He smiled as though secretly amused and lightly touched the space between her eyebrows. "Stop fretting, Annie."

"I can't help it."

"When was the last time you kissed a man?"

She felt her face heat and Nick supplied his own answer. "Not since Ronald?"

Annie shook her head, sending her hair falling forward from behind her shoulders.

Nick tucked a lock behind her ear, his fingers

lingering at the lobe, caressing it. "You have nothing to be ashamed of."

"I'm not ashamed."

"But you're worried."

Her ear tingled. "I thought you were going to kiss me."

"I am."

Annie leaned toward him, but Nick shook his head. "Not yet."

"When?"

He moved his knuckles down her jaw and Annie fought to keep from turning her mouth toward them. "When your feelings have been awakened. That's all that's happened to you—your feelings have been asleep."

"More like in a coma."

"And instead of kissing them awake, I want to celebrate their awakening with a kiss." He smiled and spread his fingers to the side of her neck, then brought up his other hand to cradle her face. Slowly, he kneaded the knots at the base of her head—knots she hadn't known were there. With his thumbs, he outlined her ears.

"Did you know that ears have a language all their own?" he asked, his voice a mesmerizing whisper.

"Do they?"

He nodded. "My guess is that right now, you have a headache."

Her head did feel tight and heavy, although it wasn't exactly a full-fledged headache.

"If I squeeze here, your head should feel better." He did so.

To Annie's amazement, the discomfort receded. After a few moments he released the pressure. Though still not perfect, she did feel better.

"This spot alleviates hunger." Nick squeezed a place higher up on her ear. His fingers continued to trace her ears, stopping at different points as he named the parts of her body they would affect.

Annie felt herself relaxing until he outlined the shell of her ear and lingered at the lobes. Awareness prickled down the sides of her neck.

"Desire," he whispered.

All over Annie's body, nerves deep inside her were awakening.

But Nick still didn't kiss her. Instead, he eased his hands down her neck, gently massaging the tendons and muscles. The echoes of his touch lingered as he slowly moved his fingers across her upper back.

Annie liked watching his face and the banked passion in his eyes as he gazed deeply into hers, silently coaxing her long-buried emotions to the surface.

This was a very different Nick from the man who'd tempted her on that long-ago visit. Then, their kisses had been quick, hard, and impatient because they'd been so wary of being caught. Also, their fevered passion had made it easier for Annie not to think about what she was doing.

Now, Nick was forcing her to be aware of herself and of him with his patient, erotic ministrations.

His hands closed over her shoulders, working out the kinks. Annie closed her eyes, her head falling back.

"Does that feel good?"

"Mmm."

"In order to feel desire, you must be open to it. I want yours to flow freely, not be stopped by knots or blocked by pain."

Annie could feel little blocked doorways opening all over her body. "Where did you learn to do this— No, don't tell me," she added as a vision of a long-legged Swedish masseuse running her hands over a prone Nick popped into her mind. She tensed at the unexpected spurt of jealousy.

"Relax," he murmured close to her ear, his breath tickling her still-sensitive lobes. "That's it." He worked his way down her arms.

When he reached her hands, he lifted them and placed them on his shoulders.

Annie inhaled and opened her eyes.

His gaze scanned her face and he gently touched the spot between her eyebrows. "You're not worried anymore."

She shook her head. "But I am impatient."

"So am I, Annie. So am I." And with heart-pounding slowness he lowered his mouth to hers.

As soon as their lips touched, it was as though a dam burst inside Annie and liquid desire began flowing through her. She felt herself begin to shake and was helpless to stop.

"Annie…?"

She drew his mouth back to hers, discovering that his kiss was at once familiar and new.

It was better, deeper, richer.

She shivered, but clutched him to her, unapologetically using Nick to erase all traces of Ronald. It didn't take long at all, she was delighted to discover. Nick's kiss had the same forget-about-everything-else quality it had always had.

His hands cupped her face and she mirrored his actions, discovering a tiny scar next to his hairline that she was sure hadn't been there before.

She loved the way his thick hair curled around her fingers, loved the tautness of his jaw, loved the way her fingertips tingled when she drew them across his beard-roughened skin. She loved the feel of her heart beating and the building desire.

She could *feel* again—feel in a way she'd thought was lost to her—and to top it off, she was in the arms of a strong sexy man.

You've still got it, Annie, she thought, and laughed.

"What is it?" Nick breathed, drawing back to look into her eyes.

"Thank you," she said simply. "I don't know how you knew what I needed, but thank you."

"Maybe because I need it, too."

He leaned down to kiss her again, but Annie shook her head. "That was quite a kiss. I...need time to absorb it."

Long moments passed as Nick gazed down at her. "All right, Annie," he finally agreed, slowly sliding his hands down her arms. "But I'm not going to let you take seven years this time, understand?"

Heart thudding, Annie nodded, but she wondered just how much time she did have. Nick had already been at Deena's for a month—an eternity for him.

She didn't want to ask, so she blinked down at the notebook that had been in her lap all this time.

Nick shifted away from her. "We should hurry up, here. It's almost two and we want to be away well before dawn."

Annie drew a calming breath. "There are other papers in the box." She handed it to Nick. "Take a look at them while I see what I can find out from the diary."

Though it was tempting to read the entries around the time she'd caught Ronald in bed with Lynn, Annie didn't.

The recent entries predictably discussed HI-Com's limping performance and the effect it might have on Ronald being named Wireless Communications Businessman of the Year. She'd just read a puzzling reference to "victory being all the sweeter next year," when Nick spoke.

"Annie? Look at this." He'd unfolded a paper with an official seal.

Annie stared. "These are the Articles of Incorporation for Texafone!" She ran her fingers over the seal. "It's the original." Flipping to the second page, which listed the officers of the corporation, Annie sucked her breath between her teeth. Then her hands began to shake.

"Whoa, careful there." Nick took the paper from her.

"He—he—he—"

"He owns Texafone," Nick finished. "I suspected he might."

"He made her co-owner!" Annie was outraged. "Where's the camera? We need a picture of that— No, better yet, let's take it with us."

"Why? It's not a crime for a man to start another company." Nick tossed the papers back into the strongbox. "That's where his money is. It looks like Jenny's out of luck."

"No! Don't you get it? He talked about something like this before we were divorced," Annie told him. "I thought he'd dropped the idea when I said I didn't want any part of it." She threw the notebook back in the box. "I don't even have to read this. I know exactly what he's doing and if it isn't illegal, it should be."

"Wait until I get the camera, then explain it to me."

Annie didn't wait. "He *is* going to bankrupt HI-Com!" she shouted. "He'll get out from under the contracts, and then Texafone will buy the assets."

"Shh." Nick returned with the camera.

"My stock will be worthless!" Annie raged. "No wonder he didn't protest about giving it to me in the divorce settlement, even though it must have infuriated him that I owned so much of the company."

"Annie, I know you're mad right now, but you've got to keep your voice down." Nick spread out the Articles of Incorporation and photographed them.

Annie was being absolutely no help and she knew it. "This has to be illegal. Lynn is good, but she isn't that good."

"Just arrange the papers so I can get photos of them. We'll show everything to a lawyer and see what can be done."

"I'm going to get him," Annie vowed. "Up close and personal." She stood.

"Annie, where are you going?"

"To the kitchen for pepper. I don't care what you say, I'm putting pepper in their underwear. I'm putting pepper in the bed, I'm putting pep—"

Nick grabbed her ankle and yanked. Annie tumbled on top of him and he covered her mouth with his hand.

She heard a motorized rumble and metallic groaning. In the distance, Poopsie barked.

"That's the garage-door opener." Nick released her and turned off the light. "We've got company."

CHAPTER SIX

"DO YOU THINK THAT'S Ronald and Lynn?" Annie scooped up the papers and shoved the box back under the bed.

"Sounds like it." Nick grabbed Annie's backpack, then pulled her to her feet.

"They're not supposed to be here!"

"Do you want to tell them that?"

She shook her head. "What'll we do?"

"Head for the closet," Nick said as the back door opened and Poopsie barked frantically.

Annie didn't know if they were being quiet or not because her heart was pounding so loudly in her ears.

Fortunately, the master-bedroom closet was a double walk-in. Nick hustled her straight to the back where they sandwiched themselves between Ronald's suits and a garment bag.

For the next several minutes, Annie couldn't hear anything but their own breathing and Poopsie's high-pitched barking.

"Will you make that damn dog shut up?" Ronald bellowed.

"He's upset because you put him in the utility room."

"I did not!"

"Mommy's poor baby didn't have any water or food." Poopsie's barks were reduced to whines as Lynn talked baby talk to him.

"This is a whole new side of Lynn," Annie risked whispering. "And not an attractive one."

"Shh." Nick backed against her, pressing her farther against the wall. "If they find us, you stay hidden. I'll draw them away and you get out however you can."

"But—"

"*Do it.*"

"Okay."

"Good girl," he barely whispered, then dropped a light kiss on her forehead.

It was a funny thing about that kiss. One minute, Annie was worried that her ex-husband would catch her hiding in his closet, and the next, all she could think about was Nick and the fact that a large area of his body was pressed against hers.

It felt good. Very good. And the darkness of the closet made it even more exciting and intimate.

Annie began to enjoy the mere act of breathing. That vest of his could do with a few less zippers, but all in all, this was not a bad position to be in.

NICK HAD OFTEN fantasized about being in the dark with Annie's curves plastered against him. How-

ever, they were usually horizontal, not vertical—
though vertical was proving more interesting than
he'd thought it would be.

Annie took a deep breath and Nick bit his
tongue to keep from turning around and picking up
their kiss where it had left off.

His awareness of Annie was drowning out Ronnie's voice. She shifted against him, perfecting
their fit, and he hoped her hearing was good, because his nerves were screaming and he couldn't
hear a thing.

"CAN YOU HEAR WHAT they're saying?" Annie
whispered.

"No," Nick whispered back.

Bracing her hands on his shoulders, Annie
turned her head and stood on tiptoe, trying to hear.

He had nice, solid shoulders, just the type made
for leaning on. He smelled good, too. Vaguely foreign and exotic, with a little bit of leather. Annie
imagined the scent came from Nick slinging his
leather bag over his shoulder when he wore the
vest. She leaned forward—hoping he couldn't
guess what she was doing—and inhaled.

Their balance shifted and Nick took a jerky step
forward. Embarrassed, Annie leaned back, steady-
ing Nick as he straightened. Ooh, nice arms. She
gave a little exploratory squeeze. How had she
missed Nick's arms before this? Probably the shirt.
With arms like that, he shouldn't wear a shirt.

She ran her fingertips lightly toward his shoulders, following the definition of the muscles. The vest and no shirt—that should be the look for him.

Although when she curved her arms around his waist—his flat waist—and ran her hands up his rib cage—

"*Annie.*"

Oh, right. She should be scared. They were on the brink of being discovered. Professional embarrassment, financial ruin, et cetera, et cetera.

Instead, Annie wanted to prance out of the closet, leading Nick by the hand and singing "Look what I've got!" to Lynn.

And Annie would point out Nick's flat middle to Ronald.

And the full head of hair.

She wouldn't have to point out anything to Lynn.

Annie was so taken with the thought, so pleased that Nick had kissed her earlier, and that things were finally heating up once more in her life, that she stood on tiptoe intending to kiss whatever she could reach. He was too tall for her to reach anything without his active cooperation, so she had to settle for extending her tongue and giving his earlobe a lick—just a little one.

Nick's breath caught in a shudder, and without warning he moved, his hands latching on to her shoulders and his mouth unerringly finding hers in the dark. He kissed her with an urgent thoroughness that reminded Annie of the young, impatient Nick.

By now, she was feeling fairly impatient herself, and tugged his shirt out of the waistband of his pants so she could run her hands over his skin.

"An-nie…" Nick murmured, but since he murmured it while their lips were locked together, he might have been saying, "Don't stop," which was how Annie chose to hear it.

Now, *this* was the way to play hide-and-seek.

They were going to have to stop before things got out of hand—or maybe things should get out of hand first, and then they could stop. The problem was that she was here in the dark, surrounded by Nick—his touch, his scent and his taste. And she didn't want to stop.

"For the last time, I didn't *know* you were supposed to book the suite bedroom separately!"

Lynn's voice sounded like it was in the closet with them. Annie started and bit her lip—or maybe that was Nick's lip she bit.

"I'm *sorry*, Ronald. But we're here now, so can't you just forget it? *You're* glad we're back tonight, aren't you, Poopsie?"

Poopsie let out a high-pitched yap.

"How could you not know to book the bedroom?" Ronald's voice was so full of contempt that Annie winced, even though it wasn't directed at her.

"Well, I told them I wanted the Presidential

Suite—at those prices, I figured the bedroom would come with it.''

"Annie always managed to get it right.''

Annie smirked to herself.

"Then maybe you should have had Miss Perfect book it this time, too. Next year, you can handle all the details. Isn't that right, Poopsie? Next time Ronsie-wonsie can book it himself.''

Ronsie-wonsie. Annie buried her face in Nick's shoulder so she wouldn't burst out of the closet hooting "Ronsie-wonsie.''

"Lynn…honey…''

"I'm tired of you bringing her up every time there's a glitch. Don't you remember just how big a glitch *she* was?''

I'll show you "glitch," Annie thought, and felt Nick put out a restraining hand.

"You're right. She was too perfect. It was exhausting being around all that perfection.''

"I'll bet she wasn't perfect in bed.'' Lynn's voice had taken on a husky quality.

"She tried, I'll give her that.''

Oh, the humiliation. Annie felt herself shrivel.

Poopsie yapped.

"*Put down that damn dog!*''

"Ronald!''

"Out!''

Poopsie whined.

"Oh, for the love of—''

"You scared him!''

"Either control that dog, or find some doggy diapers for him to wear!"

Lynn's voice sounded farther away. "If you hadn't yelled at him, he wouldn't have had an accident. You should feel him—he's trembling, poor baby."

"And so *I* get to clean up the mess?" Ronald was obviously talking to himself.

They heard him go into the bathroom, then slam the cabinet door. "Lynn! Where's the carpet cleaner?"

They heard a faint response, and Ronald left the room.

Nick rummaged in his vest. "Quick—what's the number here?"

Annie recited it, then saw the green glow of a cellular telephone.

"What's the name of the night security guard at HI-Com?"

"There's more than one."

The telephone rang.

"Pick one!"

"Ed."

The phone rang again, then Ronald answered it.

Nick spoke very fast. "Mr. Haggarty, this is Ed. There's been a break-in here at the office. I thought you'd want to know before the police get here. Yes, sir. Well, I'm not real sure— Hey, got to go." Nick disconnected the call.

Annie was impressed, even before she knew whether Nick's plan would work or not.

"Lynn!" Ronald bellowed, his voice sounding clearly throughout the house. "We've got to go to the office. Someone broke in. I want you there to find out what's been disturbed while I talk with the police. Make sure nothing gets seen that shouldn't be seen."

Within minutes, they were gone.

"Come on," Nick said, holding her hand.

They emerged from the closet, with Nick tersely giving orders. "Look over the contents of that box once more while you straighten out the papers. Make sure we've got copies of everything we need. I'll take a final sweep through the house to check that we haven't left a trail."

Annie heard him as if from a distance. She stood at the foot of the bed, staring at it.

"Much as I know you don't want to, arrange the pillows the way they were before." Nick scanned the area as he spoke. "Watch your step." He left the room.

"She tried, I'll give her that," Annie's ex-husband had said. *But hadn't succeeded,* was the implication. Had it ever occurred to the ego-swollen Ronald that he might be partly to blame? Maybe a big, selfish part?

In fact—she smiled, remembering the closet—maybe Ronald was entirely the problem.

Nick appeared in the doorway with the metal

lamp Annie had armed herself with earlier. "Where did you get this, Annie?"

Slowly, she turned and looked at him. Just looked.

He looked back, waiting.

"Ronald triggered a lot of memories." Annie spoke clearly and resolutely. "Memories I don't want anymore. Memories you can help me forget."

Nick dropped the lamp and walked steadily toward her. "Ronnie and his wife will be back in the time it takes to drive to HI-Com and drive back, plus maybe ten minutes. Thirty-five, forty minutes at the most."

"That's a half-hour more than Ronald ever needed."

Nick stopped in front of her, his chest rising and falling. "I'm going to unbutton your blouse one button at a time. You have until the last button to change your mind."

"Nick?"

"Mmm?" Unblinking, he stared into her eyes.

"I'm wearing a turtleneck."

He blinked. "Then time's up." With breathtaking speed, he peeled it off.

Annie shook her hair back into place to find Nick regarding her, the look in his eyes dark and dangerous—and exciting.

"You're wearing black lace. I love black lace." He stepped forward, slipped one satin strap off her shoulder and planted a warm, gentle kiss on the spot where it had been.

"I wore a black suit this evening," Annie explained, dazzled by the pace Nick set. "This went with it."

"Good choice." They were moving fast, but it was Nick-fast and not Ronald-fast. There was a huge difference, Annie discovered, as his tongue traced the throbbing pulse in her neck while his hand drew down the other satin strap.

"I love lace," he murmured from the depths of her cleavage. "It hides and reveals. It teases." He ran his tongue over the lace inserts.

Annie's knees went wobbly.

"I like the way it's rough on my tongue...then my tongue becomes more sensitive and I can fully appreciate the feel of your skin...."

And her skin was on fire. Annie buried her fingers in his hair as Nick took the lace edge between his teeth and tugged it downward.

"Look how beautiful you are," he whispered and stepped behind her so that Annie saw herself in the oval mirror over the vanity.

He'd peeled down one lace-and-satin cup, revealing almost her entire breast. She looked like a modern version of some pagan statue.

That's me. I can't believe that's me.

"So beautiful," he murmured against her ear.

As she watched in the mirror, he reached from behind and cupped her breast with his hand. The contrast of Nick's hand against her white skin mesmerized Annie as much as the heated expression in his eyes.

"How do you feel, Annie?" he asked, tracing erotic circles with his fingers.

"Hot," she answered, hardly believing she'd had the nerve to say that.

"I want you steaming," Nick said. He unhooked her bra—not that it was doing much at this point.

Annie stared into the mirror, hypnotized by the sight of Nick's hands covering her breasts, the flush on her throat, and the concentrated desire on his face as he nuzzled her neck.

"So beautiful," he murmured again, as though determined Annie should believe it.

She'd been standing there all this time like an erotic zombie, absorbing the sensual images Nick was creating for her.

Slowly, afraid she'd break the spell, Annie raised her arms and looped them around Nick's neck, then tilted her head back, giving him better access to her throat.

"Annie..." he breathed, then looked up, meeting her eyes in the mirror.

Annie's lips parted as her breathing increased.

Nick slid his hands down her stomach. Cradling her between his legs, he unbuttoned her slacks and slowly unzipped them. Easing the fabric over her hips, he smiled. "And more black lace. I do love black lace."

Annie wiggled against him. "I can tell." She was becoming particularly fond of black lace herself.

Nick trailed his finger over the lace design until Annie moaned and tried to turn around. "Not yet," he whispered.

But he must have been becoming impatient, too, because he snagged the edges of her panties with his thumbs and drew them away, as well.

She shivered.

Nick wrapped his arms around her, resting his chin on her head. "Look. Tell me what you see."

Annie swallowed. "I see that I'm naked, and you're not."

He shrugged out of his vest. "Then undress me."

In the end, Nick had to undress himself because after Annie had worked the knit shirt over his head, she was overcome with a momentary attack of nerves at the sight of his tightly muscled torso.

"That isn't the expression I'd hoped to see the first time I took off my shirt for you," he said quietly.

"Oh, Nick, it's just that you're so..." She gestured up and down. "And I'm so *not*."

He exhaled in a smile. "You're Annie, you're beautiful, and I've wanted this for a long time."

"You have?"

He nodded.

"You don't just think of me as a ripe fruit ready to be plucked?"

"That's exactly what you are. You're at your peak, ready to be consumed." And he kissed her as he took off his pants.

Well, when he put it like that...

Annie kissed him back, liking the thought of being consumed. She ran her hands over every taut inch of him, until he moaned and swept her into his arms.

He set her crosswise on the bedspread. Instead of joining her, he walked over to the mirror and tilted it. "What do you see, Annie?"

Her reflection appeared in the mirror. "Me."

Nick smiled and joined her. "Now what do you see?"

"Us."

He leaned on his side and began to caress her. "You see us on the bedspread, don't you?"

Actually, she had a glorious view of Nick's tight buns, but she nodded her head so he wouldn't move away.

Not only did Nick not move away, he used his hands and mouth to ensure that Annie's memories of this bed were breathtaking. Wherever the expert touch of his hands led—her breasts, stomach, between her thighs—the damp heat of his mouth followed.

He was so unabashedly sensual, reveling in all the senses and exhorting her to do the same, that

Annie nearly wept, thinking how close she'd been to having never experienced lovemaking with Nick.

He tapped into depths of passion Annie hadn't known she had. She thrashed, she moaned, she clutched, she scratched, and she might even have bitten.

"Nick...please!"

"Steaming, Annie?" His voice was hoarse.

"Does 'sizzling' come before or after 'steaming'?"

"In this case, before."

"Before?" she panted. "There can't be more than this. I'm going to evaporate!"

"Take me with you, then," he said, and entered her in one bold thrust.

Annie gasped and looked straight into Nick's eyes. He didn't move and neither did she. Then he turned his head to the mirror and she knew he wanted her to look, as well.

And Annie stared at the picture they made—joined together, the blue-and-white bedspread crumpled around them—and knew that this picture would be the one to replace the other one that had been burned into her mind.

"Thank you," she whispered.

"Don't thank me yet." He grinned and began to move.

Annie turned away from the mirror. "Nick, don't take this personally, but I can't..." He *did* feel really good. "I mean, I probably won't...but that doesn't mean I haven't thoroughly enjoyed this."

He raised an eyebrow. "You haven't thoroughly 'anything' yet." Shifting his weight onto one arm, he moved his hand between them.

Annie sighed inwardly. She appreciated the effort, really she did, but was disappointed that Nick, with all his fabulous traits, was going to force her to fake it.

He kissed her neck. Annie liked his kisses. She thought she'd give him a little preliminary moaning as positive reinforcement.

"Ohhh, Niiick, that feels—" She broke off when Nick's fingers applied a subtle pressure. Her next moan was completely unrehearsed. She moved her hips and he increased the rhythm. This was wonderful. This was incredible. This had real promise. Annie felt like she was gathering herself for a sprint up a hill. Then she *was* sprinting.

Oh. My. Gosh. Oh my gosh. Oh-my-gosh. OH-MY-GOSH Oh— "Nick!"

And Annie didn't have to fake anything.

Judging by his shout, Nick didn't have to, either.

"Oh, Annie," he breathed, then touched his forehead to hers.

It took several minutes of hard breathing for Annie to be able to speak. "Thank you. Again." The words were inadequate, but she felt compelled to say them anyway.

"You're very welcome." He smiled a satisfied male smile.

But then, he had every right to be self-satisfied.

Annie glanced into the mirror, surprised to see her flushed face and the dampness around her hairline—and even more surprised at the sense of total liberation she felt.

"Do you like what you see?" he asked.

He'd been asking her about what she'd seen and how she'd felt all along, but this time, there was something else in his voice. "Yes," she answered.

"I do, too." He turned away from the mirror and gazed down at her. "We're good together, Annie."

"Very good."

He didn't speak for a moment, searching her eyes with his. "Then let's stay together."

"What are you saying?" Did he even know?

"I'm saying forget about Ronald and his sleazy business tactics. Come travel with me, Annie."

"Come travel with me, Annie." Nearly the same words, the same challenge, as before. Annie was moved more than she could possibly say, but she recognized a fling when she saw one. "Nick, you don't have to make this into anything more than it is."

"But I *want* to." He gently kissed her. "Come with me."

Annie found herself even more torn than she'd been seven years ago. "I can't."

"Why not?" he murmured, nuzzling her neck.

"My job, for one thing." Sitting up, Annie drew the edge of the bedspread around her and turned her back to the mirror.

"I'll provide everything we need," Nick said.

Smiling, she touched his jaw. He captured her fingers and kissed them. "I have a responsibility to the people who'd lose their jobs if Ronald destroys HI-Com. And what about Jennifer and Kevin?" she added.

"We'll tell Deena's lawyer what we found and let him go after Ronald. If Jennifer sits out a semester, it won't be the end of the world."

He was right, Annie knew.

"As for HI-Com, why bother?" he continued. "If Texafone's rates are too high, then someone else will start another company."

Simplistic reasoning, but nevertheless accurate. Annie was aware of how much business HI-Com had lost and how much effort would be required to save the company at this point. And why should she want to? Though she owned a chunk of it, it was Ronald's company, not hers.

She'd been making excuses to avoid telling Nick the real reason she couldn't go with him: She wanted love, and he wanted fun for as long as it lasted.

"Now, what's the other?" He sat up next to her and wrapped his arms around her.

"Other what?" Annie's resolve was weakening.

"The other reason you won't come with me."

She owed him honesty. "I don't want 'temporary.'"

He gazed at her. "Who says it has to be temporary?"

"*You* do. You don't stay in any place long enough to put down roots. I need roots. I need stability and commitment and security."

He shook his head in frustration. "You need to *live*."

"But if I'd drifted through life like you have, then I'd have nothing."

"If Ronald succeeds in bankrupting HI-Com, you'll have nothing now. At least I've learned about the world and the people in it. I've got experience and memories. And a little money in a Swiss bank, besides."

Annie closed her eyes, realizing that he was right. What *did* she have? A few pieces of furniture, sinking stock, a broken marriage and stress-filled, joyless days. She didn't even have money in the bank.

"Come with me, Annie. You can be my stability and my roots." His voice dropped to a hoarse murmur. "I need you."

She shouldn't have opened her eyes. The expression in his was... "Oh, Nick," she wailed, "don't make me fall in love with you, unless you love me back."

He gripped her hand tightly. "What do you

think this has all been about?'' he asked fiercely. ''I loved you seven years ago and I love you now. I've traveled all over the world looking for a woman to replace you, Annie. And no one can.''

He loved her. *He loved her.* ''For seven years?''

He smiled crookedly. ''Yeah.''

''Oh, Nick.'' She clung to him, about to agree to follow him anywhere, when a thought occurred to her. ''But what about your job?''

''What about it?''

''Well, I mean…Nick…aren't you some kind of spy?''

He ran his hands up and down her arms. The longer he was silent, the faster Annie's heart beat. ''I've done some unofficial favors for people,'' he admitted slowly. ''In my research for the guidebooks, sometimes I discover pieces of information that I can't use.''

Annie groaned.

''And…there are a couple of countries where we *probably* shouldn't go.''

''Nick!''

''Shh. I'll never hurt you and I'll never put you in danger.''

''But I'd worry about *you!*''

His knuckles grazed her cheek. ''Then I won't do any more favors. I won't have to. The danger was what helped me forget about you. But now you'll be with me, won't you, Annie?''

Annie stared at what life was offering her—she

could either work herself into the ground fighting her corrupt ex-husband, or she could take time off to travel with a great-looking man who loved her and wanted to show her the world.

No contest.

She looped her arms around Nick. "Why didn't you tell me you loved me seven years ago?"

"Would you have believed me?"

"Probably not," she admitted. "I wouldn't have believed it was possible to fall in love with someone in such a short time."

"Do you love me now?"

She nodded and grinned. "Yeah."

He leaned forward to kiss her. "Then you know it's possible."

It had been some night, Annie thought, and she put a little extra into her kiss.

Nick pulled back. "Careful, unless you want them to find us."

Ronald and Lynn! "I forgot!" Annie jumped up and scrambled for her clothes.

"I'll take that as a compliment." Nick stretched lazily.

"How much time do we have?"

"Not a whole lot. I didn't look at my watch when they left."

They dressed quickly, smoothed the bed, and Annie checked the box containing Ronald's memoirs before locking it.

"You know," she said, "I hate the idea that Ronald is going to get away with this."

"He won't. We've got enough to trigger an investigation."

"But he'll try to weasel out of it and spend everything he's got in the process. Then there really won't be any money left."

Nick touched her shoulder. "Do you feel like gambling?"

"I'm going away with you, aren't I?"

"That's not gambling, that's a sure thing. Let me see the key."

Annie dropped it into his hand and Nick unlocked the box. "How is Ronnie at dotting i's and crossing t's legally?"

"He misses a few, probably on purpose."

Nick shuffled through the papers. "You know, we could confront him with what we know and offer him a deal. Depending on how legally airtight all this is, he might take it."

"What kind of a deal?"

Nick headed back to the office. "Let's see what we can bring to the table."

CHAPTER SEVEN

AFTER RAIDING THE FILES, Annie and Nick raided the refrigerator, finding only Asti Spumante and green olives. "When we get to Italy, I'll feed you real olives and Asti," Nick promised.

Annie was sitting in the living room reading passages from Ronald's memoirs aloud to a highly-amused Nick, when Ronald and Lynn arrived home.

"Poopsie, your mommy's here." Annie urged the snoozing dog off her lap. Poopsie barked sleepily as the back door opened.

"This has not been the best of nights, Lynn, so please drop it!" Ronald snarled before seeing Annie and Nick. He came to a frozen halt.

"Hi, Ronsie-wonsie." Annie waggled her fingers.

"Ronnie!" Nick stepped forward and took his hand in a hearty shake. "Good to see you again. And this must be your lovely wife, Lynn." He shook her hand, too. "Nick Mandola. I'm Deena's brother. Come on in. Sit down. Can I pour you a glass of wine?"

Ronald's mouth opened and closed.

So did Lynn's, but she actually spoke. "Ronald? Ronald, what are they doing here?"

"You see them, too?" Ronald turned to his wife. "I'm not hallucinating?"

"Don't be ridiculous." Lynn walked into the living room and confronted Annie. "How did you get in here?"

"Through the door," Annie answered. "Olive?"

Lynn's gaze was suddenly riveted on the various files and papers Annie had arranged in a neat display. They exchanged looks. "No, but I'll have that drink, now." Lynn quietly sat in the nearest vacant chair.

"What's going on here?" Ronald demanded.

"I think a little fraud and a little embezzlement are going on here." Nick took his seat on the sofa and threw his arm across the back.

"And what makes you think that?"

Nick gestured toward Annie's display. "Your files make interesting reading."

Ronald put on his game face. "Those are private files—copies of correspondence, contracts, and the like. Nothing illegal."

"You sure about that?" Nick asked pleasantly.

Ronald glanced over at his current wife. Lynn raised her wineglass and drained it.

Nick made a tsking sound. "It's a crime to treat a wine of such quality that way. But I suppose if that's your only crime, we can forgive you." He smiled.

"But Nick, darling, you're forgetting all about Texafone—she owns part of it, and is acting as counsel. It's conflict of interest in direct violation of her employment contract with HI-Com, at the very least." Annie gave him a sappy smile.

He gave her one right back. "You're absolutely right, sweetheart." Turning to Lynn, he said, "Sorry, you're out of luck. I must insist that you treat that wine with all the respect it deserves."

Lynn yanked the bottle away from Annie and poured herself another glass.

"Lynn?" As Ronald watched her drain the second glass, his game face slipped. He stared at the papers, then at Annie. "Well, now that you've gone to such trouble to bring this to our attention, I'm certain Lynn will immediately sever her connections with HI-Com."

Nick laughed. "Ronnie, that's a case of shutting the barn door after the horse has escaped."

Annie liked visualizing Lynn as a horse. "Especially after you used HI-Com to finance Texafone."

Ronald looked pleased with himself. "That will be difficult to prove."

"Not really," Annie said with a bored sigh, and withdrew Ronald's memoirs from beneath her chair cushion. "You've finally written something people will be interested to read."

In the entire time they'd been married, Annie had never seen Ronald's face turn that shade of gray. Fear was very attractive on him. It complemented the circles under his eyes.

"Ronald?" Lynn asked sharply.

He sent her a silent look.

"Damn it, Ronald!"

"Olive?" Annie popped one into her mouth.

"Ask them what they want," Lynn ordered him.

"I could use some crackers," Annie said.

"What do you want?" Ronald asked Nick.

"Crackers work for me, too."

Ronald sat down.

"We don't have any crackers," Lynn said in a thin voice.

"Too bad." Nick leaned forward and steepled his fingers. "You'll just have to give us money, then."

"We don't have money, either," Ronald said.

"No, but you have this." Nick held out Texafone's Articles of Incorporation.

Ronald and Lynn exchanged looks. "What are you going to do?"

"Not what you deserve to have done," Nick replied, all affability wiped from his voice.

Annie spoke. "Ronald, I find that our corporate vision is no longer compatible, so I'm asking for a divorce."

"But—"

"A professional divorce. Here's the deal—Bring

Texafone out into the open. Buy out Hi-Com, and hire the employees. Give me fair value for my stock, pay back my loan, and make good on Jennifer and Kevin's support.''

''Now, just—''

''Ronald,'' Lynn interrupted, then turned to Annie. ''And in exchange, you will…?''

''Leave.'' Annie got up from her chair and joined Nick on the couch. ''I will resign and give up all interest in Ronald's business.''

''And start a rival company with inside information!'' Ronald snarled.

Annie put her arms around Nick. ''I'll be too busy traveling.'' They grinned at each other.

''I don't believe you. Work is your life, Annie. You'll be bored within a month.''

Annie snuggled closer. ''I don't think so.''

Ronald gaped at them. ''Do you actually expect me to believe that you're willing to walk away from HI-Com to bum around with him?''

''Yes,'' Annie said, looking at Nick.

Support came from an unexpected source. ''Annie's naive, Ronald. She isn't stupid.''

''Thank you, Lynn.''

Lynn lifted a hand in a dismissive gesture.

''Better give this deal some thought, Ronnie,'' Nick said. ''Everyone can understand a husband and ex-wife severing business connections. And when Texafone takes off, you'll remind everyone just what a savvy businessman you are. Maybe you'll finally get elected as Grand Pooh-Bah.''

Ronald's eyes lit up and Annie could see him mentally writing the climax to the story of his life. "You've certainly made a very interesting offer."

Nick gave him a nudge. "Did we mention that it was a limited-time offer?"

"Well, we'd have to—"

"You won't leak any of this to the press?" Lynn interrupted.

Lynn's legal doings must have drifted over into very shady territory. Annie wondered if Ronald knew—or cared. "Leak what?" Annie asked.

Ronald stared at her. "You've changed." There was a spark of interest in his eyes.

"No, I haven't." Annie and Nick stood. "I was just never in a position where I could fully explore my own sensuality." She put her arm around Nick's waist and they started toward the door. "Lynn understands. Don't you, Lynn?"

Lynn's face could have been carved from ice.

Ronald spluttered. "We—we haven't talked money yet! Where are you going?"

Nick swung Annie's backpack over his shoulder. "I'm taking Annie exploring."

"Exploring? Exploring what?"

Lynn glared at him. "Shut up, Ronald."

"We'll be in touch," Nick said and opened the door, urging Annie through it. "Oh, one other thing.'' He gestured toward the papers. ''We have copies. Bye-bye, now.''

Once outside the door, Annie clung to Nick. ''Do you think he'll go for it?''

''Looks that way.''

''I can't believe it worked.''

''Shh. Let's get out of here.'' Nick led her down the front walk.

''Shouldn't we stick around and get an agreement in writing?'' Annie asked. She wouldn't put it past Ronald to figure a way out of this.

''Not necessary,'' Nick said. ''Did you watch Lynn? They have been *very* naughty. We'll let them stew for a while and come to the conclusion that we know more than we do. By the time we talk numbers, they'll agree to anything.''

Annie drew a deep breath. ''So, now what? I've just turned my life upside down. I don't know what I'm supposed to do.''

Nick slipped an arm around her. ''You're supposed to come with me.''

''Where are we going?'' Annie was a little nervous about striking out into the world of no rules.

''We're embarking on a grand exploration.''

''But...I don't have a passport.''

''You'll get one later.'' Nick leaned down to kiss her. ''I'm the only passport you need for this kind of exploring.''

EPILOGUE

Provence, two years later

AFTER A MORNING SPENT shopping at the weekly market, Annie arrived back at the charming stone farmhouse where she and Nick had stayed for the past month. She was almost sorry that it was time to move on. Almost.

She had the same mixed feelings she always had at the end of one of Nick's guidebook assignments—sorry to leave, yet eager to see what new part of the world she could come to love.

Pushing open the door—no one locked doors in this tiny village—Annie set her shopping basket on the massive wooden table that dominated the kitchen and unwrapped the bunch of flowers she'd bought.

She was snipping the ends off the stems and putting them into an earthenware pitcher, when Nick's moped put-putted into the yard.

Annie stopped her flower arranging and leaned out the kitchen window to watch him. She could never get enough of Nick and his love for life. How wrong she'd been about him! But, every time she moaned about all the years together they'd lost, he'd tell her that she wouldn't have appreciated him if she'd gone off with him the first time. And then he'd candidly admit that he wouldn't have appreciated her, so Annie guessed things had worked out the way they were supposed to.

He propped the little bike in the shade against the side of the house, hung his helmet from the handlebars, then saw her. Blowing her a kiss, he jogged up the stone steps.

"Did you get a chance to call Gene, or did you just mail off the packet?" she asked.

"Both." He grabbed her around the waist and kissed her fully on the mouth. Nick never settled for a chaste peck on the cheek. "I also picked up the week's mail," he told her some moments later. "Interesting stuff this time."

"Interesting good, or interesting bad?" Annie swept away the bits of stems and Nick slung his backpack onto the far end of the table.

"Texafone filed for bankruptcy."

"Finally." Annie took a deep breath and allowed the feeling of satisfaction to wash over her. "Ronnie hung on longer than I thought he would."

Nick unzipped his backpack and shoved an envelope toward Annie. "Deena sent clippings. She put smiley faces on them."

Annie pulled the bits of paper out of the envelope and laughed. "She's entitled. She's worked hard running CelStar for the past year."

"You both have," Nick said.

Shrugging, Annie scanned the articles. "I just told her what to do. She and Jennifer are the ones who actually did it. Ooh, Ronnie's a sore loser. Listen. 'Haggarty attributed the failure of Texafone to the devious and underhanded business practices of his two bitter ex-wives, owners of the rival CelStar. Haggarty, a past nominee for Wireless Communications Businessman of the Year, made the comments at this year's banquet, at which one of those ex-wives, Deena Haggarty, was awarded the honor.'" Annie chortled. "I'll bet Deena's winning the first year she was nominated got to him."

"Is Lynn mentioned anywhere?"

Annie quickly read through the rest. "At the end, there's a comment about the current Mrs. Haggarty saying they'll start over again—you know the drill."

"Standing by her man. You've got to hand it to her."

"They deserve each other."

"Speaking of deserving...I have a present for you," Nick announced.

"What?" Annie couldn't suppress her excitement. Nick's presents were always exciting and unusual.

"How would you like to spend our first anniversary in Monaco?"

"Monaco?"

"Correction—Monaco on an expense account."

Her mouth dropped open. "Gene gave you the assignment?"

Grinning, Nick nodded.

"But Niles always gets the glitzy assignments." Niles looked good in a dinner jacket—but not as good as Nick, she thought, eyeing her husband's flat stomach and broad shoulders.

"I insisted this time, and I've got the seniority."

"Oh, Nick." He'd done it for her.

For the past two years, she and Nick had researched travel destinations off the beaten path. It was their specialty. Annie had loved their life far more than she'd ever dreamed she would, but occasionally, she longed to dress up and experience the glitter and noise of the big city. She'd never said anything to Nick, though. How had he known? "Thank you. It's a perfect present."

"For a perfect wife."

Annie sat on his lap and kissed him.

"You've been shopping," he said after a long and languorous kiss. "Did you buy cheese?"

"Yes," Annie answered.

"I'm going to miss the local cheese." He poked through her basket. "What's in the bottom of the basket here?"

"A bedspread."

"Another one? I thought you'd already bought your Provence bedspread."

She smiled. "We've practically worn it out."

"Just getting it broken in."

Annie stood and retrieved the bedspread from the basket. Sometime during each assignment in whatever locale they found themselves, Annie bought a bedspread. Each was filled with memories.

Except this one.

She shook out the French country blue-and-yellow print and held it up. "What do you think?"

Nick stood. "I think I need to see it on the bed."

Laughing, Annie headed for the bedroom, where she and Nick floated the spread over the ancient mattress.

And then they made more memories.

Night Fire
Elda Minger

To Phyllis Kaelin,
who loves to walk on
the wild side as much as I do!

CHAPTER ONE

HE'D BEEN WATCHING HER for a long time.

Steve McKnight had a routine for his evenings after he got off work. He'd long ago decided that this was probably because the nature of his work was so highly unpredictable. Being a detective could be rough, so after he left his job, he wanted—no, he actively *desired*—a little predictability.

That was why, after a long day, he headed for Bud's Café.

Bud's was really an old-fashioned diner. But in order to survive in ultratrendy Los Angeles, the red neon sign said Bud's Café.

Steve had been coming to the restaurant for years. Bud, who actually worked and cooked there, had become something of a friend. In his late sixties and a bodybuilder, Bud knew enough about human nature that when a man came in looking exhausted and defeated, he told his waitresses to simply hand him a cup of coffee and a menu and leave him alone for a while.

He also knew enough about men to hire some

of the best-looking women in southern California as waitresses.

One of them, Amy Robbins, had been on Steve's mind for months.

She worked evenings, and she looked tired. He suspected she had another job, although they'd never talked about it. He'd been watching her for about three months, since she started at Bud's, and their brief conversations had been confined to what he wanted to order, a few comments about the weather, or some bit of news making headlines on CNN.

He wanted to get to know her better, but he knew she was gun-shy, or rather, guy-shy.

You could tell. Or at least, he could. You didn't spend years watching people, suspecting their motives, wondering how they could have done what they'd done without gleaning a little bit of knowledge about human nature.

Tonight, after a long and particularly grueling stakeout, Steve had come into Bud's knowing exactly what he wanted. A bowl of Bud's world-famous chili and a cold beer—not exactly the kind of meal that would send him off to a peaceful sleep, but Steve wasn't sure he wanted to drift off to sleep, anyway.

He deliberately sat in Amy's section, a row of booths by the large front windows that looked out on Sunset Boulevard. The diner was located in West Hollywood, just a few blocks short of the famous Sunset Strip, with its colorful billboards, hotels, restaurants and comedy clubs.

Amy brought his coffee right away, the way he liked it—black. Then she handed him a menu and, without a word, turned on her heel and headed back toward the kitchen. He watched her backside—a very cute backside. As tired as he was, just watching this woman walk gave him a rush.

She was cute. Just over five feet, with wavy, dark red hair she tried unsuccessfully to keep restrained in a ponytail. And she had the most beautiful face: gorgeous green eyes, an elegant little nose, and a lush, full mouth. And, most unusual in his estimation of redheads, not a single freckle on those high, beautifully shaped cheekbones.

He'd spent a lot of time on stakeouts, while trying to stay awake, wondering if she had a single freckle on any other portion of that curvy little body.

That body, encased in a pink waitress's uniform with a crisp white apron, approached his table.

"Hi, Steve, what'll it be?" She was cute and sassy and did everything short of snap her gum.

"A bowl of chili and a beer. A Bud," he said, setting down the plastic-coated menu and wondering, as he had for many nights, how he was going to get past their waitress-customer relationship and get to know this woman. However it happened, it wasn't going to be easy. He saw that wary look in those green eyes.

"That's all? The Dutch apple pie's terrific to-night."

He smiled. She was really, really good at her job. "Maybe later."

She turned on her heel again, walked briskly behind the counter and called out to Bud as she clipped the order slip up above the warming counter, "A bowl of red, a bullet, and save me a D.A."

Steve smiled as he watched her. Bud had turned his diner into a neighborhood hangout. One of the ways he'd given the place a distinct style was by reviving some of the calls that had been used in the coffee shops of his college days. The locals were used to it; they liked the sense of place it gave them, the identity. The tourists loved it, and jammed the immaculate restaurant in the summer months before they took off for Universal Studios, Malibu, or Disneyland.

Steve stared out the window, trying not to be too obvious about watching Amy while she worked. He'd already tried the more obvious routes in getting to know her. He'd asked Bud about Amy on one of the few nights she hadn't been working, but the older man had been curiously tight-lipped. Bud, with his thick salt-and-pepper hair and muscled forearms, simply didn't talk when he didn't want to.

"Maybe you'd better ask her yourself," was all he'd said.

Steve knew Bud was right. How one petite redhead with an attitude could make him feel so nervous, when he was used to tracking down suspects and dodging gunfire, simply amazed him.

There was only one small comfort in watching Amy as she efficiently went about her work. She might not be letting him get any closer, but as far as he could see, she wasn't letting any other man get to know her either.

AMY BROUGHT STEVE HIS chili and a cold beer, all the while trying to study the man without his noticing her.

She liked his looks. But then again, she'd liked Lenny's looks, and look where that had gotten her. Yet there was something about Steve McKnight that made her think about trying again, made her dream about how wonderful life could be with the right man.

Highly unlikely. Keep him as a friend. It's safer.

"It's good tonight," she said as she placed the bowl of chili in front of Steve. "I think Bud was inspired." Bud's chili was the one erratic item on the extensive menu. The man refused to work from a recipe when it came to chili because, as he often said, "I just have to be inspired."

"That's a relief," Steve said, reaching for his spoon. "But it always is. Different, maybe, but good."

She took a deep breath as she set the bottled beer

down on the speckled Formica tabletop. "Rough day?"

"You don't want to know."

"Well," she said, surprising herself by gently patting his muscular forearm, "that chili will warm you right up." Before she could make even more of a fool of herself, she turned and went to check on her other customers.

STEVE TRIED NOT TO STARE after her.

She'd touched him.

She'd touched him, and it had been as if internal fireworks had gone off. And he knew that, no matter what it took, he was going to get at least one date out of this woman, maybe two, so he could figure out exactly what was going on between them.

He hadn't reacted to a woman's touch like that in— Forget the years. The word he was searching for was *never*.

AFTER MAKING SURE HER other customers were all right, Amy asked Bud if she could take her break and retreated to the employee lounge. Bud had furnished it with a large fridge, a comfortable couch, a few overstuffed chairs and a small color television. But she didn't turn the TV on, and didn't reach for anything to eat. Instead, she sat down in one of the chairs and wondered what had possessed her to actually touch Steve McKnight.

He'd felt wonderful. She'd felt wonderful—that little zing of electricity zipping up her arm, startling her. And if just touching his arm had felt like that...

Let's not go there.

Amy leaned back in the chair and closed her eyes. She'd liked Steve the minute he'd walked in the door. Oh, she was a sucker for a black leather jacket and hair just a little too long, brushing the back of his collar. That, and the well-worn jeans over decidedly muscular legs. And the boots. And that *voice*. He had a bedroom voice, deep and rough and gravelly.

But it was his eyes that had really captivated her. They were the most beautiful shade of blue gray. His hair was a very dark brown, almost black. His skin had the slight tan of a man who spent a great deal of time outdoors but didn't always bother with a sunscreen. His height—a little under six feet—had intimidated her at first. The way he carried himself was different from that of any other man she'd ever met.

She noticed little things, like the way he checked out a room before entering it. How he kept his right hand free, even his entire right side. The slight bulge beneath the black leather jacket told her he carried a gun. She was sure he knew how to use it.

She'd asked Bud about him. And Linda and Alexis, two other women who waitressed at the diner. They'd all told her the same thing: an ex-cop, who now made his living as a private detective. She'd guessed as much, had known Steve had to work in some field like that. Since her divorce, she'd been a lot more observant about people.

Yet even knowing all this about Steve, she liked him. She liked the way the tiny lines around his eyes crinkled when he smiled at her. She liked the way his large hands looked, cupped around a mug of coffee. And she really liked the way he entered Bud's, checked the place out, then looked for her, and smiled. Right at her. As if she were the only person in the place.

At first his attention had scared her. The last thing she wanted, after her messy divorce from Lenny, was to get involved again. At twenty-six—a very *old* twenty-six—there were ways in which she felt her life was over. Or at least that part of her life—the part in which she felt like a woman again, with a man.

There were plenty of other things to fill her time with. Like work.

Amy leaned back and rested her feet on the hassock in front of her. It felt so good to take the weight off her legs. Sometimes, after working all day cleaning houses and then coming to the diner at night, she felt so worn-out and defeated. But she'd never been a complainer. If life had dealt her a hand that wasn't exactly to her liking, then she'd make the best of it.

After her fifteen minutes were up, she went back out on the floor and immediately glanced at Steve's booth. He was still sitting there, the chili finished, the beer in his hands as he stared out the window into the October night. This stretch of Sunset was lit up with a lot of neon—a strip joint down the street, a bookstore a few doors over, a Thai restaurant with its specials written in the window.

She approached his booth.

"Still interested in that pie?"

He hesitated for a moment, as if he were about to say something. She held her breath. Then he simply said, "Sure."

LATER THAT EVENING, AMY lay in bed, listening to a talk-radio show. She was restless, couldn't sleep. When she got into one of these moods, it seemed to her that nothing in her life was as it should be.

Not even her bedroom, which was really just a corner of her studio apartment separated from the rest with screens. When she remembered back to the heirloom bedroom set that had once graced the light, airy room in Illinois, the fresh flowers she'd put in vases every day, she wondered how she could have fallen so far so fast.

This pseudo-bedroom—in a small, stucco apartment building off Sunset, with its courtyard of enormous tropical plants—seemed so different. She'd furnished the room with garage-sale castoffs, inexpensive wicker and pressboard furniture. Her thin mattress felt lumpy most of the time, and the large window that overlooked the courtyard had black iron security bars running across it. Usually the rather ugly curtains were drawn, as she didn't really want any strangers walking through the courtyard area looking in.

Light and airy, it wasn't.

There were a few pieces from her past she'd been able to save. The afghan her grandmother had crocheted for her. A vase that had once been on her mother's table. Several exquisite doilies she had carefully packed away. Photo albums filled with pictures that seemed as if they'd been taken a long time ago—only years ago, but sometimes it felt like lifetimes.

These all had tremendous sentimental value for her, as did her feelings about home and family. But there wasn't much else she'd been able to salvage. She felt that way about her own life sometimes, and the energy she had to devote to making it better. There were days when nothing seemed like it would ever change.

Resolutely determined to change her mood, Amy concentrated on the radio show.

There were a lot of lonely souls in the City of Angels, and tonight it seemed as if most of them had found their way to this man's program, "In the Midnight Hour."

"Tomorrow night," the radio host's disembodied voice said, the tone warm and smooth, "we're going to do something special. Right at midnight—not quite day and not quite night, that magical, unpredictable hour when anything can happen—I'm starting a show-within-a-show called Midnight Kisses. And I want all of you people out there to call in and tell me your secret fantasies, intimate thoughts you can't even tell your closest friends, your husbands or wives. Fantasies, sexual or otherwise, that you've always wanted to try but never quite had the nerve to do."

Amy closed her eyes as she lay on her double bed. Her hand went out to pat the silky coat of the cream-colored Pekingese lying next to her. There was a part of her that still yearned for fantasy. She remembered long, cold Illinois winters, and springs devoid of all color except for lead gray skies, brown mud, and dirty white snow. She'd sat in the safety of her father's house, looking out the window and wondering why there couldn't be more color in her life. More excitement. She'd wanted vibrancy in her life. After her father's death, when Lenny had come to town, she'd been more than ready to fall for his selfish schemes.

He'd left her with nothing but a mountain of both debts and regrets. The last thing she wanted to do was get involved with someone else. Yet those fantasies, those silent yearnings were still there, teasing her, right on the edge of consciousness, demanding to be heard....

She shifted in the lumpy bed, still petting the little dog's silky fur. And she thought about Steve, and the way she'd fantasized about him. For just a moment, she'd been tempted to call in to this new radio show. At the same time, fear told her it would be far more comfortable to stay in her safe little space, to not push herself out of her comfort zone—for now.

Yeah, right. I can't even make up my mind whether to talk to Steve at the restaurant, and I'm going to spill my guts to a guy over the radio? No way.

But she continued to listen.

THE NEXT DAY, HER ONE DAY off a week, Amy cleaned her small apartment, did all her grocery shopping, her laundry, and took her two dogs, Ming the Pekingese and Joe the elderly golden retriever, for a long walk around the neighborhood. If she'd had her car, she would have taken them to Griffith Park and really let them run, but her aging Toyota Tercel was in the shop getting its brakes fixed.

That same day, Steve slept in until one in the afternoon, got up, showered and shaved, checked his mail, and reported to work late in the afternoon. He and his partner, Martin, had been shadowing a deadbeat dad who had mysteriously disappeared, but whose wife believed was still alive. The guy had just walked out of her life, leaving her with two young children and several creditors who regularly hounded her to pay his bills.

Through some careful sleuthing, Steve thought they'd nailed the house he was living in. Now it was just a matter of Steve and Martin sitting outside that house as unobtrusively as possible and waiting for this loser to show himself.

It was long work. Sometimes boring work. You couldn't read in a darkened van, couldn't do anything that might call attention to yourself.

Thank God for the radio.

AMY LAY IN BED, BUT SHE couldn't sleep. Joe, stretched out on the rag rug by the side of her double bed, snored softly in his sleep. His furry legs twitched as he dreamed of chasing squirrels. Ming, still awake, watched her intently from his perch by her pillow, his black eyes button bright in his wrinkled little face.

Amy was restless. Couldn't read. Couldn't sleep. Couldn't do any needlepoint. She'd folded and put away all her laundry, the groceries were carefully placed in the fridge or her pantry, and she'd even scrubbed the small kitchen floor. By all accounts, she should have been exhausted, ready to fall asleep in preparation for her long day tomorrow.

Yet here I am, wide-awake....

She wondered what Steve was doing. Probably right around midnight, he'd roll into Bud's and order something to eat. Steve's life as a detective sounded romantic and exciting to her. Much more exciting than cleaning houses by day and working as a waitress into the wee hours of the night.

She had no one to blame but herself. If she hadn't been naive enough, in love enough, to believe all her ex-husband's lies, and if she hadn't allowed him to run up a massive amount of debt, she wouldn't be working two jobs in order to pay everyone back.

She'd believed in love. Once.

Never again.

Fiddling with the radio dial, she came across the talk show she'd listened to the previous evening.

"Hey, here we are, 'In the Midnight Hour.' And tonight, I'm going to do something a little different during that most dangerous of hours. Not quite night, and not quite day, a time when anything might happen and often does..."

She smiled at the talk-show host's buildup. It was fun, actually, to think of some excitement coming into her life. Sometimes her days were so utterly predictable that she felt as if she were drowning from the weight of it all.

"Tonight," continued the talk-show host, "I'm going to open up the phone lines for anyone and everyone to call in. I don't want any of you out there to be shy. I want you to *talk* to me—in total anonymity, of course—and really tell me what your little heart desires. Take down this number—555-KISS—think about calling 'cause, folks, this is a brand-new segment within our regular show, called Midnight Kisses. I hope we'll talk about all the other things we like to do in the dark.''

Amy reached over to scratch Ming's head. The Peke gave a satisfied, doggy grunt.

"MIDNIGHT KISSES?'' Martin repeated, after taking a sip of what had to be his eighth cup of coffee. "What kind of new show is this?''

"It's got to be more entertaining than sitting here waiting for Joey the Rat to show up,'' said Steve, his attention on the small frame house across the street.

"Good point.'' Martin, slender and balding, with calm hazel eyes and a gentle manner, reached into the white paper bag on the seat between them. "You had the cake doughnut with the sprinkles, right?''

"Take whatever you want.''

Martin lifted out a chocolate éclair and took a generous bite, while Steve continued to watch the house. The night felt strange to him; the moon was enormous and full, the sky cloudless. The digital display on the small clock in the dashboard of the van told him it was almost exactly midnight. Crazy things happened at midnight. Even crazier things happened during a full moon.

The van they sat in, parked across the street and down from the house in question, was a dirty white vehicle—more of a grimy gray—that hadn't seen the inside of a car wash for many months. Faded lettering on the sides proclaimed, Kelly's Expert Exterminators—We Hunt Down Roaches and Rats So You Don't Have To! This had amused Steve when he'd bought the van, as he'd known exactly the type of vermin he and Martin would be hunting down.

They had their stakeout routine down pat. It was so different from what was depicted on television or on a movie screen. Stakeouts could be boring, but not when you thought you might be nabbing a deadbeat dad who had abandoned his children. Unfortunately, they were usually children who still adored their father, and couldn't understand why Daddy no longer lived with them—or cared about them.

Though the outside of the van looked grimy and completely forgettable, the inside was impeccable, completely fitted with the latest in state-of-the-art surveillance equipment. More than once, Steve thanked the gods for the fact that his partner was something of a genius when it came to computers, cameras, and everything associated with them. Martin had joined his detective agency within months after Steve had left his job at the police department, and both men now pulled down a much better salary than they ever had previously.

There were only a few rules, as both men were rather easygoing. The front-seat area was fair game for wrappers, food, drinks and the like. Martin usu-

ally had a vast selection of fast-food wrappers beneath his feet at any moment in time. But once
either of them moved back toward the equipment
in the enormous van—their "home away from
home" as they so jokingly referred to it—their focus had to be on work, not food.

But stakeouts were about food. And radio
shows. Music. Anything to keep their spirits up.

A few seconds after wiping chocolate icing off
his mouth with a paper napkin, Martin said, "Why
do I have a feeling your mind isn't on this stakeout
tonight?"

Steve sighed. His partner knew him all too well.
His mind had been on Amy.

"But I take it you don't want to talk about it."

Silently blessing Martin for his tact and under-
standing, Steve nodded his head.

AMY EYED THE PHONE, wondering if she dared.

The sound of a helicopter broke into her
thoughts, the blades whirring as it made its nightly
run far above the city. Someone laughed in the
courtyard, and Amy remained still. One of the
things she missed most, living in such a huge city,
was the complete lack of privacy. In Los Angeles,
you had to have money to pay for that privilege.

On the radio, she'd already listened to a woman
complain about how her husband ate garlic and
onions before bedtime, and a young male teen
whine about how badly his girlfriend treated him.

The talk-show host, who had specifically asked for sexy, private fantasies and not complaints, was practically begging for someone with a new and original take on their love life to call in.

Something inside her grew very calm as she lifted the receiver off its cradle and dialed 555-KISS. She had to talk to someone; she'd kept so much inside for so very long. Perhaps this was the best way—with total anonymity. No one would ever know. After all, who did she know who would be listening to a Los Angeles radio talk show at such an ungodly hour?

She was put through swiftly, and found herself talking to the show's host, an affable young man named Frank.

"WHAT'S YOUR NAME?" Frank said.

Steve took a long swig of black coffee from his takeout cup as he listened to the radio. Sexual fantasies. This could get interesting. And it might work far better than caffeine at keeping him awake and alert.

"Amy."

He almost choked.

"And what would you like to tell me, Amy?"

Steve almost stopped breathing. He knew that voice. He knew whom it belonged to. And he knew that a carefully contained woman like Amy was taking quite an emotional chance in calling a radio talk show.

"I think I know what a lot of women would like, including myself."

"And how do you know this, Amy? Other than the obvious, you being a woman and all."

"Well, I guess it's because when I was growing up, I didn't think my life would turn out this way."

"What, you mean no guy, no 2.5 kids, no little house in the suburbs with a white picket fence, a rose garden, and a golden retriever with big brown eyes?" Frank, the host, sounded genuinely intrigued.

"Hey, I've got the retriever." Amy paused, then added, "But nothing else. Though that's not to say I've totally ruled children out of my life."

"Just marriage," Frank said.

"Good guess," Martin said, munching on Steve's cake doughnut with the sprinkles as he peered at the house in question with high-power, infrared binoculars. Martin loved messing with the newest in equipment any chance he got.

"Yeah…I think so," Amy said, in response to the radio talk-show host.

"Want to tell me what happened?" Frank's voice was deep and soothing.

"It's pretty boring. The same old story. He was very good-looking, and I was totally infatuated, and by the time I realized Lenny was incapable of loving anyone but himself, he'd left me with a pile of debts."

"Was there another woman involved?" Frank asked.

Steve tensed. No wonder Amy seemed so wary of men.

"Isn't there always? You know, when I finally realized what was going on, there was almost this sense of…relief. I almost felt sorry for her, because she was going to have to deal with Lenny and all his problems."

A short silence ensued, then Frank said, "Amy, let's deal with you and your problems."

Amy laughed. "I don't have any man problems, Frank. I'm okay. I made this decision—no more relationships in my life until I'm debt free, period. So for now, I'm content with fantasy."

"How much do you still have to pay off?"

She named a sum that made Martin whistle through his teeth. Steve winced. Even Frank seemed stunned.

"Amy, I want to get back to what you said a while ago, about knowing what women want. That intrigued me, and I'm sure it's intrigued our audience. What exactly did you mean when you said, 'I think I know what a lot of women would like'?"

"Just that— Well, when you're sixteen and lying in a hammock on a summer afternoon in Antioch, Illinois, you just don't picture your life the way mine has turned out."

"How old are you, Amy?" Frank asked.

"Twenty-six."

"And what did you think your life would be like?"

"I don't know. I mean, something a lot more exciting than this. An adventure. I thought I would wake up each morning, eager to face my day. Not knowing that each one would be exactly the same."

"What do you do, Amy?"

"I clean houses during the day, and waitress in the evenings."

"And you're paying off all those bills."

"Yeah."

"Is Lenny helping you at all?"

Steve leaned forward. Now he was really curious.

She laughed. "I married a guy who used a false ID. I don't even know if Lenny was his real name. I don't know where he is, or who he's with. Or what he's up to. No, Lenny's not helping me pay any of the bills."

"Whew. Tough break."

"Yeah. But I'm making it. In about three more years, I'll have everything paid off, and then I'm going to rethink my entire life. Maybe go back to school or something."

"But for now, all you can see in front of you is day after day of work, work, work." Frank's voice had softened.

Steve cradled his coffee in his hands, his eyes on the small, dingy house across the narrow street.

But his mind and heart were with Amy on that talk show.

"Yeah, that's—" Her voice had started to break, and after a short moment of silence, Steve heard her say, "That's it in a nutshell."

"Is there any guy in your life right now, Amy, or do you still consider yourself in recovery from your ex?"

Steve held his breath. He could sense that Martin had been drawn into Amy's story, as well. His partner remained totally silent as he listened.

"No, there's… Well, there's this one guy, but I really don't want to talk about him on the air."

"Fair enough. I'm just glad there's someone else you're talking to besides me. Now, about what women want—could you be a little more explicit for our listeners?"

"I want some excitement."

"Okay."

"I want to go out and walk on the wild side."

"Yeah!" Now Frank sounded really interested.

"I'm tired of playing by the rules, of being this nice girl that nothing ever happens to. I mean, I don't ever want to *not* be nice, but once in a while I'd like some adventure."

"And does this adventure include a man?" Frank prompted. "Perhaps a couple of midnight kisses?"

There was a slight hesitation from Amy, then, "Yeah."

"What kind of man?"

"The kind of man who's not afraid to be romantic. To go all out."

Steve was listening so intently he was forgetting to breathe.

"This sounds great, Amy," Frank said. "Okay, now describe your dream date. Pull out all the stops. Go for it, girl!"

"Okay."

Steve smiled into the darkness. It sounded to him like Amy was really beginning to open up and enjoy herself.

"He would come over and pick me up in his car—"

"A mere car, Amy?" Frank asked.

"Well…"

"This is your fantasy," Frank reminded, his voice soft and mellow, encouraging her. "I want you to go all out. Nothing is too much in your imagination—you know what I mean?"

"Yeah." She hesitated, and Steve felt himself practically leaning into the radio.

"Okay," Amy said after a pause. "Okay. He picks me up in a limousine."

"Black or white?" Frank said.

"Oh, black. It's so much more elegant. And not one of those really long ones, just a regular limo."

"So you and this guy—" Frank said, encouragingly.

"Oh, no. He's not in the limo. The driver comes

to my door and tells me that the limo is ready, and I come out and walk to the car. He opens the door, and there's a red rose on the seat. A single red rose. With a note. A note that tells me how badly this man wants to see me, how much he's looking forward to our evening together, and how much he wants to please me.''

"Wow," said Frank softly.

"Wow," said Martin softly, before taking another long swig of his coffee.

Steve merely listened. Carefully. If there was one thing he excelled at as a detective, it was details. Details often led to plans, and the start of a plan was just beginning to formulate in his brain. He had a feeling that Amy was going to give him all the details he needed.

"So," Frank continued softly—and it was clear to Steve that the talk-show host was a smart man; he didn't want to break the spell he'd woven, didn't want to break Amy's train of thought. "What happens next?"

"We drive through a darkened city," Amy said. "Los Angeles at night is a city of sparkling lights. It's quiet inside the limo, I can't hear any traffic sounds. We come to a restaurant—"

"What kind of food?" Frank asked. "Pick your favorite."

"Oh, Italian," Amy replied quickly. "It's a small, romantic little place, overlooking the ocean. The man who has arranged all this is waiting inside. I walk into the dining room and he's bought out the entire place, so there's just one table set, overlooking the ocean. That table is surrounded by white candles—the only light is candlelight. Then he escorts me to my seat, pulls out my chair, the whole thing. He kisses my cheek, but doesn't say a word.''

"Rich and dumb, that's what most women like," Martin muttered. Steve—knowing that Martin was currently separated from his wife, and that the majority of their fights had been about money—wisely said nothing.

"We order dinner," Amy continued, "and he tells me how wonderful I look. There's that…you know, that electricity between us. Chemistry. I can barely eat my food, my stomach is fluttering so fast, because throughout the entire dinner, we both know what will happen afterward.''

Steve practically crushed his coffee cup in his hands. How could the sound of her voice, and what she was describing, have such an erotic effect on him? He could visualize the entire experience, could see Amy sitting at a table across from him, her hair up in some sort of elegant style, wearing a sexy little dress with barely any back and not all that much covering her front. He could barely keep his concentration on the house across the street from their parked van, because all he could think about was this dinner with Amy.

"Do you even make it to dessert, Amy?''

"Oh, he doesn't rush me. Even though we both know how the evening is going to end…how it *has* to end. He lets me enjoy every single moment. We have coffee afterward. Cappuccinos. And tiramisu, that Italian dessert."

"I know the one," Frank said. "Now, can you tell me how the rest of this dream date goes, or am I asking you to be more explicit than you want to be?"

Amy hesitated.

"Just remember, Amy." Frank spoke very softly, as if talking to a frightened horse ready to bolt out of the corral. "There were no last names given. You could be any woman in Los Angeles. Or every woman. And I'm sure many of our listeners have had some of the same thoughts."

"I know." Still, she hesitated.

Steve held his breath.

"Come on, Amy," Martin muttered under his.

"We…we dance," Amy finally said.

"Dance?" Frank repeated. The radio host sounded disappointed, as if he'd expected more.

"Dance. There's nothing more romantic, to me, than dancing after dinner. But this kind of dancing, it's more like…foreplay."

"I get it," said Frank, sounding relieved. "Please continue."

"We dance. We get all…turned on. He kisses me, and it's like…over the moon."

"Oh, yeah," Frank said.

"He's not taking any commercial breaks," Martin said, worried.

Steve shushed him with a gesture. He'd given up all pretense of watching the house, and was riveted to what was happening on the talk show.

"And after this kiss on the dance floor, is there a little dirty dancing afterward?" Frank asked.

"We drive back through the city, in the darkened limo. We can't keep our hands off each other. We practically make love in the back seat, but he keeps building the anticipation, making me wait...."

"I can't take much more of this," Martin said.

I know the feeling.... Steve closed his eyes, needing to hear only her voice.

"We finally get to his place, and he carries me to the door, practically kicks it open, carries me up the stairs to the bedroom, throws me down on the bed, rips off his clothing and mine, and...we do it."

"Wow," Frank said.

"Wow," Martin echoed. "Why can't I meet a nice, uncomplicated girl like her?"

"Thank you, Amy, for sharing that fantasy with us," Frank said. "You've started off this first evening of Midnight Kisses with style."

"Thank you, Frank," Amy replied, her voice sounding shy and unsure. Soft. "I think... I think I needed to say all of this. It kind of helped me. You know what I mean?"

"Yeah. You take care now, babe, and don't settle for anything less than that guy who's going to take you straight over the moon...."

Steve saw a movement out of the corner of his eye, right by their targeted house.

"Martin! He's moving!"

"What?" His partner was clearly thinking of Italian restaurants by the sea, and long, dark limousine drives.

"Joey the Rat is making his move."

"Right."

Both men exited the car and closed in on their quarry. For the moment, Steve had to put Amy out of his mind, because he was absolutely determined that this was one deadbeat dad who wasn't going to get away.

LATER THAT EVENING—rather, early that morning—Steve fell into bed, exhausted. Joey the Rat had been captured; another piece of what Steve considered human vermin had been made to face up to his responsibilities and act like a decent human being. But before Steve closed his eyes and practically passed out from lack of sleep, he wondered what he was going to do about Amy. He knew what he wanted to do, but he wondered if what he wanted was best for her.

It was pretty clear she didn't want a man in her life after what she'd been through with that guy. Yet he'd heard the genuine yearning in her voice when she'd described her fantasy. And the hurt when she'd detailed the reality of what life had handed her. He'd also heard the absolute determination in her voice when she'd stated that she had no intention of getting involved with anyone again until she'd paid off a considerable amount of debt. Twenty-six thousand dollars, to be exact.

No wonder she was working two jobs. He was surprised she even had the energy or the desire to smile back at him as he walked into Bud's Café.

He thought about her life, and wondered why there were Amys in the world, and why there were Joeys. Joeys ran at the first sign of trouble, like rats racing off a sinking ship. The Amys of the world stayed, fought, tried to change their lives and make them better; even had a tendency to clean up other people's messes.

Steve stared up at the ceiling, unable to sleep because he couldn't stop thinking about her. He liked her style, her feistiness, her courage in the face of odds that would crush most women.

Thinking about Amy, his sense of admiration quickly turned to feelings of desire. As his thoughts became decidedly erotic, he finally fell into a deep and blissful sleep.

As STEVE SHAVED AND showered early the following afternoon, he found that he'd come to several decisions. First, Amy wasn't going to experience her fantasy with anyone else but him. It would take a little work, and some extremely careful planning, but he'd amassed quite a few favors over his years of detective work. He could call in several of them for Amy. She was definitely worth it.

He found that he wanted to do this more for her than for himself. More than anything, he wanted to put some sparkle back into her life. He wanted to erase those little lines of tension in her forehead, around her mouth, and see her really laugh.

He wanted to drive her to the ocean, eat a wonderful meal with her, dance with her, and...

"And" was the tricky part. But he would leave that part up to her.

Steve smiled into the mirror as he finished shaving. His detective's intuition told him they were both in for quite a spectacular night.

CHAPTER TWO

THE FOLLOWING EVENING at work, Amy worried about whether Bud might have had the radio blaring during the night shift, but no one made any reference to a woman named Amy baring her soul on the air.

Steve came into the diner at the usual time, looking tired and a little scruffy. But there was a gleam in his eye that made her think that perhaps a case had gone particularly well for him.

"You look happy tonight," she said as she poured him another cup of coffee to top off the piece of cherry pie à la mode he'd just finished.

"I'm getting ready to start a very special case."

"Someone important?"

"Someone very important," he replied.

"Well," she said, pleased with herself because she was actually having a conversation with this man that wasn't about the weather or what he wanted to order, "I hope it ends up working out. The way you want it to, I mean."

He smiled to himself then, with such a sexy, self-satisfied expression on his face that she almost dropped the coffeepot. As she headed back toward the kitchen, she wondered what it would be like to be the woman in Steve's life, and to be on the receiving end of that smile.

STEVE FOLLOWED HER HOME that evening, making sure she never saw him. He wrote down the address of her building, and the apartment number. He'd already started calling in favors, and planned to be ready with Amy's fantasy on her next day off. He'd recreate it perfectly, just the way she'd described it on the radio. He wanted that evening for her, and for himself. More than anything, he found himself thinking of ways to make her happy, because he sensed she hadn't had a lot of that particular emotion in her life lately. And it was up to him to change the odds.

THE FOLLOWING WEEK, on her day off, Amy heard a sharp knock on her apartment door. She glanced at the clock on the kitchen wall. Three thirty-five in the afternoon. She wasn't expecting anyone. With the wariness any woman had to possess when living alone in a big city, she left the heavy chain fastened as she cautiously opened her front door.

A man in some sort of uniform stood outside. The smile he gave her was very nice, reassuring. He seemed all of about twenty-five, with a freshly scrubbed face, thick blond hair and a good haircut. Like so many men in L.A., he looked like an out-of-work actor, moonlighting at another job.

"Amy Robbins?"

"That's me."

"My name is Tim and I'll be your limousine driver this evening."

She felt a blush start from her chest and flare its way up her neck and into her face, her cheeks stinging with color as only a redhead's could.

"Is this some kind of a joke?"

"Nope. This guy's dead serious. But, right now," he continued, "I have a delivery for you." He held out a cream-colored envelope, and a single red rose. "He told me to give you as long as you needed to get ready for tonight, but if you thought it was a bad idea, you just have to say the word and I'm to leave."

Speechless, she stared at the envelope in her hand, the rose in the other. Her fantasy. Someone had been listening to her fantasy. But who would ever connect the name Amy with her?

Bud? She instantly dismissed the thought.

Perhaps Linda and Alexis at work? The two older and married waitresses were always gently teasing her about her lack of a love life. But would they go to this kind of extreme on their tight budgets? And who would they hire to play the role of her dream date?

Then she remembered Steve's smile.

"I'm getting ready to start a very special case...."

Her heartbeat accelerated.

"Someone very important..."

Her heart, her gut, told her it was true. *Steve.*

"Steve?" she said, looking up at the limo driver through the slight crack in the door.

"You mean, Mr. McKnight? Yeah. You know, I think you should take pity on this guy, because he really wants to go out with you tonight. I mean, he told me to wait as long as it takes for your answer, unless you just said no right away, and then I was to leave and not bother you at all." He leaned forward and whispered, "But you should give the guy a break."

"Do you know where we're going?" She asked him this because she found she needed to be sure.

"Some little Italian place in Malibu."

He was giving her the fantasy. *Her fantasy.* It was right in front of her, a chance to be someone different, to do something different from the humdrum sameness of her days. He'd listened to her on the radio; really listened. Somehow, fate had contrived to have him tuned to that same station just as she'd called in and opened her heart up. And now, Steve wanted her to have her fantasy.

With him.

"Can you—can you give me about five minutes to decide?"

"Sure," said the driver. He was grinning.

"Better make it ten."

"No problem."

She closed the door and leaned back against it, the rose and the envelope still in her possession.

Then she laughed out loud.

IT WAS BOTH THE LONGEST and shortest ten minutes of her life.

Part of her—that deeply instinctual part that had actually made the call to the radio talk show—wanted to throw caution to the winds and go. Another part of her hesitated, remembering exactly how steamy and X-rated that fantasy had become. She wondered if she was really ready to take that step with Steve.

Not that she hadn't fantasized about it.

Yet another part of her remembered her ex-husband, and the all-enveloping pain that had engulfed her when she'd realized she'd given herself, heart and soul, to a man who was no better than a con.

But Steve isn't like that....

The instinctual part of her put up quite a fight. She'd been working at Bud's for the last few months, and Steve had been a regular. The other waitresses liked him. Bud liked him.

Bud...

With shaking fingers, she dialed the restaurant. Bud picked up on the first ring.

"Bud's Café."

"Bud, do you think I should go out with Steve?"

"Amy?"

"Yes."

"I think you should put that guy out of his misery."

Her heartbeat sped up again, because she already knew what she wanted to do.

"Can I trust him?" she whispered, her throat aching.

"Yeah. He's one of the good guys. Go out and have a good time, okay?"

"Okay. And Bud? Let me tell Linda and Alexis myself."

"You got it. I never spoke to you. We never discussed this."

Bud hung up the phone, and Amy reached for the envelope.

She'd put the single red rose in a small vase on her bedside table, and set the envelope down next to it. She'd called Bud first, because she'd known that if she opened that envelope before she talked to him, she was probably a goner.

"He's one of the good guys. He's one of the good guys...." She kept repeating the words over and over in her head, like a mantra, as she opened the envelope and pulled out the single sheet of paper. His handwriting was bold, strong and distinctive, much like the man himself.

Amy,
Let me make one of your dreams come true.

The limo and dinner by the ocean are on me.
The rest is truly up to you.

                                        Steve

Just as she'd thought—she was a goner.

MARY LYNN, HER FRIEND who lived down the hall,
was a struggling makeup artist. Amy had met her
a while back in the apartment's laundry room, and
now didn't waste any time calling her.

"Sure, I'll make you up. I'll be right over. What
are you going to wear?"

Amy wasn't exactly sure. Nothing in her simple
wardrobe came anywhere close to a fantasy like
this one. But, like Cinderella's, her problem was
solved within minutes of its arrival.

When Tim the driver came by exactly ten
minutes later, he had a large, flat, white package
in his hands with a huge red bow. This time, after
she glanced through the security peephole, Amy
opened her door fully without using the security
chain.

"In case you say yes," he said, a grin on his
handsome face.

"What is it?" she asked, but she'd already
guessed.

"A surprise. Go ahead and open it."

She did. The dress was stunning—sleek and
black and sexy, totally suitable for dancing the
night away. And so much more beautiful than any

piece of clothing she'd owned in a long time. The enclosed note said, *To see you in this dress is one of my fantasies. Say yes.*

"He's really going all out," Tim said. "You have to admire the guy."

She made the decision that fast, and it had nothing to do with the dress or the rose. It had everything to do with the first note—and the man.

"Could you pick me up at about six?" she said.

"Sure you don't want any more time?"

"What do you think?"

Tim gave her an adorable grin. "I told you you should go out with this guy, but you shouldn't make it too easy for him. Why don't I pick you up at seven? We'll miss rush-hour traffic, and I'll get you to the beach by around seven-thirty. A late supper."

"I like the way this man thinks," Mary Lynn said. The petite blonde was sorting through pots and tubes of color, and selecting her brushes.

"Seven it is," Amy said.

AT THE RESTAURANT, STEVE thought about how useful it was to have friends in high—and sometimes low—places.

Carmine had owed him big time, so the Italian restaurateur hadn't even blinked when Steve had asked him if he could have the use of his most elegant restaurant for a night—minus the other customers.

"She must be one special lady, eh?" Carmine had said.

"That she is."

Now he sat out on the balcony of the restaurant, overlooking the Pacific Ocean. Gulls wheeled overhead, and the salty, fresh smell of seawater filled his senses. But all he could think about was whether or not Amy would accept his invitation.

His cell phone rang, and he immediately answered it.

"Steve," he said shortly. His emotions were on edge; he wanted her answer to be yes. It had to be yes.

"It's Tim. She was really surprised, but she said yes."

"Great. What time will you be here?" Steve was surprised at how nervous he was. More than anything, he wanted everything to be perfect for Amy.

"I'm picking her up at seven. She wanted a little time to get ready. If traffic's light, we should be there in about thirty to forty minutes."

"Call me immediately if anything changes. Are the flowers in the back of the limousine?"

Tim laughed. "Everything's fine."

BY THE TIME MARY LYNN had finished making up her face, Amy didn't recognize herself. But it wasn't like a department-store makeover. She looked spectacular.

"I love what you did with my eyes," she said. "They look like cat's eyes."

"Just shadows and liners," her friend replied. "I'll take care of your puppies tonight in case you get in really late. You look perfect—that dress is perfect. Just go on out there, get in that limo, and stun this guy into submission."

SITTING IN THE LIMOUSINE, in the darkness and silence, Amy thought about what she was going to do.

She'd already made up her mind she was going to sleep with Steve. The way she responded to his slightest touch had convinced her they would be good together. Another motivating factor was the fact that she'd been a virgin when she married her ex-husband. Though their sexual relationship had been sort of exciting at first, Lenny's innate selfishness had colored everything in the end—even their relationship in bed. She'd stopped trusting him long before she'd stopped loving him, and a part of her had shut off in the bedroom.

She'd lost a part of herself that she cherished, and now she longed to get it back. And she had a feeling Steve could help her find it again.

Closing her eyes, she sank back into the leather seat. The fragrance of flowers filled the luxurious car—an effect of the dozen red, long-stemmed roses that had been waiting for her when she stepped inside, along with a full bar stocked with several bottles of extremely expensive champagne. She'd asked Tim to open one of the bottles, and now proceeded to drink a glass, the sharp bubbles tickling her nose.

Just a little champagne—for courage.

They were driving along the Santa Monica Freeway, toward the beach, but she kept her eyes closed, breathing deeply. She tried to still the racing of her heart. All he wanted was her company for dinner. That was all.

"The rest is truly up to you...."

Well, for once in her life, she was going to walk on that wild side. As the saying went, with a slight modification, *No More Ms. Nice Girl....*

SHE KNOCKED HIM OUT. Totally. As she entered the restaurant, he noted that the little slip of a black dress he'd selected with her in mind barely covered the essentials. Lots of leg, lots of bare back, and a knockout front view. High heels. And her vibrant red hair exactly as he'd imagined it, up in a twist, with a few pieces escaping, framing her face. On Amy, the style didn't look severe, just...elegant.

She hesitated in the doorway, and Steve knew why. He was sure she'd expected them to be dining at a public place, with other people. She hadn't truly expected her total fantasy, with the single table by the window overlooking the beach, surrounded by white candles.

"Amy," he said, as he reached her side. Then,

remembering that the guy in her fantasy didn't talk all that much—at least, not right away—he led her to their table, slid out her chair, seated her, then kissed her on the cheek.

He couldn't resist saying one more thing.

"You look absolutely beautiful."

FOR THE LONGEST TIME in her fantasy, the man had remained nameless. Faceless. Any man would have filled the bill, as long as he adored her. But when she'd spoken of it on the radio talk show, she'd thought of Steve. He'd definitely been the front runner.

Here, at this moment, in this candlelit restaurant, the reality was so much better.

Scarier, but better.

She wondered what he thought of her as he seated her. His fingers scarcely brushed her bare shoulders as she sat down, and little bursts of electricity shot through her. Amy had done enough reading to know that the human body had an electrical field surrounding it, but this was ridiculous.

She had the strangest urge to burst into tears as she glanced around the darkened restaurant, lit only by dozens of white candles. The result was a dreamily soft ambience. Outside, the stretch of beach with waves surging against the sand was lit by strategically placed lights. As she glanced out over the ocean, all she saw was endless blackness as the water met the horizon, somewhere.

She turned her attention back to Steve.

Devastating—that was the word she'd been searching for. He looked absolutely devastating in a dark, well-cut suit and a white shirt; a classic look. His hair hadn't been trimmed or skillfully styled for the occasion, and she was thankful he'd kept that part of himself still slightly rough around the edges. It made him more familiar.

The whiteness of his shirt set off the darkness of his skin. The way he was looking at her as their waiter approached their table caused her breath to hitch in her throat.

She had to keep reminding herself that all Steve expected was dinner. What scared her was what she wanted.

"Wine?" Steve asked her, and she nodded her head. She knew nothing about fine wine, and simply watched as the waiter poured a small amount into Steve's glass, waited while he tasted it and signaled his approval, then filled both their glasses and discreetly vanished.

"You know wines?"

"No," he said. "Don't be impressed. I just know what I'm supposed to do. But I do know that Carmine has an impressive wine cellar."

"This Carmine is a friend of yours?"

"You could say that." He paused for a moment, then said, "I thought in your fantasy we weren't supposed to talk a lot."

She could feel her cheeks start to burn. "It's

okay. I'm...I'm kind of nervous, so...if it's okay with you, I'd like to talk.'' She couldn't imagine going through the rest of the evening if this man remained a stranger. Talking, getting to know him, would help.

''You choose the topic,'' he said softly.

She picked up her wineglass. ''That's easy. You.''

''Ask anything. I'm an open book.''

''Where do your parents live?''

''They don't. They died when I was a baby. A car crash.''

''My God.'' Now she was sorry she'd asked.

''Don't be upset. It happened a long time ago.''

''Who took care of you?'' The thought of a baby, alone and helpless, was overwhelmingly sad to her.

''The state.'' He gave her the name of a local boys' orphanage, in one of the poorer areas of Los Angeles.

''Steve,'' she said, not sure how to react.

''Hey, they kept food in my mouth and a roof over my head.''

''But it couldn't have been pleasant.''

''What did I know?'' He took another sip of his wine.

She hesitated, wanting to change the subject. ''How did you get to be a detective? Bud said something about you being a cop.''

''I was.'' He hesitated. ''I blew out my left knee

in a chase. Fell down a hill after tackling this guy. When we came up for air, it was pretty badly twisted. Even after surgery, it didn't ever heal correctly. I couldn't stay on the force, so I decided to do the next best thing and start my own company.''

Totally impressed with his initiative, Amy took another sip of her wine. Their waiter had appeared again only moments before, and set down a tray of appetizers. She selected a piece of bruschetta, and a few black olives.

"So you're happy doing what you do?"

"Yeah, I like it."

"It sounds so exciting."

"It has its moments," he said.

"It must be better than cleaning houses."

"You want me to track down that creep for you?"

It took her a moment to realize he was referring to her ex-husband, Lenny.

"Could you do that?"

"I could give it a try."

She thought about this. In some of her other fantasies—spun out while she lay in bed and couldn't sleep for worrying about the bills—she'd thought about going after her ex and making him pay for the debts he'd run up. Now Steve seemed determined to make that fantasy a reality, as well.

"I don't know," she said. "Even if he were forced to pay by a court, he's the type of guy who'd manage to sneak away, get out of it, leave the country. On one level, it's easier for me to pay it off myself, get my credit rating back, and start over.''

Steve took another sip of wine as the waiter served their salads. ''You impress me, Amy. You've got guts.''

She was startled by the salad. Menus hadn't appeared, they hadn't even ordered.

''I took the liberty of ordering for both of us,'' Steve explained. ''There's not a whole lot not to like on Carmine's menu.'' His brow furrowed, and for just a moment he looked worried. ''You like seafood, don't you?''

''Love it.''

Clearly relieved, he sat back. ''We should be just fine.''

They concentrated on their salads, then small bowls of garbanzo-and-vegetable minestrone soup. Amy finally got up the courage to ask the question she'd wanted to ask from the beginning of their evening together.

''How did you hear me on the radio?'' Nervous, she fiddled with her napkin. ''I mean, how did you know it was me?''

''The name, first of all. And I recognized your voice.''

His eyes were so warm as he studied her, his gaze so appreciative.

''Where were you? At home?''

"On a stakeout. Downtown L.A. With my partner."

"Oh." She considered this. "So you listen to the radio on stakeouts to pass the time."

"It beats getting bored waiting for our target to arrive. Contrary to popular belief, and to what the entertainment world would have you believe, a lot of detective work is quite boring. But the payoff's always worth it."

"Did you find this person?"

"Oh, yeah. We found him."

"What happened?"

"Well, he owes his wife a lot of money—" He stopped, and she felt the color rise in her cheeks, washing her face with a sensation of prickling heat. Money. If Steve had listened to the entire radio show that night, he knew the enormity of her debt.

Twenty-six thousand dollars.

"I'm really a good person," she began.

"I know that," he said, and his voice was so gentle she almost wanted to cry. "I admire you, Amy, for having the guts to call in and voice that fantasy. And I admire you for facing your problems and paying off a debt that isn't really yours. Working two jobs. Taking responsibility. A lot of people wouldn't have. A lot of people would have gone straight to bankruptcy."

"I couldn't do that. It didn't feel right. Lenny fleeced people out of their money under false pretenses. Including me." She hesitated. "But those bills still have to be paid. And I want you to know, Steve, I had absolutely nothing to do with any of it, except I was too naive to see it. Actually, I didn't *want* to see it—especially what he was doing to me.''

''I know.''

''I've come to the conclusion that my relationship with Lenny was like a fantasy—but a bad one.''

They were silent for a short time, neither touching their food, before Steve said, ''I liked listening to your other fantasy.''

''You did?'' Now she didn't feel as insecure with him. After all, he knew almost everything about her, even the shame of being in debt. And he still thought she was a good person; he didn't blame her for what Lenny had done, or for not having been able to see through him.

''Yeah. I liked the way you had the whole thing all thought out.''

''Really.'' This fascinated her.

''The details. I was amazed. You have an extremely active imagination.''

She smiled at him, suddenly feeling quite daring. ''I have the feeling you do, too. After all, you were able to appreciate my fantasy.''

''I did.'' He broke off a piece of bread, reached for a pat of butter. ''I think fantasies are crucial. They keep people alive. When I was lying on my couch at home recuperating, watching those talk shows, my knee hurting and elevated on a pillow…hey, my fantasies were all that kept me going. I saw myself walking again with no pain, even though I knew I'd never be able to go back to work with the department.''

"That had to be hard.''

"It was,'' he said. "And I also had this crazy fantasy about starting my own business, and here I am. So don't ever discount all the crazy things your mind can come up with. Or even your dreams. There's genuine pay dirt there.''

She laughed, feeling relaxed and happy.

"That was the main part of my fantasy,'' Steve said softly. "I wondered how you'd look if you really laughed. I wanted to make you laugh.''

His simple statement touched her deeply.

When their pasta arrived—linguine with all sorts of seafood in a creamy sauce—Amy was in heaven. But it wasn't entirely because of the food, or even the restaurant. This evening was far more magical than anything she could have dreamed of. She loved sitting across the small table from Steve and talking on such an intimate level.

It was almost better than sex. She blushed as that thought surfaced, and tried to concentrate on her food.

"This guy can really cook,'' she said, twirling her pasta on her fork and stabbing a piece of lobster meat onto the tines.

"One of Carmine's many talents—one that doesn't seem to get him in too much trouble."

She was tempted to ask, but didn't really want to talk about Steve's friend.

Dessert appeared directly after dinner. Tiramisu and cappuccinos, just as she'd described on the radio show. And as Amy spooned a little sugar into her Italian coffee, she realized that the time had come to make her decision.

She realized it didn't matter what she and Steve had talked about, because far more important than any of the conversation that had flowed between them, she sensed that this was a man who could reawaken her sensuality. She felt safe with Steve. Protected. He was the sort of man who would protect whomever he was with. Bud had told her Steve was one of the good guys, but her feelings went deeper than that. He was a man who'd been dealt a pretty tough hand—like her—but he hadn't complained. He'd simply rolled up his sleeves and gotten on with it.

They had more in common than she'd originally thought.

But there was also that little matter of chemistry. She felt more *alive* with Steve than she had with any other man in her life. If she were honest with herself, she'd been sizing him up since the very first day he'd walked into Bud's diner.

He was handsome, but that wasn't the total appeal he had for her. There was something wild and a little reckless about him. Amy had the feeling that if she went to his place, if they made love, some of that wildness would find its way into their relationship.

She wanted to be alone with him. She wanted the evening to end with lovemaking. She wanted to feel alive again.

"This is wonderful," she began. "It's been wonderful."

He set his coffee cup down. "But—"

"No buts." She drew in a deep breath, trying to relax the tight, excited feeling in her chest. "I want you to take me home."

He cocked his head, eyed her closely. That expression, in those intent eyes, almost robbed her of breath.

"With you," she whispered.

Comprehension dawned in the beautiful, blue-gray eyes.

"Steve, I want you to make love to me."

HE HAD TO MAKE SURE he was actually hearing what he thought he was hearing. Because he'd wanted her to say those exact words so badly, he couldn't be sure he wasn't hallucinating.

"You want me to make love to you."

She nodded her head, that gorgeous red hair reflecting the candlelight.

"You don't want to dance with me."

"Are you disappointed? Steve, you didn't hire an orchestra, did you?"

He grinned. "There's a discreetly hidden stereo system."

"Good. Then we can leave, right?"

He noticed her voice was shaking, and covered one of her hands with his own.

"Amy, are you sure you want this?"

She swallowed, and he saw the conflicting emotions racing over her beautiful face.

"I want... I want you to...sweep me off my feet."

"Ah." Now he understood. There was nothing he wanted more.

"I want you to...want me."

Intuitively, in his gut, he knew the real damage her ex-husband had done to her. Amy might never have felt wanted in her marriage, but she would feel wanted tonight.

"I do." His voice roughened as he lowered it, tightening his grip on her cold hand. "I've wanted you from the very beginning. From the moment I walked into Bud's and saw you in that uniform, all I've thought about was unzipping that front zipper and taking it right off you."

He wasn't sure if his words would shock or frighten her. But they were honest. The absolute, raw truth. He watched as her pupils widened, her lips parted. And he ached with the need to kiss that mouth. But not here. Not now.

"Before I saw you, I went into Bud's once a week, maybe twice. After I knew you were there, I figured out the nights you worked and never missed one."

"I wondered about that," she whispered.

Steve had already arranged to pay for dinner beforehand, so he knew their waiter wouldn't be coming back to their table except to ask them if they wanted another Italian coffee or perhaps an after-dinner liqueur.

But the way he was feeling, dinner was over.

He leaned closer, moved his chair next to hers at the small round table until he could lean to brush his lips over one perfect ear.

"Amy, you can't even imagine the thoughts I've had about you."

Her soft intake of breath pleased him.

"I'm going to take you home with me, and you're going to have no doubts in your mind that I want you."

He walked her to the limousine, opened the door, and eased her inside. Then he strode around to the driver's side, had a few quiet words with Tim, and then came back around to the darkened interior of the limousine.

He left a little space between them on the leather seat when he sat down, and she was grateful. Her heart was racing so fast; she didn't know how she would have reacted if he'd suddenly grabbed her.

But he was obviously taking it slow. Building

the tension. Opening another bottle of champagne, he poured them each a glass.

"To tonight," he said, his voice low. "To you, Amy."

She felt tears sting her eyes as she accepted her glass. It had been a long time since *she'd* felt safe in the presence of a man, let alone contemplated anything sexual. She was trusting Steve with her heart—her battered little heart—and she knew he wasn't going to disappoint her.

They sipped their champagne as the driver eased the long, sleek car out of the parking lot and onto Pacific Coast Highway.

Steve finished his champagne, then set his glass down. He moved closer, encircling one of her wrists with his fingers.

"I can't wait any longer," he whispered roughly against her ear. "Come here."

The sound of his voice did the most amazing things to her insides. She felt all fluttery—all soft and liquid and yearning. She set her glass down, turned toward him, and knew she would let him do anything he wanted.

He kissed her wrist, then the center of her palm, all the while looking at her face. She closed her eyes, so thankful she was sitting down. Sensual excitement caused her muscles to relax, her body to become more receptive to the powerful pull of his masculinity. She leaned toward him, felt his fingers beneath her chin, tipping it up, and knew he was about to kiss her.

It had been so long since she'd been kissed. Amy had always thought that when it finally happened again she would go into it with her eyes wide-open, wary; unable, unwilling to trust. She hadn't thought it would be like this—her eyes closed, her insides melting, her body surrendering so totally in the darkness.

Her hands clenched, her fingers gripped his shoulders as his mouth found hers, and it was so good she moaned softly, a little feminine whimper. Then she fell silent as his lips parted hers and his tongue played inside her mouth.

She felt that tongue, that masculine thrust, all the way down to her toes. They curled inside her high heels. And that most feminine part of her, between her thighs, bloomed hot and wet, yearning for an even greater closeness.

She felt alive again.

He continued to kiss her, and she found she didn't even possess the energy to keep them upright. She didn't want to. She simply melted, sliding back on the leather seat, its softness cushioning her as the hardness of his muscular body pressed down on her. She wanted his body tight against hers and her hands reached up, pulled at his shoulders, pulled him closer.

Their lips never parted. He continued kissing her as the sleek car smoothly ate up the miles, the dark window between the two of them and their driver affording them total privacy.

His hands, his touch, felt sure on her body. There was nothing at all tentative in the way he stroked her, caressed her. And she knew, in the smallest part of her brain still operating rationally, that this was right. She'd sensed it. With some men, you just knew. The way they touched you, the way they kissed you—with assurance, as if you were a woman and not some delicate thing that could be broken.

But what she found most thrilling of all was that she could sense his attention was totally on her. There was nothing else on his mind as he kissed her. With Lenny, she'd always felt the wheels turning, his mind elsewhere. Toward the end of their marriage, she'd sensed he was already involved with another woman—another scam.

Whereas Steve was utterly focused on her. There was nothing else, no one else in the limousine tonight, but the two of them.

His hand slid up her rib cage, and she knew the second before he touched her breast that he was going to. She did nothing to stop him; simply gasped and finally broke their kiss as she felt his fingers find her nipple, pebble hard, beneath the sleek material of her dress. She hadn't worn a bra; the style and fabric of the dress made that item of lingerie impossible to wear.

She hadn't worn any panties, either—just stockings that stopped at mid-thigh. The thought of Steve discovering just how little she had on excited her even more.

He seemed impatient as he slid the bodice of her dress down, baring her to the waist. He sat up and discarded his suit jacket, and his shirt seemed so white in the darkness. As he came back down on top of her, she found she liked the way he smelled. He settled himself between her thighs, and she gave silent thanks that her dress hadn't ridden too far up her thighs—though she knew she really wouldn't have minded. With some men, it was impossible to go too fast.

Then all rational thought was completely obliterated as he took her nipple into his mouth.

She arched against him, almost writhing in the leather seat. How could one man make something feel so impossibly good? Her fingers threaded into his long hair and she pulled it, needed to do something to lessen the intensity of the sensation.

He kissed his way up her chest, her neck, his hands on her breasts as he whispered, "You're so beautiful."

With shaking fingers, she started to unbutton his shirt. She'd never had sex like this—wild and powerful and almost out of control. She'd never wanted a man this desperately. And judging from the expression on Steve's face, it was the same for him.

She parted his shirt, slid it back down over his shoulders, and almost ripped it off, overcome by the need to see, to feel, his naked chest and shoulders. When he finally shrugged his shirt off and came back to her, she kept touching him, restlessly moving her fingers over the powerful muscles of his chest and arms. He seemed to burn beneath her hand.

"You're so hot," she whispered, before his mouth covered hers again. This time, when he came down on top of her, she eased her legs farther apart, cradled him against her body, felt the hard, insistent ridge of his arousal pushed against that part of her that wanted him most. The pressure, the movement, was almost enough to send her over the edge.

Her dress rode up the same instant she felt his hand sliding up her stockinged leg. And Amy, barely able to catch her breath, wondered if they were even going to get to Steve's place.

His hand continued up her leg, his fingers sure and strong, caressing her calf, her knee, her thigh, and then stopping for the merest second where her stocking ended, playing with the lacy elastic band.

She caught her breath sharply as his fingers moved closer to the softness of her inner thigh. Closer, closer...

He went perfectly still for a moment when he found her, open and exposed and vulnerable, unprotected by even the merest wisp of silk or lace. Then masculine urgency took over, and she practically arched off the seat as he cupped her, rubbed her so sensuously she almost screamed, then slid two fingers inside her.

Her hips bucked as her orgasm washed over her. He eased her through it, and after she was finished, as she lay on the leather seat incapable of moving a single muscle, he pulled her dress over her head.

Amy knew she'd never had sex like this, because she was lying in the back of a limousine in only her heels and stockings and she didn't even care. She couldn't even think. She couldn't stop, and she was sure Steve couldn't. Even if someone had chosen that moment to interrupt the two of them, to open the limousine door and ask just what they thought they were doing, she couldn't have stopped.

There was a wonderful, powerful, sensual inevitability to what was about to happen, and she couldn't stop it; didn't want to.

Through half-closed eyes, she watched as Steve made short work of his shoes and socks, unbuckled his belt and slipped off his pants. Then he came back down on top of her and kissed her with a hunger that bordered on ravenous.

She wanted it all—his muscled chest pressing on her breasts, the brush of his chest hair against her sensitive flesh, the feel of him—hard and hot—against her. Then suddenly, his hands were on her legs, on her upper thighs, pushing them apart as he positioned himself.

There wasn't time to think about anything. She

only knew how good he felt as he slid inside her. Then her eyes widened because she'd thought he was all the way inside, but there was clearly more. She had to shift the slightest bit for him to push in all the way.

Her head fell back against the leather seat, her eyes closed, and she surrendered to the powerful, masculine, driving rhythm. Each thrust was like a sensual invasion, and it took her a moment to accommodate him, to get used to being so completely and thoroughly filled.

He filled her senses, as well—with his masculine scent that seemed to both stimulate and relax her; with his powerful muscles, bunching and unbunching as he ground his pelvis against hers. She was more than ready for him; he'd seen to that. She grasped his shoulders and her hips began to move with a rhythm of their own, in a desperate answer to his thrusting, a silent plea for release. His hands cupped her bottom, urging her on, harder, faster—

She climaxed again, and that sent him over the edge. She felt his movements quicken, heard the agonized, labored breathing, as if he'd run a long distance. Not wanting to simply collapse after her own release and ignore Steve, she held him tightly as his thrusting accelerated even more. Then she felt those final, urgent spasms as a powerful finish swept over him.

She looked into his face as he came, at the tightly closed eyes, the intensity of his expression.

Then she couldn't do anything more because *another* climax, her third this evening, caught her by surprise—she who had never even had *one* with a man before tonight. His excitement continued to fuel her own, and this was one wild ride she wanted to take.

She closed her eyes and fell headlong into the sensual void.

CHAPTER THREE

WHEN AMY OPENED HER eyes again, the limousine had stopped. Steve was lying next to her, his large body curled around hers. She moved her head just enough to see his face, and realized he was watching her.

"Hi," he said, his voice soft and low. Intimate.

She swallowed against the sudden tightness in her throat. What he'd given her was indescribable. She felt...lighter. Happier. Sexier. Her body felt...right. Certainly a lot less tense. But it was more than that, and had been more than just a physical experience. She'd been living up in her head, trying to deal with her pain by shutting herself off; trying to ignore what her life had become. Steve had given her back her faith in her body, and had touched her emotions, as well. He'd given her the faith to try to connect with another person in one of the deepest ways possible.

She didn't know if she wanted another relationship right away. At the same time, she knew that that was her scared self talking. In Steve's arms, right now, she felt happy and free and whole again in a way she hadn't since her divorce.

"Hi," she said, then reached out and touched his arm.

He kept looking at her, and she knew he was waiting for her to say something, to let him know how she felt. He was waiting for her to set the pace.

First things first.

"What time is it?" she whispered.

"Close to midnight."

"Where are we?" she whispered again. She couldn't hear a sound. No traffic noise, not a single helicopter sweeping through the night sky. That was strange, in the middle of a city like Los Angeles. Everything was so very still.

"We're back home," he replied.

"Your place?"

"Sort of." He sat up and reached for his suit pants. When she sat up and reached for her dress, he handed her his jacket.

"This might be a little warmer. It's cold outside."

She didn't argue. As Amy slipped the suit jacket around her bare shoulders, she could smell his scent on the fine material. Strangely, it reassured her. She gathered up her dress—little more than a handful of soft material—and cautiously stepped out of the limousine, following Steve.

The house looked like an Italian villa, set far back from the main road, with an enormous circular cobblestone drive.

"Where *are* we?" she asked, whispering again. Somehow, she was reluctant to break the silence. How could Steve afford a place like this on a detective's salary? Unless his business was doing extremely well...

"A friend of a friend," Steve said, taking her hand. "An actor."

He mentioned a well-known name, an individual she'd seen up on the big screen just a few weeks ago at the movies.

"He gave you the keys to his house?"

"We grew up together," Steve said. "I'm house-sitting for him while he's on location in Toronto."

"And he told you that you could have wild parties while he was gone."

"In so many words..." He glanced at her and grinned, and her heart did that funny little flip-flop.

"Lead on," she said, and they started up the drive.

Once inside, her first impression was that the living room had acres of carpeting. But she was used to houses like these. After all, she cleaned them almost every day of the week in neighborhoods like Beverly Hills and Bel Air. At first, the sheer amount of vacuuming and dusting had been daunting. The enormous expanses of windows to clean had been overwhelming. But Amy was one to put these things in perspective, and gradually her sense of humor had won out.

"This is his quiet little getaway, right?"

Steve laughed. "He doesn't do anything in a small way."

"Where do you live?"

"Venice."

She'd visited the small, southern California city by the sea, with its lovely little canals and individualistic shops. The minute Steve named the area, it seemed perfect for him.

"Why did you bring me here?" She wasn't at all afraid; she simply wanted to know.

He turned toward her, and her heart sped up once again.

"Because I don't have as nice a pool. Or one that's as private."

"Ah." She could see the direction his mind was taking.

"I thought we might continue the evening—now that we've finished with your fantasy—with one of mine."

"I'm a believer in equal-opportunity fantasies."

"Great, because I'd like a few for my memory book."

"Tell me."

"I have fantasies of swimming with you."

"In the nude?"

"Is there any other way?"

She was surprised at how little modesty she had with him. On one level, she'd never had that big a hang-up about nudity. She'd also reached a certain level of comfort with Steve, because of all the times she'd spoken to him at Bud's. She'd also done a certain amount of fantasizing about him herself that hadn't stopped with the single dinner date.

He'd touched her so deeply this evening, creating her fantasy for her and going to such trouble to get each exact detail correct. Now she found she wanted to do the same for him.

"What does this fantasy entail? The specifics, I mean."

"I don't think men are quite as elaborate about their fantasies as women are. It just involved you, me, a pool, and a nice night like this one."

She started to laugh. "You gave me your jacket out there because you told me it was cold."

He smiled, then gave her that look that had her toes curling inside her shoes.

"The pool's heated."

"I see." She glanced out the windows of the enormous living room, toward the turquoise swimming pool. Then, giving him a mischievous look over her shoulder, she said the words she knew he wanted to hear.

"Let's do it."

SHE WALKED SLIGHTLY AHEAD of him, clad only in her high heels and his jacket, which hit her just above the knee. Amy had never before been quite so conscious of the erotic power she held over a man. She knew from their wild lovemaking earlier this evening that Steve desired her. She also knew she was perfectly safe in his company.

It was a wonderfully heady combination of emotions that served to set her free.

She reached the edge of the pool as she thought about how she could carry this off. Deciding that men were definitely more visual in their fantasies, she quickly glanced around, glad there were no neighbors' houses in sight. This property was most definitely private.

Swiftly, she shed the jacket, folding it and carefully placing it on one of the outdoor chairs by the pool. Then, instead of walking into Steve's wonderfully warm arms, she turned away from him and began a slow, seductive walk, still in her heels, toward the diving board.

The dead silence behind her almost made her laugh. She loved creating this moment for Steve; loved the thought that he was watching every move she made, that his attention was solely on her....

She glanced at him out of the corner of her eye as she reached the diving board. He was watching her, his hands on his hips.

She stepped up onto the diving board in her heels, feeling like a wild child, the most daring girl at the party. And it was a feeling she really liked, but she knew there was only one person she could ever do this with. Steve.

Making each step count, she sauntered to the end

of the diving board. She smiled as she heard Steve call out, "You're reading my mind, Amy."

The night air felt cool against her bare skin. Not wanting to ruin a perfectly good pair of heels no matter how wild she felt, she carefully removed each shoe with the grace of a seasoned stripper, tossed them onto a lounge chair, then almost laughed as she heard the soft, barely suppressed masculine groan that floated across the flickering, turquoise water. The pool was lit from beneath, and glowed vibrantly in the night.

She glanced at Steve. Their gazes locked. Suddenly, she didn't feel the cold.

"I think you have too many clothes on," she said.

Her voice seemed to startle him out of a dream. Obviously, he'd been so caught up in watching her, he hadn't thought about removing his clothing.

She watched as he stripped off his pants, then threw them carelessly onto the chair where she'd left his jacket. She took off her stockings, taking her time, making each moment count.

"Aren't you coming in?" she called out. "Someone told me the water's really nice. Heated."

He walked to the shallow end of the pool, then down the steps into the water. "You have a real talent for this."

She laughed at that, then watched as he began to swim, cutting cleanly through the shimmering water until he was beneath the diving board, looking up.

"You going to come in?" That rough, gravelly voice did as much for her as the look in his eyes.

"Yeah." Where she got her nerve, she'd never know. Cupping her breasts in her hands, she said, "It's getting pretty cold. My nipples are really hard."

The expression on his face was her reward as she backed up, then launched herself off the board, sliced through the water cleanly, diving deep into its warm, turquoise depths.

She arched her back as she surfaced, swiping her hair off her face as she treaded water and waited for him to catch her. She didn't want to evade him, didn't want to postpone what was going to happen.

He surfaced next to her within seconds, linked his fingers with hers and started to swim to the side of the pool, taking her with him.

"You are an enchantress," he said, and she could hear the suppressed laughter in his voice.

"You think so?" And then she couldn't say anything more, because he'd eased her up against the side of the pool, a tanned, muscular arm on either side of her, trapping her. But in a way she wanted to be trapped. She could feel the hard muscles of his body against hers, the long length of him as he practically pinned her to the smooth tiles behind her.

"What happens now?" she asked, teasing him.

She loved the way he looked down at her, his eyelashes spiked with water, his breathing slightly labored. She knew that feeling, the way such intense excitement forced you to breathe more deeply.

"What do you think?" he replied, tracing the curve of her cheekbone with a finger. His deep voice caressed her, made little flutters of excitement start up in her stomach.

"I think," she whispered just seconds before he kissed her, "that we're both going to get what we want."

STEVE HADN'T THOUGHT THAT the evening would go as well as it had. He certainly hadn't expected to do more than kiss Amy good-night at her door. He hadn't wanted to push her, because he'd already decided she was different from any other woman he'd ever met.

He didn't want a few nights with her, he wanted many nights. And lots of days. From the first moment he'd seen her, he'd wanted her. He could be honest with himself about that. But over the past three months at Bud's Café, he'd seen a side of her that had intrigued him. And the night she'd bared her soul on the radio talk show, he'd known she was a kindred spirit. She wanted to live life, and to love, to the fullest. Just like him.

Now he walked her through the water toward the pool's shallow end, kissing her, keeping her naked body pressed tightly against his.

"We're not staying in the pool?" she said against his mouth.

"Trust me," he muttered, intent on getting her first to the warmth of the Jacuzzi, then into the large, king-size bed in the guest room. His actor friend would have a field day; he'd love knowing that his house had been the site of one of the greatest experiences of a buddy's life with a woman—no, with *the* woman.

He swung her up into his arms once they were outside the pool, and she gave a little shriek as the cool air hit their damp bodies.

"Hang on," he said, heading for the Jacuzzi. He'd turned on the heat before he'd left for the restaurant, hoping that he just might get lucky. But he'd never believed he'd be *this* lucky.

She sighed in delight as the hot, bubbly water closed around her body, up to her shoulders. As he joined her, he thought about how great she looked with her hair all wet and disheveled, her mascara making those little cat's eyes appear wet and smudged. Her color was high, the light in her eyes excited.

It gave him an incredible sense of pleasure to make her happy.

"Give me your foot," he said suddenly.

Her eyes widened. "This is a different approach."

"Seriously. Give it here."

She lifted her leg from the swirling water; he

placed her foot in his lap and began to knead and massage the ball of it firmly.

"Oh, my God, you should hire yourself out."

"I had a case in Chinatown once," he said, keeping his voice low, soothing. "The guy who hired me was this little old man who ran a herb shop. When I finished the case, I told him I didn't want my payment the usual way."

Her eyes had been blissfully closed, her head leaning back against the edge of the Jacuzzi. Now that glorious head of red hair came up, and those green eyes opened.

"How did he pay you?"

Steve smiled lazily, still massaging her foot. "I asked him to teach me all the Oriental skills of seduction at his command. I wanted to make myself irresistible to women."

"Oh, like with those eyes and with that voice, you needed any help?"

"You like my eyes?" How strange, that he should be so extraordinarily pleased by what she thought of him.

"I like a lot about you."

"Yeah? Then I think you should show me." Taking a firm hold of her foot, he grasped her calf, then slowly began to pull her in his direction, carefully noting that she didn't offer any resistance.

He maneuvered them both until she was sitting in his lap. Lifting her wet hair and kissing the back of her neck, he said, "There are parts of you that I like."

"Oh, let me guess."

His hands were already cupping her breasts as he kissed her.

His heart almost stopped as she curled her fingers tentatively around his erection.

"There are other—" she managed to get out as their kisses deepened "—parts of you that I find quite extraordinary."

He couldn't even speak.

She stroked him gently, and he had a very strong feeling they might not make it to the bedroom this time, either. But that was okay. Curling his fingers around her thighs, he eased her over him, then found her center with his fingers and parted her, so gently. She moaned, and her head fell forward onto his shoulder, her arms came up around his neck. He recognized that feminine surrender, and slipped his fingers in a little more, making sure she was ready for what had to happen.

She was more than ready. That walk alongside the pool must have been as big a turn-on for her as it had been for him.

"I need you now," he whispered into her ear. He liked to talk to her during these sexual moments; he liked letting her know how she affected him. "I don't think I can wait until we get inside the house."

Her arms tightened around his neck, and he took

that to mean she assented. Cupping her buttocks in his hands, he lifted her, positioned her over him, then slowly eased her down on his hard, fully aroused flesh.

Then he couldn't hear anymore, couldn't concentrate on her for just that second as she tightly enveloped him. The warmth and heat, so exquisite, caressed him. He had to think wildly of other things to suppress his excitement even though he'd climaxed barely an hour ago, she affected him that strongly. Steve gritted his teeth and tried to distract himself with the details of the case he was working on. At the same time, he held her hips firmly, causing all movement to still.

"Don't move," he whispered. "Give me a moment."

That part of her that was so intensely feminine, that had him totally enveloped, gave a little flutter, the tiniest of contractions.

He groaned.

She groaned.

"Don't move that, either," he said.

She turned her head so her lips brushed his ear. If possible, he felt himself grow even harder inside her.

"That…was beyond my control."

He took a deep breath, then another, then felt himself slowly regain control. Fine.

"Okay," he whispered.

She leaned back, still straddling him, and smiled

up into his eyes. And he wanted to make her wild, to give her pleasure again, to hear her cry out his name, to know she was thinking about him at that exact moment.

"There's a guesthouse," he said. "It's closer than the house."

"You can go in there?"

"I have the run of the place for the next six weeks."

She leaned against him and whispered, "I'm putting myself in your hands."

THEY MADE IT TO THE carpet in the living room of the guesthouse. The door had barely shut behind them before Steve grasped her hand, dragged her down on the plush carpet, and covered her with his body.

Afterward they showered together, then he carried her into the bedroom, tucked her in, and curled up around her. Then finally, they fell asleep.

But not for long.

They made love again when they woke up, and he urged her to be the dominant one this time, to sit astride him. "Do with me as you will," he had said, making her laugh and ensuring most of her shyness disappeared.

Much later, he opened another bottle of champagne.

"I have a few thoughts about the way you handled this evening,'' she said, leaning back in bed against the pillows as she looked up at him.

"Such as?"

"Well, first of all, there's no time for morning-after jitters when we both stay up all night. I mean, who has time to get nervous? You don't leave a girl much chance for inner reflection."

"It's highly overrated," he said, and she tickled him in the ribs.

"Secondly...this *place*."

"Too much?"

"No. Just right. It's like living in a fantasy."

"You won't be upset when you see the way I really live?"

"No. I'm a simple girl with simple tastes." She buried her head in her pillow to muffle the laughter.

"Too much champagne?" He reached for her glass before she spilled it.

"Just enough. Oh, Steve, I've wanted to go crazy for so long, and you're just the perfect man to do it with."

"I hope that was meant as a compliment."

"It was." She opened her eyes and squinted toward one of the bedroom windows. "I think the sun's starting to come up."

"Worried about the time? Got a date?"

The ridiculousness of his question made her laugh all over again.

"No."

"What time do you have to be at work?"

"Actually," she said, moving closer to him on the large bed, "when Tim came to the door and I accepted your evening out, I canceled my morning and afternoon housecleaning appointments. I don't have to be anywhere until four, at Bud's. I decided I wanted to have some fun."

"Hmm," he said, setting down his champagne glass and taking her into his arms. "That was very wise."

"Wait a minute. I was thinking about getting a little nap in some time today—"

"There's plenty of time for sleep," he whispered, just before he kissed her. "Later."

STEVE TOOK HER HOME in his own car, a black BMW.

"I bought it during one of the years the agency did really well," he told her as he opened the passenger-side door for her.

They drove to her apartment in silence. Amy thought it had to be because they were both completely exhausted.

"You still have time for that nap," Steve said as he walked her up the front drive and into the plant-filled courtyard of her two-story apartment building.

"Only if you don't come inside," she teased. But her stomach fluttered. What if he never called again? What if this had been just an evening of fun for him—one of many—and she was only one of many women...?

"Well, I'll see you tonight at Bud's, then," he said.

Joe, her golden retriever, began to bark behind the apartment door as she inserted her key.

"You have a dog in this place?"

"Two," she answered as Ming's excited little yaps joined Joe's deeper barks. "I asked my neighbor, Mary Lynn, to walk and feed them this morning. I had a feeling I might be coming home a little later."

When she opened her door, she noticed he seemed to be studying her pets intently.

"Did you have these two dogs when you were married?"

"No. In fact, I just got them a few weeks ago."

"Where?"

She studied him. He seemed awfully interested in her two pets. Maybe he was just an animal lover, like herself.

"This woman whose house I was cleaning went away on an extended cruise and abandoned them. Her brother was going to take them to the pound, so I told him I'd take them instead. Joe's eleven—no one would have selected him for a pet. And Ming's kind of temperamental. I don't think he'd be too good with children. He's stubborn, too."

"Joe," Steve said softly, and it was perfectly

clear to her that his mind was on something other than the present moment.

"Steve? Is something wrong?"

"I'm not sure yet." He pulled her into his arms for a swift kiss, then said, "I'll see you tonight. Nothing's wrong. Don't get that worried look on your face—I'm nothing like your ex."

She had to smile. He had a real talent for seeing straight through to her emotions, almost reading what she was feeling at any given moment. This man looked deep. She hoped he liked what he saw.

SHE SAILED INTO WORK that evening, glowing. Linda and Alexis, the two women she worked with, sensed something was up. She gave them a few details about her date with Steve, but nothing too incriminating.

"Some women have all the luck," Alexis teased as she cut a slice of coconut cream pie for a customer and reached for one of the glass coffeepots. "I had my eye on him, but he had his eye on you. Just the way it goes. But I'm happy for you, Amy."

Linda seemed to sparkle with happiness for her as she let Amy know that Steve had been in and asked them what size uniform she wore.

"Sexy lingerie?" both women guessed, enjoying her evening vicariously.

"A sexy evening dress, perfect for dancing," Amy said.

"Even better!" Linda said. "He took you out."

Steve came by Bud's promptly at ten and sat in his regular booth. She poured him a cup of coffee without a word, handed him a menu, then started to walk away. He snagged her wrist and called out, "Hey, Bud, has she taken her break yet?"

"Nope," the older man called back. "But you better ask her if she wants to take it with you."

Amy slid into the seat across from him.

He patted the seat next to him. "That's too far away."

"Oh, no. I hate to think what might happen if I get within reach."

He grinned, then glanced at the menu. "Feel like a piece of pie?"

"Sure."

"You pick."

The lemon meringue was superb tonight. Bud's mother's recipe had won her many prizes, not the least of which was undying customer loyalty for her son's restaurant. Amy cut two generous slices and brought them back to their booth. A light rain had started to fall, streaking the huge glass windows that overlooked Sunset Boulevard.

"You seem a little distracted," she said, halfway through her pie.

"I'm wondering if you're going to let me walk you home tonight."

She gave him a look. "I have a feeling you want to do more than walk."

"Maybe. Or maybe we could just rest this evening. In the same bed, of course."

"You, rest? This should be a novel experience."

He calmly ate his pie. "I was in an extremely good mood all day today, Amy. Even my partner, Martin, remarked on it."

"I'd say so. I can hardly stand up."

HE STAYED UNTIL CLOSING, then followed her home, followed her into her bedroom, carefully placed Ming, the Pekingese, on the overstuffed chair in her bedroom and joined her in the double bed.

"There's a little less room," Amy said as they settled in.

"Think of it as cozy," Steve said as he curled around her, spoon-fashion.

She'd already told him she didn't think she was up to more wild and crazy lovemaking tonight. She needed her rest.

"No funny stuff," she muttered as she pillowed her head against his shoulder.

"Cross my heart, but I can't speak for other regions of my body," he said, and she could hear the suppressed laughter in his voice.

They were silent for a while, lying in the dark. Occasionally they heard the sound of another tenant walking in the courtyard, or a car in the street. Then Amy asked the question she'd wanted to ask since Steve had told her about his parents' accident.

"Were you lonely in the boys' home?"

"Sometimes."

"Did you ever miss your mom?"

"I was too young when she died. I don't really have strong memories of her."

She thought about this. Amy didn't think she would sleep easily this night. It wasn't because Steve was sharing her bed; it was because she sensed his tension. He couldn't sleep; therefore it was hard for her to do so.

"Anything wrong?" she asked, after a short period of silence.

"Just thinking about the case I'm working on."

"You aren't regretting—"

"Nope. Not one minute."

"Do you want to talk?"

"Not about the case."

"How did you end up becoming a cop?"

"You mean, as opposed to a juvenile delinquent?"

"That's not what I meant."

"Hey, I know the rep that orphanage has. By the time I was a teenager, it might as well have been a juvenile home. They tried as hard as they could, but with limited funds and staffing, there was only so much they could do."

"What made the difference?" She found she had to know.

"Two people. Florence and Jimmy."

"They worked at the orphanage?"

"By then, I'd been moved to a boys' home. No, they didn't work there. They lived in Beverly Hills. But they did a lot of charity work together, and were just genuinely good people."

"How did you meet them?"

"Jimmy caught me trying to break into his car. I wanted to drive it."

Amy smiled in the dark, shifted against his shoulder. She could picture Steve as a boy, just as determined as he was now. If he'd wanted anything, he would have gone after it.

"Breaking into his car," she said. "You must have been one stubborn little boy."

"The teachers were always telling me—us—that we'd amount to no good. You hear that enough, you start to believe it."

"What did Jimmy do when he caught you?"

"He took me out for ice cream."

"He caught you trying to hot-wire his car and he took you out for ice cream?"

"Yeah. He asked if he could borrow me for the afternoon, and we went out and had ice-cream cones, then walked along the beach."

Something in the tone of his voice made her sure this was one of his very favorite memories. Now she was totally intrigued.

"What did the two of you talk about?"

"He asked me what I'd wanted, breaking into

his car like that. I told him I'd always wanted to drive a big old car like his, and he impressed me when he said that if I wanted to drive a car like his, it was a lot cooler to *own* one than to try to steal one.''

"How old were you?''

"Twelve.'' He shifted in bed, one arm beneath his head, the other around her. "It had never crossed my mind that I was even capable of owning a car like that.''

"So that's what Jimmy did?''

"He and his wife did a lot more than that. They had me over to their home all the time. They let me do yard work, feel like I was really earning money. And by the time I was ready to go out into the world and make a living, because of their good opinion of me, I decided to apply to the LAPD.''

"Do you still see them?'' Amy snuggled closer.

"Jimmy passed away a few years back. I manage to phone Florence every few weeks.''

She wasn't sure what had happened, but she knew she'd lost him again. She sensed his thoughts weren't quite on the words he was speaking, and she wondered why.

ALMOST A WEEK LATER, she found out.

Steve walked into Bud's and sat at his usual booth. When she went over with his cup of coffee, he said, "I need a favor. A big one.'' He seemed upset, and she slid into the booth beside him. This late at night, Bud's wasn't exactly bustling. And Linda and Alexis were more than willing to cover for her for a few minutes.

"Anything."

"Amy, don't agree to anything until I tell you what it is I want you to do."

She hesitated. "Steve, you're scaring me."

"Just hear me out."

"I mean, I know you wouldn't ask me to do anything immoral or illegal—"

"Don't be too sure about that."

Now he had her complete attention.

"What exactly do you want me to do? Are you in some kind of trouble?" All her instincts were screaming at her that Steve was nothing like her ex-husband, that he wasn't a con man, that he wasn't going to use her in any way, shape, or form.

But a nervous little sense of doubt slowly began to worm its way into her heart.

He took a deep breath, hesitated, then finally made his request.

"Amy, I need you to help me break into a house."

CHAPTER FOUR

"WHAT?"

"Do you have a dinner break coming up?" he said.

"In about thirty minutes."

"About an hour?"

"Yes."

"Will you give me that hour to present my case?"

The raw need in his beautiful, blue-gray eyes was what basically did her in. That, and that little part of her, the gut part, that told her this was a man who would never hurt her.

He had to be asking her to do something this bad for a reason.

HE BOUGHT HER DINNER at a little Chinese place a couple of blocks down the street. Over dinner, and finally fortune cookies, he filled her in on the case.

Amy sat back, her hot tea in hand, going over in her mind what he'd told her. When Jimmy Monroe, the man who'd caught a young Steve hot-wiring his car, had passed away, Florence had gone into something of a decline. She and Jimmy had built a fortune from nothing. They had both worked extremely hard in their bridal shop on Rodeo Drive, and had created an empire from what had started out as a dusty little storefront. They'd never had children, though not from a lack of love or desire. Their children had been all the youngsters they'd befriended at the orphanage, and later, at the boys' home.

But with Jimmy gone, Florence had a younger brother who was closing in on her, determined to get his hands on her fortune. According to Steve, this man, Douglas Bullard, had recently talked Florence out of living at her large estate and had somehow convinced her to enter an old age home. Now he was in the process of illegally signing over most of her considerable assets to himself.

"You know," Amy said, toying with the corner of a fortune cookie, "you don't even have to convince me that something like this could happen. All I have to remember is what I went through with Lenny."

"I thought you'd understand."

"But why me? I'm the last person you'd want along on a major break-in. I get scared easily, I'm a little afraid of the dark—"

"You also know the entire layout of that house because you clean it once a week."

"Which house?"

He gave her the address, and she simply stared.

"Oh my God. Steve, that was Douglas who gave me the dogs. I mean, I took them."

"I'm sure he was about to take them to the pound to be destroyed."

"I knew it!" The fine hairs on the back of her neck had risen; her instincts were working overtime. "I'd just finished for the day, and as I was leaving I noticed he had both dogs in their travel kennels. I asked him what had happened, and...he told me their owner had gone on a cruise and just abandoned them."

"So you never actually met Florence?"

"No. I was just recently assigned that house. Douglas was the one who called the housecleaning agency, and requested a maid."

"If you knew Florence, you'd know she would never abandon anyone's dog, let alone her own."

"Do you know where she is—" Comprehension dawned. "That's why you were so strange that night in my bedroom! You recognized Joe!"

"Florence had told me she had a retriever and a Peke. I'd never met Joe—he was usually out back lying on the patio in the sun when I'd pick Florence up. But it was too much of a coincidence when I saw the two dogs."

"What does Florence think about all this?"

She saw the merest flick of a muscle in his cheek before Steve finally spoke.

"I tracked her down a couple of days ago. She's so drugged up she barely recognized me. I told her to put her medication under her tongue until the nurse walked out of the room, and to hide it after that. I'm not even sure she completely understood me. I'm hoping you'll want to go to the old age home with me tomorrow, and we can bring the dogs.''

"I'm not sure about breaking and entering a house," Amy whispered. "But I'll go with you tomorrow."

Steve took her hand. "That'll have to be enough.''

THE NURSING HOME WAS IN South Pasadena, a residential neighborhood to the east of Hollywood that still had a small-town feel. But as Amy followed Steve up the drive, she felt uneasy. It wasn't a place with an atmosphere that encouraged visitors. The large building, though adequately kept up, had a lonely, neglected feel to it.

"She made millions with her bridal shop, and her brother locks her away in a place like this?" Amy whispered as they neared the double glass doors at the front of the home.

"It's a strange world. Now, give me Joe's lead and tuck Ming into your shoulder bag like we practiced.''

The small dog went willingly into Amy's over-size canvas bag, and Steve donned his dark glasses, then took a firm grip on Joe's leash.

"Dogs are not allowed—'' began an ominous-looking nurse.

Amy replied gently, "Joe is a Seeing Eye dog." They swept past the startled nurse before she could demand any proof, and Steve led the way down a dingy, dimly lit hallway painted an unattractive toothpaste green, and smelling of disinfectant and urine.

Florence's room was at the far end of the corridor. As they entered, Amy instantly saw the elderly woman who tried to raise her head off the thin pillow.

"Stephen?" she whispered.

"I'm right here," Steve said. "And so is Joe."

"Joe!"

Amy's eyes stung as she saw the elderly retriever start to prance and wag his tail. Years were erased and he was a puppy again, delighted to be with his owner.

Her bag started to move, and she realized Ming was struggling inside; the little dog wanted to get to his mistress. She lifted the long-haired Peke out of her purse and placed him gently on the narrow bed.

Ming raced up the dingy, off-white, waffle-weave coverlet until he could swipe at his owner's wrinkled face with his little pink tongue. He yapped happily, and Amy was glad that Steve had had the foresight to close the door.

"Florence," Steve said, and Amy could detect the underlying tone of urgency in his voice, "have you been hiding your medication like I advised you to?''

"It's right here," she said. "I take them out of my mouth once that nurse leaves and hide them beneath the mattress. It's a safe place. They don't change my bed that often."

Steve retrieved the pills and put them in a plastic container, then slipped that into the pocket of his black leather jacket. He'd taken off his dark glasses, and Amy could see the worried expression in his eyes, the lines on his forehead.

"Did you want to come here, Florence?" Steve asked.

The older woman hesitated, and Amy agonized with her. She knew how hard it was when someone you loved chose to betray you. She knew that, like her, Florence would find it incredibly hard to face this betrayal. You never wanted to see it in your own family; you couldn't conceive of it in someone that close.

"I...I don't remember coming here."

Amy closed her eyes as she stroked Joe's head. This was so much worse than she'd feared.

"I went to bed one evening, and...I woke up here. I tried to ask some questions, I couldn't get to a phone.... Then, with the medication and all, I don't remember much else."

Amy saw the tension in Steve's jawline. His stance shifted, and his body went perfectly still. She recognized anger. It was certainly justified.

"Have you talked to your brother?" he asked.

"No." Florence hesitated. "No one comes." The blue-veined hands lovingly stroked both the Pekingese and the golden retriever. "How did you get Douglas to let you bring my dogs here today?"

Briefly, Steve told her the story Douglas had told Amy the afternoon she'd come to clean the mansion. Amy watched the elderly woman carefully, and didn't miss the sheen of moisture that filmed her faded blue eyes, or the way her frail hands started to shake.

"Why would he do that? Why would he tell her that I was on a world cruise?"

"It's a convenient way of letting people know you won't be home for a long time," Steve said bluntly. "It stops anyone from asking too many questions. And I don't think he plans on having you return."

Florence sighed softly as she continued to pat her dogs. After a short silence, she said, "Steve, I don't know what to do."

"I do," he told her. "But I need your permission."

AFTER THEY LEFT THE nursing home, Steve drove Amy to a Starbucks on Fair Oaks with outdoor tables so the two dogs could sit with them. Joe stretched out beneath the small round table, while Ming sat in Amy's lap. Steve went inside to get their coffee.

During the brief time she sat alone outside in the sunshine, Amy thought furiously. Lenny had hurt her, but he'd never wanted to kill her, or put her in a situation where she'd just waste away. Or would he have resorted to such tactics, if she'd refused to divorce him? No, her ex had been an emotional coward, incapable of dealing with even the smallest amount of responsibility. He hadn't even bothered to end the marriage; he'd simply disappeared. She'd had to hire the lawyer and file for desertion. Lenny hadn't been the type to do anything himself regarding a relationship—even ending it in such an evil way as Douglas was doing. But then, Amy thought as she patted Ming's soft fur, Lenny had already made off with her money, what little there had been of it.

The situation was different with Florence and her brother. There was clearly a great deal of money involved. If no one intervened, the old woman would die alone in that nursing home, and no one would ever know. Her neighbors would probably be told she'd passed away peacefully while cruising the world in first-class luxury.

No, Florence's problems were far worse than hers had ever been. And she could understand completely why Steve felt he had to step in. The elderly woman and her late husband had been like surrogate parents to him. If he hadn't met them, his life would have been totally different.

What she'd seen today had shocked her. Florence's hair hadn't been combed; her room hadn't seemed all that neat. The whole place had exuded an air of neglect. And they'd keep giving her those pills, continue feeding her minimal amounts of food, like Jell-O and broth, orange juice and weak tea, until one night—without hope or any reason to go on living, without feeling she was loved by anyone—Florence would probably pass away in her sleep.

And then her brother would get exactly what he wanted.

Amy absently patted Joe's head as she stared blindly out toward the street. How strange, what money could do to people. Lenny had come into her life right after her father had died. Later on, she'd figured out he'd probably been scanning the obituaries, and had figured there had to be a wife or child involved—someone he could scam. Lenny had made sure he'd fleeced her of her small inheritance, and then it was on to greener pastures for him, leaving her with a pile of debts.

She'd been duped, plain and simple. Her love for her ex-husband, her need to have someone in her life after her father had died, had made her vulnerable. Weak. She recognized that same need in Florence—the need to believe that someone she loved had her best interests at heart, even if all the evidence pointed toward the opposite.

Amy also knew that if she'd had Steve in her life, even as a good friend, while the whole mess with Lenny had been going down, her ex wouldn't have stood a chance.

Florence did have Steve in her life. She'd given him permission to break into her Beverly Hills mansion, to break into her bedroom safe and remove several crucial items. Without those items, Douglas couldn't go through with his devious plans.

Steve had been tailing Douglas carefully, following every move the man made. Steve had also been talking to his various reputable contacts throughout the city and had learned that Douglas's scheme involved the quick sale of Florence's valuable stocks, bonds, and jewelry, after declaring her incompetent to handle her vast estate. And, of course, there would be an account in his name at a Swiss bank, or perhaps at one in the Cayman Islands. Douglas, having orchestrated his wealthy sister's move to the dingy nursing home, was planning to split and leave her—without her wealth—to the mercy of social services.

He had to be stopped. The first step was retrieving those stocks, bonds, and pieces of jewelry from Florence's home, getting them out of reach of Douglas's grubby hands.

And Steve was asking Amy to help him; to go outside the law to right a terrible wrong. "The police won't get involved in a family dispute like this one," he'd told her as they'd left the old age home. "I've seen cases like this come into the agency.

Most of the time, the relatives in the right leave it for too long, and the person who's after all the money gets away with it, and more.''

It wasn't as if Amy liked the situation. She hadn't wanted to leave Florence at the home, but Steve had assured her the woman was in no real harm as long as she continued to fake taking her medication. ''And if we move her now,'' he'd said on the way to Starbucks, ''her brother will suspect something's up. No, this has to be an inside job.''

She could see his logic, and had to admire the way his detective's mind had swiftly put together all the necessary pieces.

Amy glanced up as Steve approached their table, balancing two coffees and two slices of carrot cake with cream-cheese frosting. Joe looked up hopefully, his doggy eyes gleaming; he loved sweets.

She had made up her mind before Steve seated himself.

''The safe,'' she said quietly as she picked up her double latte, ''is in the master bedroom, behind a Chagall—a real one. I was vacuuming one day and I saw Douglas open it. Will you know how to get into it?'' She'd wondered about that. Florence had still been too woozy from medication to remember the exact combination.

Steve grinned as he picked up his coffee. ''You bet.''

THEY MADE THEIR PLANS that evening, then went over them once, twice, three times. Then once again. Amy had to admit that Steve had thought of everything.

They talked as they lay in bed—talked long into the night after they'd made love, going over their plans yet again.

Steve had been watching Douglas since he'd first learned that Florence had been put in the home, and he had the man's habits and routines down pat.

"Every Thursday night there's a big poker game that goes on for hours at a neighbor's down the street. A group of guys just get together and have fun, but a lot of money's involved. Money that this guy just doesn't have."

"But when he gets into debt with his gambling, he begs his sister for a loan and promises to pay her back, right?"

"How'd you guess?" Steve asked.

"Oh, some things never change."

According to Steve, they had a safe window of time of about an hour and a half. A lot would depend on just what kind of security system he had to dismantle, and how long it would take to figure out the combination of the safe and open it.

"Now that I know where the safe is, you don't have to come with me if you don't want to," he said, after she'd finished drawing him an elaborate diagram on a paper napkin with a ballpoint pen. "I don't want to put you in any danger, and I don't think this is what you meant when you said you wanted to walk on the wild side.''

"Steve." She put her hand on his forearm. "Just try to keep me away.''

AMY STILL HAD SOME doubts. Oh, not about what she and Steve were planning to do. These doubts were far more complicated. They were about their relationship.

She'd told the radio talk-show host that she only wanted the fantasy. She'd also said she was off men for the time being—until she got her life in order and repaid her considerable debts.

Had Steve taken her literally? Had he only wanted this fantasy time with her, and nothing else? What kind of a relationship did he want with her, if he even wanted one at all? He certainly couldn't feel that enthusiastic about saddling himself with a woman who had her amount of debt. She didn't want to be a burden to him.

She also wondered if she needed a little more time to heal. Amy knew she'd learned from her marriage to Lenny, and it had been one of the most painful lessons of her life. Her marriage had ended over a year and a half ago, and it had been dead six months before then, so she felt she had two years' perspective on that time, and was more than ready to move on.

Amy also knew what she had to do to get her life back in order, but she didn't know if she felt right asking another person to come along on her particular ride.

It was all so complicated.

In the back of her mind, where all her deepest doubts lived, Amy was sure she was destined to be merely another man's good time.

"He's one of the good guys." Bud's words came to her at odd moments, and comforted her. She knew Steve wouldn't let her down, but she also knew this was not the time to have the dreaded "relationship talk." She hated having to insist on that talk, anyway. Why couldn't men just get it together and lay all their cards on the table?

What made it all worse was that Steve was so decisive. He made decisions in a split second, then acted on them. So why did she have the uneasy feeling he was taking his time with her? What was he deciding about their relationship? More than anything, she wished she could read his mind on this particular issue, just for a moment.

Yet, the way he made love to her... That alone would silence any rational woman's doubts forever. But Amy was a worrier, and nothing was going to stop her from worrying.

She had her priorities straight, however. Florence's predicament had to come first. The elderly woman was so dear, and didn't deserve what had happened to her. In light of Florence's predicament, her and Steve's problems were miniscule.

And of course, there was the issue of how she

felt about the matter. Did she even want a man in her life until she was firmly back on her feet and all her debts were settled? She wasn't sure.

All she knew was that three years of paying off her debts looked a lot longer to her—and so much lonelier—since she'd met, and made love to, Steve McKnight.

STEVE STILL HAD SOME doubts, because he had no idea what Amy wanted. In the beginning, it had all been about fantasy. She'd been adamant on the radio show that she didn't want a man in her life, that she wanted to reach a certain stage of independence and financial security before she even thought of having a relationship again. He'd heard the feelings beneath the words, and had realized that Amy needed to learn to trust before she would ever feel safe with a man again.

He found himself wanting to be that man, but wasn't sure if he had the right to rush her into a relationship before she was ready.

Steve prided himself on being decisive. But he was like any other man when it came to being rejected by a woman he cared deeply about. He was unsure of Amy's feelings, so he decided to wait until things were fixed for Florence; then he would observe Amy and try to figure out what it was she wanted.

He already knew the future he desired. He couldn't imagine a life without Amy. So Steve decided that he would give her all the time she needed, as long as there was the smallest chance they would be together.

He'd always been good at taking chances, at playing the long shot and winning. Only this time—when his heart was involved—he found that he didn't like that long shot at all.

THERE WAS ONLY ONE LAST tiny detail.

There always was.

"Remember I told you that Florence had a few pieces of jewelry?" Steve began, two nights before their planned break-in.

She nodded, sensing something was up.

"Well," Steve said, "there's this necklace. And a pair of earrings."

He hesitated, and she simply looked up at him.

"And a bracelet," Steve continued. "Jimmy bought them for Florence on their fiftieth wedding anniversary. He'd always told her he wanted to cover her with diamonds, and...well, he did. I was there when she unwrapped them."

Amy swallowed. This was getting more and more complicated, but she wasn't going to back out now. "What kind of diamonds are we talking about?"

"Have you ever heard of the Night Fire diamonds?"

Her eyes widened. "I read a magazine article about famous gems a few weeks ago. There was a picture of the set. They're incredible." Now she felt suddenly light-headed at what they were about to do.

"They're in the safe?" she whispered.

"Yep. All ten-and-a-half million dollars' worth."

"Ten million dollars?" She covered her mouth with her hand.

"We're talking hunks of diamonds, in the necklace and the bracelet. Jimmy was so proud. The necklace alone is worth six-and-a-half million. The bracelet, one and a half."

"And the earrings," she said, remembering. "Beautiful pear-shaped drops."

"Two-and-a-half million right there, for the pair."

She had to take a moment to register all this. Now she realized what Douglas had been doing at that jewelry shop on Rodeo Drive that Steve had followed him to. The prospect of Florence's younger brother opening a secret Swiss bank account and skipping out of the country seemed that much more a certainty.

Suddenly the stakes looked so much higher.

"So this is basically a diamond heist?"

Steve nodded his head. "If they're still even there."

AMY CLEANED FLORENCE'S mansion the day before D Day, or Diamond Day as she privately called it. When she was dusting and vacuuming in the master bedroom that now housed Douglas's possessions, she found herself continually glancing at the Chagall on the far wall.

Tomorrow night, she and Steve would be breaking and entering, then trying to unlock a safe and steal several important documents. Oh, and diamonds worth ten-and-a-half million dollars.

It boggled the mind.

If someone had told her what one little call to a radio station would do to transform her life, she never would have believed that person. If someone had told her what she and Steve were about to do, she would have laughed.

Then she thought of Florence, alone and afraid in that dark, dingy room. She remembered the way the woman's eyes had teared up when she'd seen her dogs, and how she'd looked at Steve in utter confusion as he'd told her what her brother had been doing. And Amy knew her resolve in this matter wouldn't falter.

She'd made up her mind.

"CAN'T SLEEP?" STEVE whispered in the dark. They were sleeping at his actor friend's mansion in Beverly Hills. Conveniently, it was located only four blocks over from Florence's estate.

"No." The digital display on the alarm clock showed that it was just after midnight.

"Too nervous?"

"I just... I can't seem to shut off my mind."

"I know a good way to get your mind off tomorrow night." His hand moved slowly over her back, caressing her bare skin.

It worked.

She turned toward him, felt herself drowning in that sensual ocean of feeling that this man so effortlessly drew her into.

STEVE WASN'T ALL THAT calm about what they were about to do the following evening, either.

Though he'd told Amy all about his past, and the hard way he'd come up in the world, he'd still needed to do some serious thinking. Breaking and entering was serious business. Even though he'd received Florence's permission and he knew he was doing the right thing, he still realized how devastating the consequences would be if either he or Amy were caught. But they were Florence's last chance. He couldn't fail the woman who had been like a loving grandmother to him.

He didn't plan on getting caught, of course. But then, no one ever did.

Taking Amy along made it that much riskier. At first, he'd thought he needed her with him, but when she'd sketched him such a perfect layout of Florence's mansion, along with the exact location of the wall safe, he'd tried to talk her out of it. It was one thing if he got caught; he couldn't bear to think of anything happening to her.

But he'd seen the resolution in those beautiful green eyes, and how everything had changed after she'd seen Florence alone in that narrow bed in the nursing home.

Now, lying in bed with Amy, Steve reached for her as a lover.

He needed to relax, but his motives went far deeper than that. He hadn't come to Amy an inexperienced man. Far from it. But he'd found something with her he'd never had with any other woman.

He'd sensed it from the first moment he'd seen her, though he wouldn't have been able to articulate it if someone had asked him. There had been something different about her, something that had set her apart. He'd wanted her, then come to care for her. Deeply. Now he knew he'd fallen in love with her—the kind of love that made a man think about forever.

Yet he was asking her to face danger with him, and this was not even counting the diamond heist. If he asked Amy for forever, he'd be asking her to accept what he did for a living, and the element of risk that many of his cases demanded. She'd already been through so much with that ex-husband of hers.

Was he being fair?

All of this raced through his mind as he began to kiss her, holding her head in his hands, parting her lips, deepening the kiss. There was an edge of desperation to his lovemaking as he eased her on top of him, cradling her small body against his, holding her closely while they kissed. He stroked her hair, he cupped her breasts, all the while kissing her. There were times in life when words couldn't convey what a person felt, and this was one of those times.

She responded so beautifully, so swiftly, catching fire the same way he did. Little signs let him know she was swiftly reaching the same level of arousal he was—her sharp intakes of breath, her soft sighs as one kiss broke off and another began, the way she molded her body to his, pressing against him with absolutely no urging from him.

He slid down her body, cupped one of her breasts, covered the hard nipple with his mouth, and pulled on it—and was rewarded by the low moans that came from her throat. Just the sounds she made could send him over the edge. He took time with her—first one breast, then the other— trying to go slow for her. Always, for Amy.

He'd meant to take more time, but found he couldn't when he felt her hands on his buttocks, urging him up over her, into her. She held nothing back in his arms, and that gift, that sensual trust, both amazed and humbled him. That she should be so giving after what life had taken from her was nothing short of miraculous.

He didn't want to wait, so he eased her legs apart, then settled between them.

Hot and wet and tight, she enfolded him as he entered her. He groaned, then covered her mouth with a kiss, his tongue creating a second intimacy. She shuddered against him in response, and something very male and primitive answered back, triumphant in the knowledge that he could do this to her, make her feel this way.

She tightened herself around his arousal, the sensation almost bordering on pain, it was that intense. He thrust deeper, again feeling her respond. The way she took him inside her body was the ultimate sensual drug. He couldn't get enough of her this way, and his movements reflected this, becoming harder, deeper.

Still, she matched him, taking everything he could give.

She reached her climax quickly. Tonight couldn't be a prolonged session of lovemaking, not when their feelings were running this hot. He felt that incredible sense of inevitability come over him, then drove into her, deep and hard. His climax washed over him and he collapsed on top of her, his breathing erratic, his body shaking as if he'd been running for a long, long time and had only now come home.

He felt her hands come up his back, smoothing over the sweat-slick skin. He loved the way she touched him after it was all over. This woman loved the life of the body, and, not for the first time, Steve wondered how her ex had ever been able to let her go.

But Steve was so glad he had.

AMY HAD THOUGHT SHE'D be terrified on the night of their heist. Did it make her something of a lunatic that she found herself totally excited by what was to come? She wondered at this, as Steve eased the black Mercedes along the night street. He'd borrowed it from his friend's garage, planning to legally park it along one of the alleys close to Florence's mansion. Then they had to go in the back way, over a high brick wall.

"No guard dogs," he'd told her earlier. "Not even when Joe and Ming lived there."

She had to laugh. Though loveable, neither dog had the disposition of a canine sentry. They were more like gentle friends.

"Hey," he said, "we should be grateful Douglas doesn't seem to be all that fond of animals in general."

She'd already told him what brand of security system Florence had installed. Amy had felt the smallest moment of alarm when Steve had said, "That's an easy one to dismantle. I'll have to advise Florence to get a better one once she's home."

This was a side of Steve she'd never seen before. Though she'd always suspected he had it, she'd never seen it in action. It excited her and frightened her at the same time.

They climbed over the back wall—a high, red-brick affair with a light covering of ivy—then found themselves in the lush backyard, among various trees and bushes. At another time, Amy might have admired them, but on this dark night, moonless and overcast, she simply concentrated on staying close to Steve.

Beside her, he quietly checked his watch, then took a pair of miniature binoculars out of the pocket of his leather jacket. He raised them to his eyes with gloved hands and glanced toward the road.

"Right on schedule. There goes our boy, ready to throw away more of his sister's money."

Amy didn't have to ask him what he saw. She knew, from her days of housecleaning, that Douglas had helped himself to Florence's cream-colored Rolls-Royce.

"Okay," Steve said quietly. "Let's go."

She followed him like a silent little shadow, as close as a burr. She'd dressed all in black; jeans, a sweater, sneakers, gloves, the works. She'd even wrapped her bright red hair in a scarf that concealed most of her face.

"Like a Ninja," she'd said when she showed her outfit to Steve.

"I like it."

As they approached the back of the house, they found a few lights on, and a television set blaring. The back entrance to the family room—a sliding-glass door that opened onto the patio—was unlocked, with only a screen separating the outside from the interior. In typical southern California style, yesterday had rained like crazy, while tonight's weather remained balmy and breezy.

They both stopped at the border of dense bushes that ringed the backyard.

"Who is she?" Steve mouthed, indicating the busty blonde who got up from the comfortable couch in front of the TV and walked into the nearby kitchen. She opened the door of the huge, stainless-steel refrigerator and got out a bottle of white wine.

"His girlfriend," Amy mouthed back.

"Great."

The girlfriend was on the phone, and the bottle of wine clearly hadn't been her first. She talked so loudly and was so angry, they could both hear her quite clearly over the television program.

"Oh, he thinks he can just go out with his buddies and leave me here like I'm some kind of cheap entertainment!"

Steve grinned at Amy in the darkness, and she saw him raise his gloved fingers, two of them tightly crossed.

"He told me to stay here. But Liza, I'm so mad I could just take off!"

Steve nodded his head, then reached over and took Amy's hand. His touch, even through both sets of gloves, reassured her.

"You think so?" the blonde continued. "You think he'd wise up this evening if he came home and found me gone?"

Steve nodded his head, silently encouraging her. Amy had to bite her lip to keep from laughing, then caught herself. There was absolutely nothing funny about what they were about to do! Breaking into someone's home was serious business.

But Douglas deserved anything he got, and this was almost too good.

"You saw him *where?*" Now the blonde sounded truly upset.

A short silence ensued as Liza filled her in.

"Dougie with a brunette at Santa Anita? Yesterday? That skunk, he told me he had to go to the dentist and have a cavity filled."

There was another short silence as she listened.

"I'll bet that wasn't all that was getting filled," the blonde finally said. "That's it, I've had it, I'm outta here!"

Steve gave Amy the thumbs-up sign as the blonde grabbed the bottle of wine and her jacket and purse, then headed toward the front of the house. The sound of that front door slamming carried quite clearly in the night air.

"Unbelievable," Steve whispered. "This is going to be so easy, it's almost as if the gods are giving us their permission." He frowned, then glanced at her. "A little too easy, if you ask me.

Stay close to me, Amy, and do exactly as I tell you.''

She nodded, silently agreeing that things never came this easily. Her own life had certainly taught her that. ''She's not even going to lock the back door?''

''I don't think so. Wait here, I'll check.''

He was gone, and she marveled at the fact that he could move so swiftly and silently and not make a sound.

Steve returned within minutes.

''She's gone. Raced out the driveway in her Jaguar, so the lady's not completely short on funds. Last time I checked, neither Florence nor her brother owned a Jag.''

''Now what?''

''Now we get us some deeds and some diamonds.''

They entered the house quickly, closing and locking the sliding-glass door behind them. Steve turned off the television, telling her he didn't want anyone surprising them because they couldn't hear them. Then they started down the long carpeted hallway by flashlight, toward the master bedroom and the safe.

She was amazed—and intrigued—at the speed with which he opened that thing, using equipment with a speed and grace that told her he was used to situations like this.

''Have you done this before?'' she whispered.

"Once or twice, when a client was in the right."

"Who taught you?"

"I called in a few favors from a guy who was a professional." He said this as he rapidly emptied the safe, tucking various documents into his inside jacket pocket, along with several very large packets of cash.

The diamonds came last. Amy watched as Steve took out the leather jeweler's box, then opened it. She knew he was checking to see if the diamonds were there. Her breath caught in her throat as she got her first look at the famous Night Fire diamonds.

The necklace was comprised of big hunks of the sparkling gems, and yet the design was incredibly intricate. The bracelet was made of the same huge clusters of jewels, and the matching set of earrings were elegant, pear-shaped diamond drops.

Ten-and-a-half million dollars, right there. Breathtakingly beautiful. A symbol of the love Jimmy Monroe had felt for his wife of so many years. Together, the two of them had worked hard and been so frugal, building their business. And as Steve shut the leather box, tucked it beneath his arm and closed the safe, Amy knew they were doing the right thing. Douglas couldn't be allowed to abandon his elderly sister to a lonely death and take everything she and her husband had worked for.

"Hold these a sec," Steve said, handing her the

leather jewelry case as he repositioned the Chagall over the now closed wall safe. He'd just finished the last adjustment on the painting when both of them heard a noise.

A slamming door. Footsteps in the foyer.

Footsteps coming their way, toward the master bedroom.

For the briefest of seconds, Amy couldn't move. Her legs didn't seem to work; her heartbeat sped up so sickeningly fast she felt the chicken sandwich she'd had for dinner threaten to come back up. She couldn't think, she didn't know what to do, she—

"Under the bed," Steve said, his voice quiet. Urgent.

He pushed her under the king-size bed, and she let him, all the while shaking badly. Once she was beneath it, the leather jewelry case still in her possession, she put a hand over her mouth because she was afraid she might inadvertently cry out, make a noise.

Then the bedroom door opened, and she didn't know where Steve was. He hadn't followed her beneath the bed.

She was alone, under a bed at the scene of a robbery, with ten-and-a-half million dollars in diamonds in her possession. Her eyes filled with frightened tears, but she blinked them away as she watched two feet, clad in expensive Italian loafers, walk over the plush carpet in the direction of the safe.

Douglas. Home far too early from his poker game. Probably going to the safe to take out some of the cash Steve had already slipped into his jacket pocket.

What would he do when he didn't find it? Amy started to shake, reaction finally setting in.

He'd do what anyone would do in a similar situation, finding an empty safe. He'd call the police. He'd wait for them to arrive, all the while watching the house. They'd search the mansion, find her beneath the bed with the Night Fire diamonds. Her days of debt would seem like a two-week luxury cruise in the Caribbean compared to what would be in store for her once she was caught.

And where was Steve? Had he left her, abandoned her holding the bag—a ten-and-a-half million-dollar bag?

She watched the hand-stitched leather loafers approach the wall safe. Fear engulfed her, causing her doubts to mushroom all out of proportion, their poisonous spell totally overwhelming and obliterating her finer instincts.

Amy wondered if she'd lost her heart to the wrong man all over again.

CHAPTER FIVE

HER LIFE WAS COMPLETELY controlled by those loafers. She couldn't take her eyes off them. She watched, horrified, mesmerized, as those expensively clad feet walked with a sense of purpose, then paused—

Amy closed her eyes, waiting for the sound of an oil painting being taken off a wall, waiting for the sound of a safe being opened. Then it would only be a matter of time before—

She opened her eyes as she heard the sound of a dresser drawer being pulled out, the wooden drawer sliding smoothly; then the sound of rummaging around, then of something being unzipped. She stretched as cautiously as she could, until she could just see from beneath the bed.

She saw a man's back—it had to be Douglas—and that man was stuffing wads of bills into his slacks pocket from a private stash in his top dresser drawer.

She moved back, careful not to make a sound, one hand clutching the leather jewelry case so hard, her fingers hurt. She closed her eyes, pressing her cheek against the cool carpet, and kept her other hand over her mouth, determined not to make a single sound.

Finally, after what seemed an inordinate amount of time, she heard footsteps leave the room, then fade down the hall. A door slammed. Then there was silence.

She couldn't move. It was as if she'd lost control of her body. Total, primal fear had effectively paralyzed her. Even though she knew Douglas had probably gone back to his poker game, she couldn't make herself get out from beneath the bed.

Tightly curled up, with her eyes squeezed shut, she waited until she heard Steve's reassuring voice. Only then did she open her eyes.

"Oh, baby," he said, his voice so soft and low. Compassionate. She sensed he knew the agonies she'd been through, and even the doubts she'd had.

He eased her out from under the bed and simply held her. When she started to cry, he stroked her hair, crooned to her and told her it was over, it was all over, and she'd been so brave. Douglas had left and they were safe.

"I want you to stand up, Amy," he said after a few minutes. "We need to leave."

"I know," she replied, her voice still shaking as she handed him the leather jewelry case. He slipped it in another of his jacket's pockets. "I know, but I was so scared—"

"It's okay now," he said, taking her hand and leading her down the hallway. "It's okay."

"Where were you?" she managed to squeak out, still wiping away nervous tears of reaction.

"I was in the closet. Right behind you."

"You stayed with me?"

"Oh, sweetheart, I never would have left you alone!"

They were out in the backyard now, and Steve, after checking that they weren't being observed, gave her a hoist up the ivy-covered brick wall surrounding the estate.

"Did you think I'd left you?" He hauled himself up over the wall, then dropped down on the other side, lifting his arms to catch her. She went willingly into his arms, hugged him tightly, then almost couldn't look at him as he crooked a finger beneath her chin and gently persuaded her to look up at him.

The instant before he spoke, she saw the comprehension in his eyes.

"I'm not Lenny. I never would have left you. Never."

Tears filled her eyes again as they walked hand in hand toward the black Mercedes.

IT WASN'T UNTIL AFTER midnight that Amy felt totally relaxed. Yet she still couldn't sleep and kept going over their evening.

"Do you think he'll blame his girlfriend for everything when he finds out the safe is empty?'' she asked. She and Steve were in the living room of his friend's mansion. Steve had built a fire, opened a bottle of wine, and now they were sitting quietly, looking into the dancing flames. Tomorrow, first thing in the morning, they were going to check Florence out of the nursing home in South Pasadena. Joe lay contentedly by the fire, snoring softly. Ming was pressed close against Amy's side. The little dog had picked up on her nervousness tonight, and craved attention.

"Probably," Steve replied. "But that blonde looks like a woman who's been around the block a few times. She can take care of herself. My gut tells me she's not going to be giving Dougie any more of her time in the near future."

"And he'll probably figure it out for himself once we get Florence moved back in."

"I'd say that's a fair estimate."

They'd made it back to the actor's mansion in record time. Steve had put the various documents, the packets of cash, and the legendary diamonds in his friend's safe. He'd keep them there until Florence told him what she wanted him to do.

"I don't get it," Amy said as Steve poured her another glass of wine. "Wouldn't your friend be frantic, knowing you used his car and got him involved by putting the diamonds in his safe?"

"Nope. He would have gone with me himself if he'd been in town. But," he added, taking her into his arms as he leaned back against the couch, "you did a great job, partner. It went a lot faster and smoother because you were there."

"True," she said, feeling safe and sound now that her one and only flirtation with true danger was over.

"Douglas should be getting home any minute now," Steve mused. "I hope the poor schmuck doesn't check the safe tonight. He's going to need his sleep for what's still to come."

Amy had to laugh. "So, we go pick up Florence tomorrow and everything's resolved?"

"Yeah. I'm bringing her back here. My buddy has the greatest cook—she's from the Philippines. I want to get Florence fattened up a little, let her get some rest before she faces her brother. Without the diamonds and the various deeds, stocks and bonds, he can't do much of anything but spin his wheels."

They were well and truly done with helping Florence regain her estate and, more importantly, her life. As Amy sat looking into the flames, she again wondered where her relationship with Steve was going. Now was obviously not the time to ask. Both of them needed a good night's sleep, and Florence had to be brought home. But that still didn't stop that little nagging feeling, the worry that was her constant companion.

She wished she could just turn those feelings off, but the questions kept silently playing through her mind. Was she ready for another relationship? Something much deeper and more complete than the fantasy she'd voiced on the radio show?

After tonight, she knew she trusted Steve. He hadn't left her with the diamonds; he'd come back for her. Amy had the feeling he wasn't the type of man who let any woman in his life face her problems alone.

He was responsible in a way her ex-husband could never be. As Amy shifted and studied the dancing flames in the fireplace, she remembered the therapist she'd seen right after her marriage had ended. Something she'd said had made a deep impression on her.

"Responsibility is actually the ability to respond," the woman had told her. "Some people choose never to develop this capacity." Amy had known, before her hour session had finished, that her ex was one of those people. She'd been scared of another relationship for so long, silently judging all men by the standards Lenny had shown her; by his inherently selfish actions.

Since her divorce, Amy had looked down her nose at men. She'd acted cool and aloof, when in actuality she was scared to death to trust again. And too scared to let herself ever be so vulnerable.

But Steve wasn't Lenny. She'd seen the ultimate proof of that tonight.

Was Steve ready for the relationship she wanted? Did he want to take her on when her life was still in such a transitional state? Was he comfortable with a woman who was so deeply in debt? Her fault or not, the monetary issues had to be faced. After Lenny, Amy knew she was nothing if not a realist. She had no fears about getting to that bottom line.

What did the future hold for them?

He must have sensed how worried she was, because he tweaked her nose and grinned. "Don't get that look on your face. I've already checked with my buddy—everything's cool. He gave me permission to bring the dogs here. We can give Florence a real homecoming."

"Okay." She took a deep breath, so thankful he hadn't guessed the real reason for her anxiety. "Okay. Oh, Steve, I still can't believe what we did!"

He took her hand, pulled her closer, gave her that grin that made her heartbeat speed up. "I can. But I'd rather concentrate on what we're about to do...."

Amy offered absolutely no resistance as he lowered her down onto the carpet in front of the fire.

"OH, MY DEAR BOY, how can I ever thank you?"

Steve studied Florence as she sat out in the garden of his buddy's mansion. He liked what he saw. The pallor and the lines of tension had left her face. The combination of good, nutritious food and a few nights' peaceful sleep had done wonders. But perhaps the best medicine of all had been her canine companions. Neither dog had left her side for more than a few minutes at a time since they had been reunited with their owner.

"Your leaving that rest home is all the thanks I need." They were eating lunch by the pool, in the midst of beautifully landscaped grounds. Joe looked up at his owner with a doggy grin, hoping for a smidgen of the grilled salmon. Ming had become permanently glued to Florence's lap.

"I still can't believe..." she said softly, letting the sentence trail off.

"I know. It's hard." Steve took a deep breath. "But you're here, and the police have escorted Douglas off your estate, and now it's just a matter of time before everything gets back to normal." He reached over and took her hand. "And if you're ever in any kind of trouble again, I want you to call me. Day or night."

"I should have done that in the beginning, but I—I didn't want to face up to what was happening. I couldn't."

He understood. He also knew that Florence needed to talk a little bit this afternoon; she needed to try and make sense of all that had happened. He would be there to listen as long as she needed him.

"When I think about what could have happened to my Joe, and to Ming." The blue eyes welled up with tears as she continued, her voice breaking. "If Amy hadn't been there, and reacted as she did—"

"But she was, and she did. You had angels watching over those dogs, Florence."

"Oh, I know!" She took a sip of her freshly squeezed orange juice, then said, "I want to do something for her, Steve. I want to help her. And I need you to humor me concerning this matter. I'm just a silly old woman with an obscene amount of money at my disposal—"

"Never obscene," Steve said, grinning.

"Jimmy and I had so much fun building up our business. Those were good years. But a person only needs so much money, especially at my age." She leaned forward, and Steve noticed the conspiratorial gleam in those gentle blue eyes. "I want to make a difference in her life, Steve. Tell me about her."

"It's quite a story, actually," Steve said, ruffling Joe's head and giving the retriever a piece of his salmon. "But I think it's one you'll understand."

"HEY," STEVE SAID as he walked into Bud's Café three nights later.

"Hey," Amy said as she approached his usual booth with a cup of black coffee and a plastic-coated menu. "How's Florence?"

"Safely at home with her poochies. And very happy."

"And her brother?" Amy had to know.

"Banished to his heavily mortgaged house in La Crescenta. It'll be a long time before those two celebrate the holidays together. If ever.'' He glanced over toward the kitchen. ''Hey, Bud, can Amy take her break?''

''Why don't you ask her yourself?'' came Bud's amused reply.

''How about it?'' he said, looking up at her, and something in those blue-gray eyes tugged at her heart. He looked so...*vulnerable* this evening, like something was on his mind.

''Okay.'' She signaled to Linda, who nodded her head, indicating she'd watch over Amy's other two customers. So Amy slid into the booth across from Steve.

''Do you want something to eat?''

''Not yet. I have to ask you a few things.''

''Okay.''

''Remember how you said you couldn't even begin to think about getting serious about any guy until all your debts were paid off and you were back on your feet?''

She was totally blown away that he would remember that detail from the night she'd called in to the radio show. But then again, the man was a superb detective.

''I remember saying that.''

''Well, before I could talk her out of it, Florence insisted on paying off all your debts. This morning she went over to that office you told me about on Wilshire and wrote that guy who consolidated all your debts a check that covered everything.''

Amy simply stared at Steve. She couldn't comprehend this. Where she came from, and where she'd been, people didn't do such things. No one had that kind of money.

"I can't let her do that!"

"Well, I told her you might not like it. But she told me it was your reward for having a good heart."

"A good heart." Amy sat back in the booth, feeling as if she'd been turned to stone. She couldn't move. Debt free. The concept was unbelievable. On her own timetable, this moment would have taken three more years—at least. Now, sitting in this booth with Steve, as the idea of having absolutely no debt hanging over her head began to sink in, a feeling of lightness pervaded her entire being. A feeling she hadn't felt in a long time.

"All of it?" she whispered, still not quite believing. Still afraid someone would pinch her and she would wake up and realize this was all a dream.

"Twenty-six grand, and some change," he said, studying her.

"For having a good heart?"

"For taking those two furballs home with you instead of letting Dougie Dearest take them on that last ride to the pound. Hey, I'm telling you, the way she told it to me, it sounded like *she* owed *you.*"

"So it won't do me any good to refuse."

"Nope. Your financial counselor already has the check. She told him to cash it today. Baby, you're in the black. Debt free."

"Wow."

"Wow is right." He cleared his throat, and Amy glanced at him. Now he looked really nervous.

"Steve? Is something wrong?"

"It's like this. I was going to ask you anyway, no matter what kind of timetable you had in your life, because sometimes life just doesn't go the way we plan it, right?"

A wonderful sense of inevitability began to wash over her as he continued, because instinct told her this was one of the most important moments of her life.

"I mean, it's not like the Night Fire necklace or earrings—"

"Yes."

He frowned. "I haven't even told you what I'm asking you to do."

She smiled. "You don't have to. I'm telling you yes, because you're one of the good guys."

"Who told you that?"

She put her hand on her heart.

He stared at her for a long moment, then patted the seat next to him. "Get over here."

She slid in beside him as he took the small jeweler's box out of the pocket of his black leather jacket.

"Can you live with a man who makes his living doing the kinds of things I do?"

"Can you live with a woman who doesn't quite know what she's doing yet? I mean, I didn't see this part of my path for years to come!"

He brushed his lips against her ear. "For a woman who doesn't know what she's doing, you do it very well." Then he snapped open the ring box, and while it wasn't the Night Fire diamonds, her engagement ring was very impressive in its own right.

He slipped it on her finger and she started to cry. As Steve gently wiped the tears from her cheeks, Alexis came by and, without a word, placed two pieces of raspberry cream-cheese pie in front of them, each with a lit candle in the middle.

"It better be a yes," she said in a gruff voice, but her eyes were suspiciously bright.

"It is," Amy replied, as Steve put his arm around her and drew her close. "It is."

A week later...

"So," SAID STEVE, as he handed her a flute of champagne and a long-stemmed strawberry, "you're sure you're not upset we didn't have a big wedding?"

She nodded her head. "Been there, done that." She wondered how she could explain to Steve that when your heart was perfectly confident in the decision you'd made, it didn't matter if you were alone with the man you loved on a tropical island, or standing in a church in front of five hundred guests. If a true, deep connection was present, if there was real intimacy and love between two people, that was what made a marriage.

She'd learned that little bit of wisdom the hard way, and that made her marriage to Steve all the sweeter.

They'd had the actual ceremony late this afternoon at The Beverly Hills Hotel, whose penthouse they were presently occupying. Although neither Amy nor Steve had any real family, Bud, Linda and Alexis from the diner, along with Florence and her dogs, had come to see the ceremony.

Amy felt she now had two families—the family of friends she'd gained through marriage, and the one she and Steve would start in a few years.

They'd talked so much in the week between the diamond heist and their wedding, deciding where they would live, when they would start a family, all the things that engaged couples needed to decide. But as far as Amy was concerned, nothing mattered but the sheer contentment she found in this man's arms. Tonight, naked and feeling almost weightless with happiness after their lovemaking, she lay in the large bed with her husband and took another sip of champagne.

"Music?" she suggested.

She had one more surprise for Steve this evening. Their entire wedding day had been magical. The weather had been perfect, they'd written their own vows, and she had cried during the brief ceremony in the hotel's gorgeous rose garden.

"Sure." He fiddled with the dial of the clock radio on the bedside table as Amy surreptitiously checked the luminous digital display.

Midnight. Perfect.

Steve's hand stilled on the dial as the familiar theme music—soft, sultry jazz—for "In the Midnight Hour" came on, followed by Frank's familiar voice.

"Hey there, it's time for a few more Midnight Kisses, those fantasies you can't even tell your closest friends. But tonight, before we start, I want to offer the audience a little hope. I want to talk to all of you about how dreams do come true in this City of Angels."

"This sounds good," Amy said, hoping her voice didn't give her away. She wanted this to be a total surprise for Steve.

"Okay." He settled back against the mass of pillows, taking her with him—but gently so as not to spill the champagne.

"Remember the call we had a few weeks ago, from a woman named Amy?"

Amy began to smile as she took a bite of the enormous strawberry Steve had given her.

"Hey," Steve began, but Amy set her crystal

flute down on the bedside table and put her hand over his mouth.

"Well," Frank continued, "I received a letter from Amy the other day, and I thought it only made sense to read it on the air. She told me I could do this, because Amy believes in dreams, in fantasy, but she says—" The radio host hesitated. "You know, I think I'll let Amy do the talking. I'll just read her letter."

Steve eased Amy's hand away from his mouth, then kissed her palm. She could sense that all his attention was directed on what Frank was about to say.

"'Dear Frank,'" the host read. "'I just wanted to drop you a note and thank you for giving me a place where I could voice my deepest fantasies. I don't even think I knew what they were until I started talking to you, and then it all came out like a flood.'"

Steve studied her in a way that made Amy blush and look away.

"'I told you there was one guy I talked to, and I want you to know that he was listening that night, and within a week he made my fantasy come true. The limousine, the drive to the beach, the Italian restaurant overlooking the ocean—all of it. The entire evening was magical, but the best part of this fantasy was that it came true.'"

Frank paused. "I love this letter." Amy heard him clear his throat, then he continued.

"'It came true because we both found out that we didn't just want the fantasy. He wanted to get to know the real me, and I wanted to know him. We had some pretty spectacular adventures together right after that night, but within a few weeks of acting out my fantasy, Steve asked me to marry him.'"

Steve pulled her closer against him and whispered, "Hey, I'm no fool."

"'We're getting married this Saturday,'" Frank read on. "'I wanted you to be one of the first people to know, because in a funny sort of way, Frank, you're like our fairy godmother. Or godfather, if you're more comfortable with that.'"

The radio host laughed. "Hey, either one suits me." He continued reading the letter.

"'But what I wanted you to know, most of all, is that I really believe that what you do is important. Because dreams are important. That fantasy that I held so closely to my heart helped me get through some pretty rough times.

"'Most of all, Frank, I want to thank you for helping me during a time when I really needed that little push to get out there and back into life. And I want all your listeners to know that—even though I know it may sound corny—well, dreams really can come true. I know this, because mine did. By the time you get this letter, I'll be the happiest woman in the world, married to the man of my dreams.'"

Frank cleared his throat again. "'All my best, Amy.'"

Steve turned the radio's volume down so it was merely background noise, then pulled her even closer as he sank back down against the pillows.

"That was some letter," he said.

"I meant every word."

He smoothed her hair back from her face. "You know, you were my dream, too. Only I didn't have a clue how to start anything with you, because you had Stay Away written all over you."

"I was scared," she admitted.

"I know." He grinned. "Maybe I should write Frank a letter of my own."

"He'd like that."

Steve studied her, and Amy saw that possessive light in his eyes, that expression on his face that she knew meant their night together was far from over. Seconds before he pulled her into his arms and kissed her, she heard Frank's voice, very low, in the background.

"So call in with a fantasy, because dreams do come true, right here at midnight, that magical hour, on our magical show, Midnight Kisses. Call in, because no matter how bad things may be right now, don't ever give up on your dreams. They can come true for you when you least expect them to...."

Smiling, Amy reached over and turned off the radio.

HARLEQUIN® Temptation.

It's hotter than a winter fire.
It's a BLAZE!

In January 1999 stay warm with another
one of our bold, provocative, *ultra-sexy*
Temptation novels.

#715 *TANTALIZING*
by Lori Foster

It was lust at first sight—but Josie and Mark were both
pretending to be other people! They were giving new
meaning to the term "blind date." How to unravel the web
of deceit? And still hang on to that sexy stranger...

BLAZE!
Red-hot reads from Temptation!

Available wherever Harlequin books are sold.

HARLEQUIN®
Makes any time special ™

Take 2 bestselling love stories FREE

Plus get a FREE surprise gift!

Special Limited-Time Offer

Mail to Harlequin Reader Service®

3010 Walden Avenue
P.O. Box 1867
Buffalo, N.Y. 14240-1867

YES! Please send me 2 free Harlequin Temptation® novels and my free surprise gift. Then send me 4 brand-new novels every month, which I will receive before they appear in bookstores. Bill me at the low price of $3.12 each plus 25¢ delivery and applicable sales tax, if any.* That's the complete price, and a saving of over 10% off the cover prices—quite a bargain! I understand that accepting the books and gift places me under no obligation ever to buy any books. I can always return a shipment and cancel at any time. Even if I never buy another book from Harlequin, the 2 free books and the surprise gift are mine to keep forever.

142 HEN CH7G

Name	(PLEASE PRINT)

Address	Apt. No.

City	State	Zip

This offer is limited to one order per household and not valid to present Harlequin Temptation® subscribers. *Terms and prices are subject to change without notice. Sales tax applicable in N.Y.

UTEMP-98

©1990 Harlequin Enterprises Limited

HARLEQUIN®
Temptation

He's strong. He's sexy.
He's up for grabs!

Harlequin Temptation and
Texas Men magazine present:

Mail Order Men—
Satisfaction Guaranteed!

Available wherever Harlequin books are sold.

HARLEQUIN®
Makes any time special ™